BOOKS by KASSANDRA LAMB

The Marcia Banks and Buddy Mysteries:
To Kill A Labrador
Arsenic and Young Lacy
The Call of the Woof
A Mayfair Christmas Carol
Patches in the Rye
The Legend of Sleepy Mayfair
The Sound and the Furry
A Star-Spangled Mayfair
Lord of the Fleas
My Funny Mayfair Valentine
One Flew Over the Chow-Chow's Nest
To Bark or Not To Bark
(coming late 2021/early 2022)
~

The Kate Huntington Mystery Series:
MULTIPLE MOTIVES
ILL-TIMED ENTANGLEMENTS
FAMILY FALLACIES
CELEBRITY STATUS
COLLATERAL CASUALTIES
ZERO HERO
FATAL FORTY-EIGHT
SUICIDAL SUSPICIONS
ANXIETY ATTACK
POLICE PROTECTION
~

The Kate on Vacation novellas
~

plus Romantic Suspense Stories
(written under the pen name, Jessica Dale)
The Unintended Consequences series (sweet)
The Binding Love series (steamy)
Bartered Innocence (steamy)

ONE FLEW OVER THE CHOW-CHOW'S NEST

A Marcia Banks and Buddy Mystery

Kassandra Lamb

author of the Kate Huntington Mysteries

a misterio press publication

AUTHOR'S NOTE:

This story does mention the Covid pandemic, but does not get into the heavier aspects.

I have tried to focus on the relief and optimism as the U.S. is coming out of the pandemic in the Spring of 2021.

CHAPTER ONE

Muscles loosened that had been tense for over a year, as the nurse applied a little round bandaid to my arm.

"Now, it takes two weeks for that to be fully effective," she said with a slight Southern accent.

I beamed at her, even though she couldn't see my grin under my puppy-dog mask. "I know. My husband was vaccinated a while ago. He's law enforcement."

Her eyes smiled back. "I love this job. I've never before made so many people happy by stickin' a needle in their arms."

We both laughed.

Woot!! Two weeks and I would have my life back.

Not that my life had been particularly gruesome—especially compared to what all too many had experienced during the pandemic. For one thing, I'd already been working from home.

But among other "normal" things I would now be able to do, I could finally deliver Bear to her rightful owner, and collect my training fee.

The Chow Chow-Husky mix, otherwise known as a Chusky, had been ready for almost a year. Indeed, I'd trained another dog during the interim months for a veteran who'd had a service dog before, so we could dispense with most of the human part of the training.

But the veteran Bear had been trained for, former Air Force pilot Russell Fortham, was living with and caring for his elderly mother, who had Stage III COPD. He'd been concerned about having me come to their home to train him, for fear I'd bring Covid with me.

And I'd been equally eager to avoid social contact since I'd been trying to get pregnant, and little was known about the impact of Covid on unborn babies.

Ironically, I had been totally ambivalent about having children, until I'd discovered—after a miscarriage a year ago—that I *had been* pregnant, but now wasn't. I'd been fighting low-grade depression and a ferocious longing for a child ever since.

As I drove home from the vaccine center, my third call was to Russ Fortham's cell phone.

The first had been to my hairdresser. For months, I'd been hacking away at my long auburn hair myself, and it was, shall we say, a little uneven. The second had been to my best friend Becky. I got voicemail and left a message that I'd be coming to Williston soon for hugs from her and her twins, my godchildren.

My call to Russ also went straight to voicemail, and a mechanical voice informed me that his mailbox was full. I instructed my Bluetooth to call his home number.

His mother answered. When I identified myself, she burst into tears. "He's in the hospital," she managed to get out in a wavering voice.

My throat closed and my stomach hollowed out. "What happened?" Had he crashed his private plane?

"He was kind of depressed," her voice was still shaky, "and then his counselor said he needed a different medication." Soft sobbing noises. "She Baker-Acted him…"

Baker Act—the informal name of the state statute, which Floridians used as a verb when someone was involuntarily committed for psychological evaluation. To Baker-Act someone was a fairly drastic measure.

"He's still in the hospital," Mrs. Fortham wailed. "And they won't let me visit."

That last part wasn't too surprising, considering the pandemic.

"When did all this happen?"

"Three months ago."

"Crapola," I blurted out. That was shortly after the last time I had talked to Russ, mid-January. He'd seemed fine at the time, excited about eventually having Bear with him.

My whole body tightened with guilt—I should've gotten his dog to him sooner. I wondered how he could've sunk so low that he required long-term hospitalization.

"Who's his counselor?" I asked.

"Jo Ann Hamilton."

I let out a soft sigh. I knew Jo Ann. She'd been my counselor at one time as well, and she was good at what she did.

I promised Mrs. Fortham I'd look into the situation.

I'd left a message for Jo Ann.

Then I did some brush-up training with Bear. She's such a big teddy bear, which is how she'd ended up with her name. The shelter I'd gotten her from had been calling her Red, but when I took her to first meet Russ, he'd rubbed her head affectionately and said, "Aren't you a big teddy bear of a dog?" She'd been Bear ever since.

We were working in the backyard, but my mind kept flashing back to the phone conversation with Mrs. Fortham. Butterflies danced in my stomach, making me a bit queasy.

Bear suddenly turned toward me and jumped up, wrapping her front legs around my waist. I staggered backward a couple of steps.

The Chusky had always had a tendency to jump up. My assistant, Carla and I had tried to break her of it, but then I'd decided to re-channel it instead. We'd trained the dog to give "bear hugs" when she sensed anxiety in her human. As apparently she had in me now.

Russ was a big man, so the hugs shouldn't knock him off balance like they did me.

I signaled for Bear to get down. She did and I scratched behind her ear. "Thanks, girl. I'm just worried about your new papa."

My phone buzzed in my pocket. I pulled it out, signaling with my other hand for Bear to lie down.

It was Jo Ann. "Hey," I answered, "you're working with Russell Fortham."

"Um, I can neither confirm nor deny…"

I'd obviously taken her by surprise. "Sorry for being so abrupt. I hadn't meant it as a question, and I have a waiver of confidentiality."

"You do?"

"Yes, the agency does. It's standard operating procedure. You did know he was getting a service dog, didn't you?"

"Yes, but I didn't realize you were the trainer."

"We're even," I said with a faint chuckle. "I didn't know you were his counselor. I don't remember seeing your name in his file."

"I took over his case about five months ago."

"I talked to his mother a little while ago. She says he's been in the hospital for the last three months."

"I know," Jo Ann said, "and I'm getting worried about him."

"Getting worried?"

"Okay, getting *really* worried. I sent him to the VA medical center for an evaluation. I thought he should probably be on a different medication, something stronger for depression, not just his anxiety." She paused. "By the way, can you fax me a copy of that waiver?"

"Of course." I headed for the back door of my training center, what had once been my house and was now connected to Will's cottage next door by a large modern addition.

"His mom's under the impression that you Baker-Acted him," I said.

"No, he went voluntarily for the eval, but he got a green psychiatrist, fresh out of medical school, and he over-reacted and Baker-Acted Russ, to keep him for observation."

Inside the house, I gestured for Bear to go into her crate. Buddy, my Black Lab/Rottie mentor dog, raised his head from where he'd been napping near the crates.

I shook my head slightly, letting him know that his assistance wasn't needed, and went to my file cabinet in a corner of what used to be my living room. "I'm pulling the file right now," I told Jo Ann.

I actually had a paper copy of the paper file maintained by Mattie Jones, the director of the agency I train for. Mattie's a tad old-fashioned.

"So, how did Russ end up in the hospital for so long?" I asked.

"It started out as a voluntary week or two to get him stabilized on new meds. I was talking to him every few days by phone. He's in a private hospital near Leesburg, theoretically so his mother can visit him more readily."

"Why do you say theoretically?" I asked.

The sound of air being blown out in a long sigh. "Well, with Covid, they're not allowing any visitors. I tried myself one time. They wouldn't even unlock the door and talk to me. Some woman kept pointing to the sign on the door that said no visitors until further notice. But after the first couple of weeks, they haven't been letting me talk to him either. They said he refused to sign a waiver."

"That doesn't sound like Russ." The pilot was one of the most easy-going people I'd ever met.

"And more recently, they haven't been letting his mother talk to him either."

"Say what? Does he have issues with his mother?" The couple of times I'd met with him last year—our initial interview and then when I'd taken Bear to introduce them to each other—he'd seemed to get along fine with his mom.

"Not that he's ever mentioned to me," Jo Ann was saying. "And I asked. That's part of my intake interview, to ask about relationships with parents. Russ seemed to be genuinely fond of his mom, with no issues that I could detect."

"Good. Lord knows he has enough issues from being in combat. But can they keep him in the hospital against his will?"

"Not readily. If he wanted to leave against medical advice, they'd have to have two mental health professionals agree that he continues to be a danger to himself or others."

I had trouble imagining laid-back Russ as a danger to others. "If he's still seriously depressed after all this time," I said, "it's not a very good hospital."

A slight chuckle. "Good point."

"What are you going to do?"

"The psychiatrist at the VA center says the case is no longer his. I've talked to Russ's VA case manager a couple of times. She doesn't seem to be alarmed. She contacted the hospital's director and was told that Russ is responding to a new medication but his improvement is slow." Another sigh. "Short of breaking down the hospital's doors and rampaging through the halls, which I can't really get away with and expect to keep my counseling license, there's not much I can do."

"Hmm, you can't, but maybe I can," I said. "I'll keep you posted."

I disconnected and called Mattie Jones. When she answered, I said, "Who on our board has clout with the Veterans' Administration?"

I filled her in.

"Harumph," was her response. "I'll see what I can find out."

Using the multipurpose printer in Will's and my joint study, I faxed Jo Ann a copy of the confidentiality waiver. Then I made myself a copy.

Refiling the original, I folded the copy and stuck it in my purse. "Come on, Buddy. Let's go for a drive."

As we went out the training center's door, my neighbor Sherie Wells was stepping out onto her front porch, just twenty feet from me.

Our two houses were now surrounded by fallow fields and woods, but they had once been among a dozen cottages on narrow lots along this end of Main Street. They'd housed the African-Americans who'd worked for old Mr. Mayfair at his long-defunct alligator farm. Mr. Mayfair was also long gone, as were the rest of the cottages—rotted away, the land reclaimed by Florida's aggressive flora. But Sherie's and our houses had been built of cement blocks.

"Where are you off to, Marcia?" she called over.

"I'm going to exercise my car." That seemed easier than trying to explain my client's situation, most of which was confidential anyway.

She smiled, a flash of white teeth against brown skin that had surprisingly few wrinkles for a woman in her late sixties. "I've taken some drives to nowhere myself lately." As always, her posture was ramrod straight. *Regal* was the word that came to mind whenever I saw her.

"How's Will?"

"He's good. How's Sybil doing?"

Sherie patted her silver-streaked black hair, pulled back in its usual tight chignon. "Good in general, but this week, she's exhausted. She's been doing twelve-hour night shifts."

Sybil, Sherry's youngest, had moved back home temporarily while between jobs, shortly before the pandemic began. "Temporarily" had become "for the duration," but she was working again, for a nursing agency.

"That sounds rough."

"It has been, but she's off for the next two days."

"Tell her I said hi." I waved and headed for my car.

I was almost to Leesburg when my phone buzzed, and a text flashed up on my dashboard screen, from Becky.

At doctor w twins. Don't worry, it's only a checkup. Call u later. Can't wait for hugs!

Smiling, I went looking for the Leesburg Psychiatric Hospital. I wasn't exactly sure what I would be able to accomplish, but I wanted to see the place for myself. And I was hoping the service-dog angle might give me an entrée, or at least help me get more information on Russ's condition.

I drove around shaded side streets in the small city, my GPS insisting that I had arrived at my destination. But all I saw were ancient live oaks and large houses that seemed almost as old.

Finally I spotted a small white wooden sign that read *Leesburg Sanitarium,* and in smaller print underneath, *A Pennington Psychiatric Facility.*

"Hmm," I said to Buddy, "they've taken discreet to a whole new level."

He sat up on the backseat and gave me his *what's-up* look, a tilt of his head and a question mark in his eyes.

I parallel-parked in the shade of an ancient tree and sat for a moment, debating. To accomplish my goal, I needed to put his service dog vest on him. It was cheating, since I wasn't personally in need of a service dog... but I ended up doing it, since it would lend credibility to my approach.

The Leesburg Sanitarium was nestled on several acres, with a tall chain-link fence surrounding the campus. The fence was barely visible though, amongst the trees and undergrowth.

The gates sat open, so we waltzed in. The main building was an old mansion, refurbished with fresh siding and a shiny metal roof. Behind it was a long cement-block building, painted white. It also sported a metal roof, glistening in the sunlight.

We climbed the steps to the wide veranda-style porch of the main building. Several empty rockers swayed slightly in the breeze.

I tried the knob of the polished mahogany door. It was locked. A wooden sign next to it read *Visitors Must Sign In at the Front Desk.* Taped to the inside of the window in the door, a computer-generated paper sign said *No Visitors Until Further Notice.*

I rang the doorbell anyway, then bracketed my face with my hands to peer through the window at a dimly lit hallway.

It took three rings to get any action. A middle-aged woman in a tailored navy pantsuit came to the door but made no move to open it.

"I need to speak to my client," I said, loud enough to penetrate the glass. "Russell Fortham."

The woman shook her head and pointed to the *No Visitors* sign.

"It'll only take a moment, and it's important." I waved the face mask I held in one hand at her. "Out here on the porch, socially distanced, is fine."

She shook her head and started to turn away.

I knocked on the glass. "If I can't see him, I need to talk to his doctor." I held the copy of my waiver up to the window.

She shook her head emphatically and walked away.

Again, I bracketed my face to peer through the window. She went to the far end of the wide hallway, which apparently doubled as a reception and waiting area, and sat down at a big wooden desk.

Okay, I was getting more than a little annoyed here. I rang the doorbell again.

The woman ignored me, conveying loud and clear that our interaction was done.

Internally, the snarky part of myself that I try hard to suppress said, *Hmm, we'll see about that.* Before I could stop her, Ms. Snark pressed the doorbell button, holding it down for several seconds.

The woman glanced up, then back down at whatever was in front of her on her desk.

Harumph. Ms. Snark rang the bell again. I didn't try all that hard to stop her this time.

A man stepped out into the hallway from a side doorway. He was tall and slender, in a charcoal gray business suit. He looked toward the door and quickly walked to the woman's desk. They conferred, the woman glaring my way.

Impatiently, Ms. Snark banged on the heavy wooden door.

Settle down, I told her internally. *I'll handle this.*

The man approached the door. His face was smooth, youthful, but he had some gray in his dark hair, mostly at the temples. I pegged him for early to mid-forties.

He unlocked the door and cracked it open slightly. "Can I help you?"

"Depends," Ms. Snark blurted out. "Are you Captain Fortham's shrink?"

He frowned.

I wrestled Ms. Snark back under control. "I need to speak to either Russell Fortham or his doctor. I have a waiver of confidentiality." I handed the paper through the crack.

The man examined the waiver.

"You can keep that," I said generously. "It's a copy."

"What do you need to know?" he asked.

Again, I waved my puppy-dog mask in the air—it was a cloth one, multi-layered, made by my friend Edna Mayfair. "Could you step out here so we don't have to yell through the door?"

Technically we weren't quite yelling, but I wanted to get this guy beyond the point where he could just close the door in my face.

He paused, sighed, and reached in his pocket. Out came a disposable face mask.

I quickly pointed out to Ms. Snark that a fist pump would not be appropriate at this time.

I stepped back from the door as I donned my mask.

He came out and gestured toward the rockers. I walked to the one farthest away and turned, about to sit down. He remained standing a dozen feet away.

So I did as well. I wasn't about to give him the advantage of hovering over me, even from a distance.

"I'm Marcia Banks-Haines," I said. "I'm training a service dog for Captain Fortham, and it's time to begin the human handler phase of the training. I need to know what his status is."

"I'm Dr. Johnson, the director here." He stood ramrod straight. "Even with this waiver, there isn't much I can tell you."

"I don't see why not." I tried to keep the snark out of my tone. I wasn't sure I'd succeeded.

Suddenly, he changed tactics. Relaxing his posture, he waved again toward the rockers. He moved to the one nearest the door and sat.

So did I. Buddy settled at my feet.

"Is this his new dog?" Dr. Johnson asked, gesturing toward Buddy.

"No, he's my mentor dog. He helps me train the others. But Russ knows him. I thought if I was able to see him, that Buddy might cheer him up."

The dog responded to his name with his *what's-up* look.

But the doctor was shaking his head. "We have to be strict about the no-visitors rule. Not all of our patients have been vaccinated yet."

"I get that." I took a deep breath. "Can you at least tell me how he's doing? When might he be discharged?"

The doc was shaking his head again. "I'm afraid Mr. Fortham may be with us for a bit longer."

I leaned forward, perched on the edge of the rocker. "Here's the problem. If I can't start the human training soon, then the dog will have to be reassigned to another veteran. She's a valuable animal. We can't let her grow old, waiting on one vet. But I know the captain would be devastated if we had to do that. He's already bonded with Bear."

Reassigning the dog was an empty threat, but it sounded plausible.

"Well, we wouldn't want that. He is making progress, although slow-ly." Dr. Johnson put his hands on his knees and pushed himself to a stand. "If I can get your phone number, I can give you a call when we have a potential release date for him."

I'd hoped to get more—if not a chance to speak to Russ briefly, at least more info about his condition—but I suspected this was all I was getting. I stood and gave the doctor one of my cards.

The woman opened the front door. She gave me a sharp glance. "Doctor, Mr. Pennington is on the phone for you."

"Thank you, Mrs. Ratchette." He slipped past her.

OMG, they've got a Nurse Ratched, Ms. Snark chortled inside my head. *Straight out of One Flew Over the Cuckoo's Nest.*

I think it's a different spelling, I pointed out internally. I'd definitely heard a T sound at the end of her name.

Trying to keep a straight face, I walked past the frowning woman, still standing in the doorway.

Her glare bore into my back, as Buddy and I walked down the driveway to the street.

CHAPTER TWO

My phone rang shortly after we got home. No name and I didn't recognize the number. But I dared not ignore the call. It could be news about Russ Fortham.

I swiped to answer it. "Hello," I said tentatively, prepared to disconnect at any indication of a sales pitch or scam.

"Is this Marsha Banks?" The woman's tone was no-nonsense, and of course, she mispronounced my first name.

"This is Mar-see-a Banks." I emphasized each syllable. "Who's this?"

"This is Janice Robinson." She said it like she expected me to recognize her name.

I didn't.

"Mattie Jones said you have a concern about one of our clients. I know someone on the Pennington board of directors."

"Pennington?" I asked, confused.

"He is checking on the status of Captain Fortham," she went on as if I hadn't spoken.

Oh, yeah, Pennington. The small print on the Leesburg Sanitarium's sign, and the guy who was calling Dr. Johnson.

The tightness in my chest and shoulders eased. "That's great. Thank you."

"You're welcome." She disconnected.

My phone screen was asking if I wanted to add this number to my contacts. I tapped yes, then stared at the phone for a moment.

For a brief period, I'd been part of that upper-crust realm where contacts were everything, back when I was married to a member of the Baltimore Symphony in my home state of Maryland. It had not been a good time in my life.

I shook my head to clear it of the unpleasant memories, and decided to take Buddy and Bear for a walk. I was too agitated to do any of my other time-killing activities—exercising, reading, or taking a nap.

Mayfair continued to be the friendly little town it had always been, just from a distance now. Neighbors waved and called out greetings, but they didn't approach or stop to chat as they would have in the past.

I was looking forward to making the rounds in two weeks and catching up on everyone's lives. But for now, I waved and kept moving. "I can't wait until this blinkety-blank pandemic is totally behind us," I said to the dogs.

Bear ignored me, sniffing a bush, but Buddy cocked his head at me in his patented *what's-up* look.

I laughed out loud. "You're a good listener, boy."

As we headed back down our end of Main Street, I spotted Sybil's silver sedan, parked at the curb in front of her mother's house.

She climbed slowly out as we approached.

"Hey, Syb, how's it going?"

She turned toward me and her body language gave me my answer. She'd inherited her mother's regal bearing, but today her shoulders sagged.

"You look tired," I said.

"I am." We started up our parallel walkways. When we got to our respective porches, she dropped down to sit on the steps. "I need a minute to rest before I go in."

I gave her a curious glance and sat on my own steps.

"I just finished a twelve-hour shift at a nursing home." She glanced over her shoulder at her screen door. The inner front door was sitting open to catch the spring breeze. "When I look at those old folks," she continued in a low voice, "most of them senile, I can't help wondering if Mama's gonna end up that way someday."

I raised my eyebrows at her. "Your mother is *not* going to go senile. God wouldn't dare!"

Sybil laughed, and her medium-brown skin lost its ashen undertone. "Phew! I would not want to be around for that showdown at the Pearly Gates."

"How do you like working for this nursing agency?"

"I like it. Being a traveling nurse, as we're called—it's a great way to get experience. I'm not sure yet what specialty is right for me. This gives me a chance to test-drive different jobs and settings."

"That's cool. So, you're not big on nursing homes. What are you leaning toward?"

She gave me a small smile. "I'm considering becoming a nurse practitioner, if I can talk myself into going back to school."

"Awesome," I said with enthusiasm.

Ask her, Ms. Snark prodded internally.

Ask her what?

Then I got it. Sometimes, Ms. Snark figures things out before I do.

"Hey, have you ever worked at the Leesburg Sanitarium?"

Sybil's eyebrows went up. "I was there a few weeks ago. Why?"

"Did you happen to cross paths with a patient named Russell Fortham?"

Her expression became guarded.

"Big guy," I said, holding my hand above my head to indicate Russ's height. "Solid, but not fat. Light brown hair, buzz cut."

"Why do you ask?" she said.

I took that as a yes. "This is confidential. He's my client. I trained Bear for him." I pointed to the big red dog, lying next to Buddy on the sidewalk. "Today, I learned that he's been in the hospital for several months now, and nobody's been able to visit him or even talk to him on the phone."

Sybil's eyebrows were in the air again, but she didn't say anything.

"Did you ever talk to him?" I asked her. "Did he actually seem depressed to you?"

She shook her head slightly. "Look, patients on psych wards often put on a good front, say they're okay, because they want to go home. It's no fun being in the hospital."

"Is that what Russ did, say he was okay?"

She frowned and blew out air. "I can't say anything specific about a particular patient."

"Okay, so let me ask you hypothetically. Say a patient talked and acted like Russ did, would you think he was okay or faking it?"

"I'm not a psychiatrist or psychologist."

"No, but you are a very observant human being." I wasn't saying that to butter her up. Sybil, like her mother, was quite astute.

She pushed herself to a stand and turned to climb the porch steps. On the top one, she paused and gave me a long, hard look. "Yes, and no."

I wasn't quite sure what that meant. "Come on, please. Can't you tell me more?"

"I was there for six weeks. That's half the normal length of an assignment, but my supervisor said they don't usually keep traveling nurses for longer than that there." She paused.

I held my breath, wondering why she was telling me all that.

"During that time," she said, "your hypothetical patient showed no signs of depression. Restlessness, yes. Anxiety, some. Definitely boredom, but not depression."

She walked up onto the porch.

"Thanks, Syb."

She waved a hand over her head without turning back around. "We never had this conversation."

Back inside the house, I paced the floor for a few minutes. During the months of self-isolation, I'd had five fallback activities to fill the hours. Do refresher training with Bear, take a walk with the dogs, take a nap, read, or practice my self-defense moves and get some additional exercise in the process.

I'd already done a training session and walked the dogs, and I was way too agitated for a nap or reading, so I opted for the last alternative.

A couple of months ago, I'd discovered a series of online self-defense videos that I'd fallen in love with. The three main attractions were that the techniques really were tailored to the average woman's capabilities, the practice sessions on the videos doubled as muscle-toning workouts, and the instructor, Sophie, had a totally cool Irish accent.

I went into our study and booted up my laptop. While I waited—in rural Florida, internet service isn't always the fastest—I savored my favorite room in our hodge-podge house.

It had been the small living room and eat-in kitchen of Will's old house. We had completely renovated it. The loveseat from my old living room and a recliner created a sitting area on one side, and his and hers computer desks dominated the other. A colorful, braid rug covered most of the laminated wood floor.

I opened the bookmarked link for the first video in the series. It was my favorite, partly because it was the best workout.

A slim, short woman with dark hair in a ponytail appeared. She wore a turquoise leotard.

Cheers, ladies. Sophie here, and welcome to my Ladies Only self-defense course.

First off, all that karate choppin' and twistin' your opponent around to toss him over your shoulder—that's for men, with strong arms and shoulders.

She puffed up her shoulders.

Women's arms are weak. She shrugged. *I'm sorry, my lovelies, but it's true. Our strength...* She lifted a knee. *...is in our legs.*

We might be the weaker sex. She winked at the camera. *But our legs are the sturdiest part of us. They're designed to walk for miles in the woods and on mountains, collecting berries and roots.*

I loved the way she said *roots.*

And they're meant to be the foundation on which we build genera-

tions. We carry wee babes in our wombs on those thighs that perhaps you despise for bein' too fat.

I settled on the floor, anticipating the workout that was coming.

So, here we go, ladies. Let's explore what those thighs can do.

My phone rang. Irritated, I hauled it out of my jeans' pocket. Caller ID read *Carla.*

I wanted to ignore it, but… Why was my assistant trainer-in-training calling?

I paused the video and answered the call. "Hey, what's up?"

"Um, I need to bring Dolly to you earlier than we'd planned. Uh, as in today."

"Why?"

"Um, it's a long story."

There was something off here. I'd never known Carla to be hesitant, and yet she had used two *ums* and an *uh* in less than three sentences.

"Um, can I explain when I get there? Don't worry, I've been staying isolated."

"Sure, okay. When will you be here?"

"In about three minutes. I'm turning into Mayfair now."

That brought me up short. "Oh, okay. See ya in a bit."

I'd barely had time to click the video off and close my laptop when I heard the rumble of an engine. Buddy and I went out front.

Carla was already out of her car, her head stuck inside the back passenger-side door, releasing Dolly from her safety strap. But I couldn't actually see the dog. The driver's side of the backseat was piled high with cardboard boxes. More were crammed into the back of the small SUV.

"What's going on?" I asked Carla as she straightened and Dolly jumped out.

They rounded the front end and stopped about ten feet from me. Dolly wasn't on a leash, but the Border Collie-Australian Sheepdog mix stayed close to Carla's knee.

Carla was wearing a mask, but I could tell by the furrowed brow that she was frowning. She'd picked up some weight since the last time I'd seen her, which come to think of it, had been months ago. It looked good on her. She'd been too thin before.

Her dark hair had grown out. Instead of shortish spikes, it hung loose and wavy around her shoulders, softening the angular lines of her face. A tiny bit of gray was mixed in now—not surprising since she was in her mid-forties—and the sun had added some red highlights.

"I lost my day job," she said abruptly. "And now I'm being evicted."

"Wha'?" I realized my chin had dropped, dislodging my mask. I quickly adjusted it. "What happened?"

"I was laid off because of Covid, but I was doing okay on unemployment. Then the restaurant reopened, and they called me back." She paused, took a deep breath. "I couldn't do it. I'm high risk. But no more unemployment because now I'm supposedly refusing to work."

"You're high risk?"

"I'm a cancer survivor—*lung* cancer."

My chin dropped again. I stabbed my mask back in place. Carla was a very private person, so I didn't know much about her background—other than she was divorced. And I'd gotten the impression that her husband had been abusive, at least emotionally.

No wonder she had a bit of a sour attitude. Life had not been kind to her.

"I was paying half my rent," she continued, "out of my savings, hoping that would show I was trying. But my landlord found out I'd refused to go back when the restaurant reopened..." She trailed off. Her eyes had gone shiny.

Crapola, is Carla Cummings about to cry?

"Did you score a vaccine yet?" I knew she'd been having trouble getting an appointment. The distribution had been left up to the counties in Florida, and some, like the good-sized one I was in, had the resources to handle it. But other smaller, rural counties had been overwhelmed. Websites had crashed, phone lines had been tied up day and night. Carla lived in one of those counties.

She was nodding though. "I got my first shot two weeks ago. If my landlord had only waited another month, I could've gotten the back rent caught up once I was working again."

"Where are you going to stay?"

She shrugged her slumped shoulders. "In my car for now. I put most of my stuff in storage."

An idea had been percolating in the back of my mind. Now I blurted it out. "No, you're not. You're staying in our guest room."

I wasn't sure how my husband would feel about that arrangement. We'd only had the house all to ourselves again for a few weeks.

My mother had finally vacated our guest suite not long ago. She and her fiancé, Sheriff Clint Burns, had settled for a very small "commitment ceremony"—with only them, us, Clint's grown kids, and a priest—in Clint's backyard. Then Mom had moved into his house, over in Crystal County on the west side of the state.

Carla was staring at me, her eyes wide. "But... Will's still working, right?"

"Yes, so there is the risk he could be exposed, but we can close off the training center." As a sheriff's department detective, he had long since been vaccinated, but the verdict wasn't in yet from the scientists as to whether vaccinated people could be carriers. "The guest suite is in the back of that part of the house," I continued. "You can have that area and the kitchen to yourself."

Excitement bubbled in my chest as I warmed to the idea. Will would go along, once he realized the alternative was her camping in her car.

I shook my head slightly. Boy, I must really be missing human companionship if I was getting excited about having Carla around.

No wonder I was lonely. Will had been working a lot of extra shifts— the department was short-handed, between people being out sick and some who had quit, out of fear of bringing the disease home to their families. And my contact with my neighbors had been curtailed for so long now. For weeks, I hadn't even crossed paths with Susanna Mayfair, with whom I shared the stall-cleaning and feeding duties at the Mayfair Riding Stable. We talked by phone occasionally to exchange information about our equine charges, but that was it.

"I can pay you some rent." Carla's voice was tentative. "I have some savings left."

I waved a hand in the air. "That won't be nec–" I stopped abruptly.

What little I could see of her cheeks above her mask were turning red and she was shaking her head.

"How does a hundred a month sound?" I said quickly.

The blush subsided. "That sounds great." Crow's feet crinkled at the edges of her eyes.

Despite her mask, I knew she was blessing me with one of her rare smiles.

Eight p.m. and Will still wasn't home. I'd ordered two pizzas delivered and left one on the training center's porch for Carla.

I'd moved Bear's crate into our living area, so I wouldn't have to go into the training center at all. Our backyard was divided into two sections, one I used for training and the other we considered "our yard." The training yard was where the dogs usually did their business, and we tried to keep our side free of doggie-doo.

I could walk Bear and Buddy down the dark yard to the gate between the two sections and let them into the training yard. But I opted to take them for an evening walk instead.

Plastic bags stuffed in my jeans pocket, we set out. A half moon lit our way, with some help from Mayfair's only street lamp, down by the motel. I texted Carla as we walked slowly down Main Street, the dogs sniffing for just the right spot.

Getting a grocery order tomorrow, curbside pickup. Text me a list and I'll get yours too.

No answer by the time we reached the streetlight and turned around for home.

Then, *Okay.*

This is going to be great. I texted her. *We can work together with Dolly and still be socially distanced.*

Another pause. Bear finally decided that a palmetto bush needed fertilizer. She squatted beside it.

Yes, it's going to be fine. Thanks again. Carla even included a smiley face.

I frowned at my phone. Smiley faces were not Carla's style. Oh, I believed she was truly grateful, but I also suspected that living in such close quarters with me went against the grain for her.

The dogs and I turned onto our walkway.

"Hey, Marcia," a voice out of the darkness.

Squinting, I looked around.

"Over here."

I shifted my gaze toward Sherie's front porch. "Sybil?"

"Yeah." She walked down the steps into the moonlight and stopped.

"I thought you'd be down for the count until morning."

She shook her head. "I made myself get up a couple of hours ago, or I wouldn't be able to sleep tonight." She gestured toward the training center porch steps. "Can we talk?"

"Sure." Again, we sat on our respective steps. The dogs settled at my feet.

"I can't get what we were talking about earlier out of my mind."

I smiled. "You mean the conversation we never had."

A short chuckle. Sybil shifted on her step, so that she was facing me. In the dim illumination from her porch light, her face looked worried. "The more I think about it, the more I can't help wondering..." She trailed off, clasping her hands in her lap.

"Wondering what?" I prompted.

"If maybe Russ Fortham, and perhaps some of the other patients at that place..." She took a deep breath. "Maybe they are being kept there longer than necessary."

CHAPTER THREE

We sat in silence for a few moments, me digesting that Sybil, who'd actually been inside the sanitarium, was now sharing my paranoid thoughts.

And Sybil wringing her hands. "You see," she finally said, "if it's true, I'm obligated to report them. But Dr. Johnson has connections."

"How so?"

"He knows people in the Veterans' Administration. That's how he gets so many referrals from them. And I think he's friends with the governor."

"So if we're wrong, you could lose your job."

She nodded.

"Hey, I have an idea. Maybe there's a way to find out more."

After I'd told her my idea, she said, "That might work. And I'm off tomorrow."

"Then let's head over there, say around ten in the morning."

She nodded again. "Yes, let's."

～

I pulled over to the curb. Once again, the gates next to the small white sign were open. I got Buddy out of the backseat and we walked with Sybil to the driveway. She continued on.

My dog and I hunkered down behind a bush just inside the gates. I peeked through the branches as she stepped up onto the wide porch.

She was dressed casually, in jeans and a peach knit top that complemented her complexion. It dawned on me that I had watched Sybil Wells grow from a gawky teenager into a gorgeous young woman.

Suddenly I felt old.

The ploy we'd concocted, that she'd pretend she had lost a piece of jewelry when she'd worked here a few weeks ago, seemed to work. The door opened. She donned a mask and went inside.

A couple of minutes later, she exited a side door and walked toward the cement-block building in the back of the property. She'd told me that Russ was in that building.

I darted across the driveway, Buddy on my heels. We snuck along behind several bushes, keeping track of Sybil's progress across the lawn. She entered the building.

And we'd run out of bushes. This was as close as we could get.

Not that Sybil really needed us to be close by. But it felt wrong somehow to not be handy, in case the situation went sideways.

Buddy flicked his ear and thumped his tail.

I started to turn as a sharp voice barked, "What the devil are you doing?"

Startled, I fell on my butt.

Mrs. Ratchette stood about ten feet away, hands on her hips. Today, she wore a dark skirt and white silk blouse that made her appear rather matronly.

I stood and dusted off my jeans. "I, um, was admiring the grounds, waiting for my friend." Too late, I wondered if I should be associating myself with Sybil. Had I just gotten her in trouble?

"And what exactly were you admiring under that bush?"

"Oh, I, uh, dropped my phone." I held it up to show her I'd retrieved it. Actually, it had never left my hand.

"Found it!" a voice sang out.

The woman and I both turned. Sybil was striding across the lawn, holding up a silver necklace. The same necklace she'd had in her pocket all along, but this woman didn't know that.

"Good. Let's go." I turned and jogged toward the street and my car, Buddy loping alongside. Again, I could feel the woman's gaze boring into me. I resisted the urge to look over my shoulder.

Sybil caught up as we got to the car. "What were you and Mrs. Rachette talking about?" she huffed out.

"She… asked me what I was doing here." I couldn't bring myself to admit that the woman had found me hiding behind a bush. "I had to say I was waiting for you. I hope that doesn't come back on you."

She shrugged. "I don't like this place anyway. Fine with me if they don't want me back here."

We climbed into the car. "So, did you see Russ?"

Sybil nodded. "I gave him your note and a pen, like we talked about. He read it and wrote something on the back." Her face sober, she handed me the slip of paper.

I looked down at my own handwriting. *Are you okay? Do you know when they are going to let you out? Marcia*

I flipped the paper over. Even though it was what we'd suspected, I felt the blood drain from my face.

I'm fine, but they won't let me out of here. Help!

I'd called Mattie and told her about Russ Fortham's message. She'd said she would pass it along to Janice Robinson.

Feeling more than a little restless, I made myself a peanut butter and banana sandwich for lunch—my fave comfort food.

My phone, lying on the breakfast bar, let out Will's distinctive ring, the opening notes of *Somewhere Over the Rainbow*, the song we'd played at our wedding.

Since we'd been the proverbial ships passing in the night lately, I snatched it up. "Hey there."

"Hey," he said. "I took a chance that you wouldn't be doing any training." Normally during the day, we texted each other first, asking the other one to call when they could, in case I was training or he was chasing bad guys at that moment. He'd been chasing a lot more bad guys recently than I'd been training.

"Nope, but Carla and I will be working together soon, with our new dog, Dolly."

"Huh, how's that gonna work?"

"Oh, um, I didn't get a chance to tell you this morning." He'd been assigned not just one but two new cases and hadn't made it home until after midnight last night. And despite it being Saturday, he'd been up again and on his way out the door, when I woke at seven-thirty. "Uh, Carla's here."

"Huh? What's she doing there?"

"She got evicted," I said, then added quickly, "She lost her job, because of the pandemic. She was a waitress." I made myself stop talking before I blurted out more of Carla's personal business.

I dropped the remnants of my sandwich on the plate in front of me and held my breath, waiting for his reaction.

"I'm confused," he said. "What does her losing her day job have to do with her being there training with you?"

"No, her being here to train with me is a side benefit. I... I said she could stay in the guest suite."

"Oh, okay, now I get it. Because she's already there, it's easy to train together."

"Yeah, out in the yard, where we can keep our distance from each other."

"Gotcha." He chuckled. "About time this pandemic made something easier instead of harder. So, I was calling because Joe is back, and he's taken one of these cases off my plate."

Joe Brown was another detective with the Marion County Sheriff's Department who had once been Will's partner. He'd had Covid back in December and had decided not to get vaccinated, convinced he was now immune. But when he'd recently been exposed again during a drug bust, he'd shown some symptoms and had to quarantine for the last two weeks.

"I will actually be home at a decent hour," Will was saying. "We got anything in the freezer we can grill to celebrate."

"No, but there are a couple of steaks in the grocery order I'm gonna pick up this afternoon."

"Excellent. I should be home by six."

"Um, Will, you're not mad about me letting Carla stay here without consulting you?"

"No. Why should I be? The guest suite is in *your* training center, and I'm assuming she's gonna want to stay isolated over there."

"Well, I guess because my mom was here for so long."

"Wasn't her fault, or yours. She never figured on a pandemic delaying her plans."

"Okay." My mind scrambled for a way to end things on a pleasant note. "Six, you say? Then I'll open a bottle of wine at five, so it can breathe awhile." I said the last two words in a breathy, and hopefully sexy, voice.

"Sounds good." He signed off with another chuckle.

I stared at the few bites of sandwich on my plate, then shoved it aside. Why had I been so uptight about Will's reaction?

On the one hand, I'd known he would be okay with it, or I wouldn't have invited Carla in the first place, without consulting him. Then why the angst over telling him?

I replayed the whole phone call in my head.

"Crapola," I said out loud. Buddy, lying in his favorite spot under the big window in the living room, raised his head and cocked it in his patented *what's-up* look.

"I'm a mess," I told him.

The image in my mind's eye during the first part of our conversation was *not* that of my current husband, Will Haines. It was the frowning face of my ex, Ted Goldman.

How could a two-year marriage that ended over seven years ago still be affecting me?

Maybe it will always affect me.

That thought had me wanting to rip my brain out of my skull and hold it under scalding water in the kitchen sink.

Deciding that probably wasn't a good thing to try, I glanced at my watch. I still had over an hour before my pick-up time at the grocery store.

I texted Carla. *You busy? Want to show me what Dolly can do?*
Sure. Be out back in 5.

I called Buddy to join me, and we went out the slider and down to the gates between the yards.

Carla, *sans* her mask, brought Dolly out the back door of the training center. The Border-Aussie was a bit smaller than the average service dog, but the veteran we were training her for wasn't a big man—only about five-ten and wiry.

She was a pretty dog, black and white with some blue merle around her face that reminded me of my own freckles, although mine were tan, not bluish-gray.

Good thing you're not her main trainer, Ms. Snark observed internally. *You'd have trouble letting her go.*

Probably true.

When Dolly spotted me and Buddy, she pulled some on her leash, wanting to sniff these newcomers.

Carla held her hand out. Dolly touched her palm with her nose. "Sit," Carla said. The dog complied, no longer paying us any attention.

"Cool," I called out. "You've already taught her the on-duty signal." She'd only had the dog for two weeks. Once I'd had my first vaccine, I'd taken the risk to go to the Buckland County animal shelter, where my former assistant, Stephanie Wilson volunteered. Stephie, now a trainer herself, had called me, all excited, saying they had a dog at the shelter who would make a great service dog, but she was too busy with a new day job to take the sweet girl on.

Stephie was right. This dog was as smart as they come.

Carla gave a modest shrug. "I didn't have anything else to do since I'm not working. I taught her the first two steps in the *cover* task too."

I nodded, even more impressed. She'd accomplished a lot in a short time. Granted, those were the easiest steps, teaching the dog to sit every time her handler stopped walking, and then to turn around first before sitting, so she was facing behind her human. The last step was much tougher, training the dog to twitch her ears and thump her tail, as Buddy had this morning at the sanitarium, to announce someone was approaching from behind.

The *cover* task was a crucial one for most of our veteran clients, whose PTSD tended to make them hypervigilant and paranoid about someone sneaking up on them.

Carla put Dolly through her paces, telling her to sit, lie down, heel, stay, and the all-important *wait* signal, meaning stop whatever you're doing and wait for more instructions.

"Awesome," I called out.

"She's ready for more," Carla called back.

"Okay, tomorrow we start on the more complicated stuff." I waved to Carla, and Buddy and I went back through the gate to our yard.

My mood much improved, I headed for the grocery store.

I made it home barely in time to uncork the wine as promised. I slid open the pocket door between our kitchen and the training center just long enough to nudge Carla's two bags of groceries through it. I texted her that they were there.

Will's and my dinner on the back deck started out well. We each had a glass of wine in hand. I'd made a salad and nuked baked potatoes in the microwave.

I sat at our picnic table, watching as he flipped the steaks.

"So, what have you been up to?" he asked, after telling me about his day.

And things went downhill from there, as I told him how Sybil and I had spent our morning. I left out my little *tete-a-tete* with Mrs. Ratchette.

I realized too late that I'd given away something about my client's mental health status, which was a breach of the training agency's confidentiality policy. But I hadn't said Russ's name.

Will had been suspiciously quiet up to this point. Now, he stabbed a steak a little more forcefully than required and flipped it onto a platter.

He let the other one sizzle a while longer. He likes his steak more well done than I do.

He turned and scowled at me. "What are you getting yourself into, Marcia?"

I suspected he wanted to add "again" to the end of that sentence.

"We didn't do anything illegal or dangerous," I said, trying not to sound defensive.

He blew out air. "Other than trespassing."

"Yeah, but I doubt they could charge me with that and make it stick."

He shook his head. "You watch way too many cop shows on TV."

I wiggled my eyebrows suggestively. "I'd rather watch my own cop put on a show."

"Don't try to change the subject."

"What subject?" I gave him an exaggerated shrug. "What's left to say? Sybil and I managed to communicate with him, he said he wants out, and I passed that info on to the people who can probably get him out. End of my involvement."

"Good." He turned back to take his steak off the grill.

"Here's another topic to discuss," I said, as we started eating. "Should we start turning one of the back bedrooms into a nursery, or do you think that will jinx us?"

We'd put the trying to get pregnant on hold for the last few weeks, since the scientists didn't know what affect the Covid vaccines had on unborn babies.

Will smiled. "I don't believe in jinxes, but if it will make you nervous, we can wait. We'll have nine months' notice after all."

"More like seven or eight, from when I'll know I'm pregnant."

He made eye contact, his baby blues serious. "Are you sure about this?"

"Yes, I am." Nothing like losing a baby you didn't know you were carrying to clarify how much you want one. Ever since the miscarriage, I'd felt a yearning that I knew wouldn't go away until I held my own baby in my arms.

But even as I thought that, the niggling doubts raised their ugly heads.

"Are *you* sure?" I asked him, not for the first time.

"Yes." He took a swig of iced tea to wash down a bite of food. "I feel like my life would be fine, great even, as things are. But it would be more complete with a child of our own."

That was the best answer he'd given me yet, well thought out and no hesitation. I shoved the niggling doubts back into the dark recesses of my subconscious.

My phone purred and vibrated on the table. I glanced down at the screen. The caller ID said *Russ Fortham*.

"Oh my. It's my client! I gotta take this, okay?"

"Sure," Will said.

"Hello."

"Wow," Russ said in my ear, "I don't know what you did, Marcia, but it worked. I'm out of that place."

"Really. That's great! Are you home?"

"Yes, and Mom is thrilled. Do you like carrot cake? She's gonna bake you one."

I laughed. "Sure, but she doesn't need to do that."

"Don't worry. She loves baking. Hey, I was thinking about the training set-up. Instead of you coming here, could I come there? You said you have a big backyard. If we're outside and keep our distance from each other, would that work?"

"I think it would. Good idea."

"Would tomorrow be too soon to start? I mean, it's Sunday."

"Tomorrow would be fine," I said.

"You know, that so-called sanitarium…" His voice sobered. "I have an acquaintance in the VA office. I'm gonna talk to him, see if he'll look into that place."

"That's a good idea."

"Anyhow," his voice brightened again, "see you tomorrow morning, say at ten?"

"Sounds good." We disconnected and I went back to my steak, which was still yummy even though it had cooled some.

Will's eyebrows were in the air. "What's a good idea?"

I chewed and swallowed. "Russ thinks there's something fishy going on at that hospital. He's gonna get a friend in the VA to investigate."

Will gave me a mock glare. "Better them than you."

My smile was a little forced. "Don't worry. Not my business."

"That's rarely stopped you before."

I put down my fork, bracing for an argument. Then I caught the gleam in his eyes.

"Oh, you're teasing me."

He grinned and poured us more wine.

CHAPTER FOUR

The Russ Fortham standing on my front porch the next morning looked as happy as I'd ever seen him. The crinkled crow's feet beside his hazel eyes told me he was smiling, even though his mouth was covered by a mask.

Six-four and well over two-hundred pounds—the cardboard cake box appeared tiny in his big hands. "For you and your husband, from Mom."

I took it from him and directed him to the side gate into our yard. "I'll meet you around back. And tell your mom we're very grateful. I haven't had a home-baked cake in eons."

I hurried inside to put the carrot cake in the fridge, then joined him on our deck. Once through the gates into the training yard, we spread out.

Carla and Bear came out onto the small back porch of the training center. My assistant wore a mask and blue latex gloves.

"Wow, she's even bigger than I remembered her," Russ said, with affection in his voice.

I assume he's talking about the dog, not Carla, Ms. Snark commented with a snicker.

I did not give her the satisfaction of a response.

"Does she still jump up?" Russ asked.

"Only under certain circumstances. If you want her to play, signal she's off duty and then pat your shoulders. There's another time when she'll jump too, but we'll get to that."

I waved toward Carla, who was coming our way. "You remember Carla Cummings, my assistant?"

The crinkles next to his eyes were back, and was that a slight pink tinge on his upper cheeks?

"Good to see you again, ma'am," he said. The pink darkened to a rose color.

Ms. Snark wanted to roll her eyes but I wouldn't let her. "Carla will put Bear through her paces so you can see what she can do for you."

Carla had stopped ten feet from us. She waved. "Good to see you again too, Captain Fortham."

"Please, call me Russ." He ran fingers through his hair. His light brown buzz cut had grown out into two-inch waves. They curled behind his ears.

He must've noticed my scrutiny. "They didn't do such a great job of haircuts in that place."

He'd said it in a normal tone, but Carla heard him. "What place is that?" she called over.

I paused, giving him time to answer if he chose to. When he didn't— the blush deepening—I said, "He's been staying away from home so as not to contaminate his elderly mother."

Carla's cheeks paled above her mask.

"I'm not sick," he quickly said. "I've been vaccinated, as a matter of fact." To me in a lower voice, "One good thing about that place, they took Covid seriously. And you could eat off the floor in there."

I chuckled softly at the somewhat old-fashioned saying, one my mom might have used.

I signaled for Carla to show us Bear's stuff, and she did a great job, explaining each task as they performed it.

When they were done, I called for a short break. Carla went inside, leaving Bear with us.

I gave the dog the off-duty signal and she trotted over to where Russ had settled on one of the wire chairs beside my small bistro table on the training center's tiny deck. I worried a little that the flimsy chair might not hold him. He looked like he'd been working out.

Bear put her head on his lap and he stroked her ears. She closed her eyes, a blissful look on her face.

I sat down on the concrete back stoop. Buddy, who'd been snoozing under the magnolia tree nearby, came over and settled beside me.

Russ, being a gentleman, offered to change places.

I waved a hand in his direction. "No, this is fine. So, did they have a gym in that place?"

He nodded. "It's actually a very nice hospital, if you need to be there. But I saw maybe a dozen patients that got better, and then seemed to go into a fog again." He shook his head. "After the first few of them, I wondered if they were being tranquilized. I stopped taking the other pills they brought me, except for the one that I knew was my antidepressant."

He gave me a small grin. "It works wonders, by the way, so I can't say that I totally regret the whole experience. It's really nice not to be depressed anymore."

"They let you refuse the other drugs?"

"They didn't know I wasn't taking them. I palmed them." He twisted his hand around like a magician making some object disappear. "After that, I slowly became more energetic. I tried to burn the extra energy off in the gym so they wouldn't get suspicious. I didn't realize how foggy my brain was, though, until it cleared."

"Wow, they're drugging people to keep them subdued?"

Or this guy is super paranoid, Ms. Snark quipped inside my head.

I hadn't ruled out that possibility.

"And so they can report that the VA patients are still depressed," Russ was saying, "and keep them hospitalized longer to make more money off of them. All the people I saw get better and then get lethargic again were veterans."

I felt a bit queasy at the thought of such fraud being perpetrated at the expense of veterans. "Did you talk to your friend at the VA?"

"Yeah, we had a long chat last night." He shook his head slightly. "I wouldn't say we're good friends. We used to butt heads sometimes when we were in the fraternity at the university. But he said he'd look into it."

"You all ready?" Carla's voice from the kitchen doorway behind me.

"Sure." Russ's crow's feet crinkled again as his eyes smiled at her.

I got up and brushed off the seat of my jeans. We went out into the yard. Carla followed.

Again, I stayed back, letting her take the lead as trainer.

Two hours later, Russ had the hang of the on-duty and off-duty signals, and he and Bear were already starting to work as a team.

"Great job, all of you!" I called out.

"Thanks," Russ said.

Carla's stomach grumbled loudly.

Russ laughed. "Can I treat you ladies to lunch?"

"Sure," I said, "but carry-out from our local diner is all we have to offer in Mayfair."

"A grilled cheese sandwich and some of Jess's wonderful tomato bisque works for me," Carla said.

Russ nodded. "Sounds good to me."

"Me too." I texted my friend Jess Randall, owner of the Mayfair Diner, with our orders.

Meanwhile, Carla had grabbed one of the wire chairs and dragged it out into the yard. She gestured for Russ to take the other one, beside the bistro table. I once again settled on the back porch, and we chatted while waiting for our food.

After a moment, Carla took off her mask, since she was at least fifteen feet from either of us.

Russ took off his as well and gave her a big grin. "I wondered if I was ever going to see the rest of your face again."

Her cheeks pinked. "I'm high risk, so I have to be extra careful."

"Oh." Russ's cheerful demeanor deflated some.

After an awkward pause, I said, "So, have you been to check on your plane yet?"

Russ's private plane, a Cessna I think he'd said, was his pride and joy.

"Not yet. Hey, I was gonna ask you about that. Would it be too soon for me to take Bear up with me, to see how she deals with flying?"

"I don't see why not." Best to find out now if she had any problems with it, so we could work on them, before turning the dog over to him.

"Wow, wish I could go," Carla said wistfully. "I love to fly."

"Really?" Russ's grin was back. "Have you ever been up in a small plane?"

"No, but my mom was a flight attendant. We flew a lot. I love watching everything get smaller and smaller as the plane climbs."

First I'd heard of any of this. And Carla was more enthusiastic than I'd ever seen her before.

Russ slapped his hands on his thighs. "Great. Then I'll take Bear up with me tomorrow. You're welcome to join us, Carla."

Her cheeks pinked again. "Maybe once this crazy pandemic is over..."

"Sure." Russ's big shoulders slumped a little.

"Where is your plane?" I asked.

"At a small private field not far from here."

"Okay, I'll bring Bear over there, say around ten in the morning? And Carla can do some work with our newest dog, Dolly."

Carla nodded, but her slight smile didn't reach her eyes.

As I headed out the front door the next morning, Bear and Buddy in tow, Carla was standing on the training center's porch. "Um, I'm gonna go too, in my own car, so I can watch him take off at least." She ducked her head. "I gotta get out of the house for a while."

"Sure. Why don't you take Bear with you?" I dropped the dog's leash, and Carla called her over.

We both loaded dogs into our cars, clicked on safety straps and drove out of town in tandem.

The Pine Hills Airport wasn't particularly impressive. It was basically a large field, with three strips of concrete for runways, and a squat rectangular main building. Up close, its faded terra cotta paint could've used some freshening, but in the bright Florida sun, anything surrounded by palm trees looks exotic.

There was another long cement-block building with huge garage-type doors sprinkled along the front—hangers, no doubt. But several airplanes were parked outside, at one end of the runways. Beyond was a strip of woods, mostly Southern pines.

So that's the Pines in the name, Ms. Snark commented internally, *but I don't see any hills.*

I ignored her.

"Why don't you stay here with the dogs?" I said to Carla. "I'll go find out if Russ is here yet."

Donning my mask, I entered the building. It was maybe forty by forty feet, the front area set up with lounge chairs on one side and a chest-high counter separating them from a bullpen of several desks.

I paused for a moment and sucked in air. The view through the floor-to-ceiling plate-glass across the front of the building was spectacular—blue sky above the line of trees and the brightly colored small planes tethered to the cement slab on which they sat. A red and white plane taxied to one of the runways and quickly picked up speed. It gently lifted into the air like a bird. I half expected it to flap its wings.

"That never gets old." A male voice.

I turned around. The desks were unoccupied but a man stood behind the counter, his elbows on it.

"Kin I help ya?" His Cracker accent was pretty intense. That and his leathery skin said he was a Florida native, and that he probably didn't bother much with sunscreen.

He was wiry, about six-two, and could've been anywhere from late thirties to early fifties. Tattooed biceps bulged slightly below the short sleeves of his navy tee shirt.

"Have you seen Russell Fortham?" I said. "We're supposed to meet him here."

He scratched the side of his head, making his short dark hair stick out some. "Ole Russ. I haven't seen him in weeks. Thought he was on some kinda trip or somethin'."

"Um, he has been, but he's back."

"Well, his timin' couldn't be better. Charlie just went out to give his plane a safety check. He's been keepin' an eye on it, takin' it up now and again, so the engine don't get all gunked up from sittin'."

I smiled, then realized he couldn't see my mouth behind my mask. I nodded instead. "If you see Russ, could you tell him that Carla and Marcia are out in the parking lot?"

"Mar-see-a," he dragged out the syllables of my name, "that's a real pretty name." He grinned at me.

And it dawned on me that he wasn't wearing a mask. But we were a good distance apart. "Thanks." I took an additional step back.

He gestured toward the wall of glass. "I've been fascinated by airplanes since I was a little shaver, and now I get to watch them take off and land all day. Lordy, I love this job."

I nodded again, sketched him a small wave and walked outside.

Carla had gotten the dogs out of the cars and the three of them were standing at the edge of the parking lot. Carla was shading her eyes, watching the airfield.

I stopped a bit away from her and followed her line of vision.

Another plane was taxiing on one of the runways. It was a gold color, like the plane in the photo Russ had proudly shown me the first time we'd met. I'd chuckled to myself at the time. He'd acted like the plane was his child.

The plane was picking up speed, and then it was in the air. It circled around.

We swiveled slowly, watching its graceful arc.

"That's a beauty," Carla said, her voice kind of breathless.

"I think that's Russ."

She dropped her gaze and glanced at me. "Really? I thought he was taking Bear up."

I shrugged. "Maybe he figured he'd do a test run first."

Her eyes lit up. "Or he just couldn't wait to get that baby in the air."

I watched the tiny Cessna dip and waggle its wings, and I laughed out loud. Russ was having fun. I turned toward Carla, to share the excitement.

Her face had paled. Her eyes went wide.

A loud rending sound of metal ripping apart. The ground shook.

I whipped my head back around.

A massive whoosh, and a ball of flame erupted above the pine trees.

CHAPTER FIVE

At least a dozen people were yelling and running around, most toward the fire, some away from it. A siren wailed from a megaphone-shaped speaker on the corner of the building's roof.

The man from the counter bolted out of the building, jumped into a white pickup, and raced toward the crash.

Heat waves made the images of the parked planes waver. Some of them broke ranks and taxied quickly to the other end of the runways, away from the flames now shooting high above the trees. People exited those planes and ran back for more.

Buddy barked, just as a fire engine erupted into the parking lot. We all jumped back. It raced past us and turned onto the gravel roadway leading to the runways.

Some shared instinct had Carla and me running for our cars, the dogs beside us. Sanity set in, sort of, by the time we got there. We shouldn't both go racing out there, getting in the way.

I turned to Carla. The skin on her face was translucent for lack of blood. She looked like she might faint.

I handed her Buddy's leash. "Keep him with you," I yelled. "I'm going to see if I can find out what's going on."

I doubted she heard me over the deafening siren, but she nodded and started loading the dogs into the back of her car.

I considered taking my car, but with my track record with vehicles—a burning tree would likely fall on it. I took off running instead.

By the edge of the second runway, I had a stitch in my side. Ignoring it, I kept running full out.

By the time I got near the crash site, the flames were no longer shooting above the trees. They were flickering between them, silhouetting firemen and hoses... and a gold airplane tail wedged between the branches of a tree.

Tears and smoke stung my eyes. I leaned over, huffing for air. When I could breathe again, more or less, I straightened.

The man from the building—the airport manager, I assumed—was coming out of the trees, covered in soot and little flecks of foam. He dragged a large red fire extinguisher behind him, on its own built-in hand truck.

"What's happening?" I asked him.

A black hose was looped over one shoulder. He swiped the other shoulder across his cheek, his navy tee smearing the sweaty soot around. Then he stared at me out of red-rimmed eyes, as if trying to figure out who I was.

A small light went on behind those eyes when he remembered. "We got the fire out in the plane. Firemen are moppin' up in the woods."

Another soot-covered man came out of the trees, lugging an oversized yellow fire extinguisher. He hefted it into the bed of the pickup.

I noticed a star shape with a large D inside it on the extinguisher's side. It brought to mind the star-shaped patches on Will's dress uniform. I wanted more than anything to be home with him right now, instead of here. This couldn't be happening.

"Thanks, Ron," the manager said.

"No problem," the other man mumbled in a mournful voice and walked away.

"What's that?" I said, pointing to the star. It was a totally stupid question under the circumstances, but my brain was in babble mode, stalling, not wanting to ask the much more important question.

"It means it's a Class D extinguisher, for metal fires."

"Metal burns?" I asked, incredulous.

"Sometimes, if it gets hot enough." His voice was grim.

My head swam. I couldn't even imagine that level of heat. I made myself ask the critical question. "The pilot?"

He shook his head. "They haven't gotten him out yet, but no way he survived that."

My stomach roiled. "Who was it?"

His eyes softened with sympathy. "It's Russ's plane."

I managed a small nod and quickly turned away, not wanting to break down in front of him. I trudged back toward the airport building and parking lot.

My mind was a jumble, which was just as well. I really didn't want to think right then.

After a few moments, the white pickup pulled up next to me and stopped. "Wanna ride?" the man said through his lowered passenger window.

I was about to say no, when I looked up and realized how far away the building and parking lot still were.

"You can hang your head out the window if yer afraid of my germs." He gave me a lopsided grin that flashed eerily white across his soot-blackened face.

I climbed into the passenger seat. "Thanks," I said, while trying to keep my head turned away from his maskless face.

"I'm Sonny."

Of course you are, Ms. Snark sniped internally.

I mentally shushed her as I glanced his way, not sure what to say.

"You a good friend of his?" Sonny asked.

I shook my head. "I'd only known him a little while, but I really liked him."

"Most people do. He's…he was a nice guy." He drove in silence for a few seconds. "You sweet on him?"

I shook my head again and held my left ring finger out in the space between us. "We were friends. I'm married." I almost choked on the words, trying to figure out how I was going to tell Carla, whom I suspected was "sweet on him."

"That don't always stop folks," Sonny said.

When I didn't answer, he fell silent. At the building, he parked the pickup. "You gonna be okay?"

I nodded, even though that was probably a lie. "He waggled the wings." I imitated the movement with my hands. "I thought he was playing around." My voice choked again.

"Most likely he was havin' engine problems," Sonny said gently. "The sheriff's people'll be here soon. They'll wanna talk to you."

I groaned softly. That meant we would be here a good part of the day. Not that I begrudged the time on Russ's behalf, but the adrenaline was wearing off. I was suddenly exhausted and only wanted to go home.

"Can I leave you my name and number for them? They can call me."

He looked me up and down. "I guess that'd be okay."

I followed Sonny into the building, wrote down my number on a small pad he shoved across the counter, and then gave him a small wave goodbye.

"You take care, Miss Marcia," he called after me in a sympathetic voice.

I nodded and kept walking, tears streaming down my face, out to the parking lot.

"Carla–"

Beside her car, she shook her head, her lips pressed tight in a thin line.

"I–"

She shook her head again, more vehemently. "Meet you back at your place." Her shaky voice betrayed her. She paused, cleared her throat. "You want Buddy with you?"

I glanced in her backseat. Despite the safety straps hooked to their vests, the dogs had managed to stretch out lengthwise on the seat, ying-and-yang style. Their eyes were closed.

"Don't disturb them," I said. "See you there."

Carla pulled out ahead of me. I closed my eyes for a few seconds, gathering myself, before I turned the key. Maybe I should've gotten Buddy out of her car. It suddenly felt quite lonely inside mine.

I drove slowly out the half-mile-long gravel airport road. I was almost to the paved county road when something moved in the rearview mirror.

I automatically assumed it was Buddy.

Wait, he's not with me!

I slammed on the brakes and jerked my head around.

The old dark blanket that usually resided on the car's floor was now across the backseat, something quite lumpy under it. The lumps moved.

I screamed and grabbed for my door handle.

A head popped up. "*Please, Marcia!* Keep driving. I'll explain later."

I gaped at the pale face of my client.

CHAPTER SIX

Carla's reaction, when Russ climbed out of my car, was priceless. Her hands flew to her masked mouth. She ran to him and threw her arms around him.

Then she must've realized what she was doing. She backed away, hands once again over her mask.

"What the heck happened?" I demanded of Russ, for about the twentieth time. In the car, he'd just kept shaking his head. A couple of times he'd said, "I don't know."

Now he nervously looked around. "Can we go in the backyard?"

Our dead-end section of Main Street was deserted, but I shrugged and led the way to the side gate. We settled on the large deck behind the main part of the house, where we could all sit a good distance apart.

I gave the dogs the release signal and they romped off, mock biting at each other. For a second, I worried about Buddy's reaction when his playmate of over a year now was suddenly gone.

I turned to Russ. "Now, *what happened?*"

He took a deep breath. "I was running a little late. I pulled into the parking lot and saw my own plane in the air. I almost ran into a parked car. And then the plane went down." He shuddered. "I was in shock for a few seconds. Then I was going to drive out to the crash, when it occurred to me that someone might have sabotaged the plane."

"Why in the world would you think that?" Carla asked.

He glanced her way, his eyes softening. "I saw you putting the dogs in your car and wanted to tell you I was okay..." He trailed off.

"But what made you think of sabotage?" I asked.

He shook his head as if to clear it. "Yesterday, when I left here, someone tried to run me off the road."

I experienced a momentary unpleasant flashback. People had tried to run me off the road, and one almost succeeded at getting me squashed by a tractor-trailer.

"At the time," Russ was saying, "I thought they must've been drunk or something, but now... I made a snap decision to let everybody think I was dead, until I could get more information."

"What kind of information?" Carla asked.

I was still trying to decide if Russ was being paranoid. Or was he legitimately in danger?

"The cause of the crash, for one thing," he said.

"And who was in the plane?" I suggested.

"Oh, I've got a pretty good idea who it was. Charlie Butler was taking care of it for me."

I nodded, my chest tight for this Charlie, even though I'd never known him. "Sonny said something about him taking it up occasionally."

"I'll never forgive myself," Russ said in a forlorn voice, "for not calling him. If I'd told him I was coming to the airfield today, he wouldn't have taken it up."

"But you would have," Carla pointed out.

He shook his head slowly. "Yeah, but it's hard to get excited about being alive, when you know someone died in your place."

Carla leaned forward, her hand outstretched, then she pulled it back. If she'd been close enough, no doubt she would've patted Russ's hand or arm. "You can't blame yourself. Either it was a freak accident–"

"Or it's the saboteur's fault," I finished for her. "Who knew you were going to the airfield today?"

Russ shrugged. "I didn't specifically tell many people, but anybody who knows me could guess I'd go there soon, after getting out of the hospital. The thing is, not many people knew about that."

"About what?" Carla said. "What hospital?"

Russ's eyes darted back and forth for a second. Then he sighed. "Jo Ann's been telling me there's no shame in it."

"She's right," I said, at the same moment as Carla snapped, "Who's Jo Ann?"

I held up a hand. "His counselor. Let him tell it in his own way."

She shot me a glare.

"Carla, this is part of the training. How to communicate with clients." I sharpened my tone slightly. "More listening, less questions."

Her eyes were still hard with anger, but then she deflated. "Oh." She dropped her gaze. "Sorry," she said to Russ.

"No problem." His body wasn't as tense as it had been. Apparently, our little interchange had given him time to prepare himself to talk about it. "I was in the hospital," he said in an almost nonchalant tone, "to get my meds adjusted, for depression."

Carla audibly sucked in air. "I am so sorry. I'm the last person who should be making you feel self-conscious about that. I'm on antidepressants too."

"I guess this pandemic is making us all a little crazy," Russ said, with a self-deprecating chuckle.

I suspected Carla's issues were no more related to the pandemic than his were, but I let that slide. "So, assuming for now that someone did sabotage your plane, who would want to kill you?"

"I haven't got a clue."

"Anybody at the airfield who dislikes you?" I asked.

"Not that I know of. I've always thought the only enemies I had were those who were trying to shoot down my plane in the Middle East."

"How about this Charlie?" Carla said. "Could somebody have it in for him for some reason?"

"I can't imagine why. Charlie is…was a harmless enough fella."

"Tell us about him," I said.

"An older guy, around sixty." Russ sighed. "He used to have a lucrative charter business, until one of his private passengers smelled booze on his breath and reported him. His business tanked fast and he lost his pilot's license for a while. Sonny gave him a job at the airport, helping out. I guess he felt sorry for him. He's been sober now for a few years, got his license back about a year ago."

"Is it standard operating procedure," I asked, "for airport staff to take people's planes up for them when they can't do it?"

"No. When they Baker-Acted me—before they took my phone away —I called him and asked if he'd take care of it for me. It's an older plane that I refurbished. It's not good for it to just sit around, and I wasn't sure how long I'd be in the hospital. Turned out to be a lot longer than I ever imagined." He shook his head, and his eyes grew shiny. "And I wanted to show Charlie that I had faith in him...in his sobriety...." His voice had grown hoarse. "I never should've asked him."

"You couldn't have known," Carla said. "Who would even imagine that someone would sabotage the plane?"

He nodded, looked away, then cleared his throat.

"Hey," I said, "you'd better call your mother, before she hears about the crash."

Russ turned back, his face pale. "That would not be good." He pulled out his phone and called her. "Mom, if some–"

She'd apparently interrupted him—I could make out her frantic tone even from this distance, but not her words.

"Mom, Mom…" he was trying to break in. "Mom, the rumors of my death are grossly exaggerated."

More frantic noises.

And I felt an echo of my old anxiety about having children. Do you ever stop worrying about them, even when they're in their forties?

"Okay, you're right," Russ said, "I shouldn't make light of it. I'm really sorry you got a scare like that, but I need you to not let on to anyone that you've talked to me. Act like you believe I'm dead." Another pause. "I know, but it's complicated. I'll explain when I get home… I know…" His voice softened. "I love you too, Mom. See you soon."

He disconnected. "Hmm, how am I going to get home? Does Uber come to Mayfair?"

I snorted.

"I take that as a no."

"I'll take you home," Carla quickly said.

"Is that a good idea?" I asked.

"It'll be fine with our masks on. He can sit in the backseat and we'll leave the windows open."

"Okay." I turned to Russ. "Let us know if we can do anything to help you figure this out."

I meant it in a generic let-us-know-if-we-can-help way, but he said, "I may take you up on that. I hear you have some detecting experience."

I grimaced. "Mostly I have experience with getting into hot water whenever I've investigated anything."

"You said your husband wanted to go private. Do you think I could hire him?"

I shook my head slightly. "He hasn't done anything about that yet, 'cause he's been working so many hours. The sheriff's department's shorthanded right now."

"Oh." Russ's shoulders slumped. "I'm not sure where to go from here then."

I thought for a moment. "I can get some background checks run for you. One place to start is the airport. Can you make me a list of everyone there who could conceivably have a beef with you, no matter how small?" I glanced at Carla, recalling her entranced expression earlier, right before the crash. "Including any women who might have shown an interest, especially if they were all star-struck about your flying or military experiences."

Carla was giving me a hot look. I ignored her.

"Why would a woman who's interested in me try to kill me?"

"Motives for murder aren't always rational," was all I said. The thought that had crossed my mind was that a woman who thought of him as a big, strong military man might become seriously disillusioned if she found out he was in a mental institution. It was a stigma my clients came up against all too often.

And if she was a little unhinged to begin with....

He gave me a half smile but made eye contact with Carla. "No, I don't have any groupies."

"Okay, but if you think of anyone who might fit that description, add them to your list. Then I'll get background checks done on them. What's Charlie's last name again?"

"Butler."

"I'll go ahead and order one on him, see if there's anything in his background that might make him a target. But this could get expensive." I told him the going rate for background checks. "Plus an extra fee if you want them fast."

"Oh yes, we want them fast," Russ said emphatically. "Spend whatever you need to."

"The other possible motive," I said, "would be the investigation into that hospital. Did you tell anyone besides your contact at the VA about it?"

"No."

"Not even your mother?"

"*Especially* not my mother."

Carla had been watching us, her gaze flicking back and forth.

"I'll explain on the drive home," Russ told her.

I was silently pleased that she seemed to have learned her lesson and wasn't so quick to demand answers this time.

Russ turned back to me. "I'd be surprised if the hospital thing is related. I just talked to Wes about it Saturday evening, and he wouldn't have been able to even start looking into things until the VA opened this morning."

"And the sabotage was likely done last night," I said, "or very early this morning."

"Besides," Russ added, "how would anybody at that hospital even know where my plane was kept, or how to sabotage it?"

"Did you tell anyone there about your plane?" I asked.

"Only Dr. Johnson, but I never said where it was."

"Probably a long shot, but I'll get a background check done on him too. What's his first name?"

"Robert." Hands on the picnic table, Russ pushed himself to a stand. "I'll get that list to you this evening."

He and Carla left through the side gate, and I looked around for the dogs. They were now snoozing in the shade of a big crepe myrtle bush.

Fighting my own exhaustion, I went inside and to our study, to send off an email to Elise, the owner of the background check company I'd used in the past. I gave her what I had on Charles Butler and Robert Johnson and told her it was a rush order.

Got it, came back immediately.

I sat back in my chair, thinking about Elise. I'd used her services, off and on, for several years, and she'd almost always responded quickly. I imagined her hovering at her computer all day, waiting for an incoming request. But my image of her might not be at all accurate. I'd never met her in person, even though I felt like I "knew" her fairly well.

Odd how we could now have friends online, or friendly acquaintances at least, whom we'd never even seen in the flesh.

My phone announced an incoming text, from Will. *Heard about plane crash. Were u there? U ok?*

Crapola, I'd forgotten that I'd told him my plans for this morning.

Yes and yes, I quickly fired back, getting up and pacing into the living room.

Pilot your client? Bear wasn't w him, was she?

The rushed, somewhat cryptic messages said he was probably in the middle of something. My heart warmed. Still, he was concerned about Bear as well as me.

No and no, I answered. *It's complicated.*

I half expected him to call at that point.

But instead, *Phew! Gotta go. Love u.*

Love u too.

Yup, he was in the middle of something. Some bad guy was about to have a very bad day.

I'd wandered to the slider. The dogs were now standing on the deck, tongues hanging out. I let them in, put Bear in her crate, and flopped down on the buttery-soft leather sofa. I was asleep in less than a minute.

I felt more normal after my nap, which made me realize just how rattled I'd been earlier. It's not every day that one witnesses a fiery plane crash.

Bear was gone from her crate. I started to panic, then thought to peek out front. Carla's car was there. She was already back from taking Russ home.

She must've come and gotten Bear to do some refresher training with her.

After a peanut butter and banana sandwich as a late lunch, I decided to take a walk.

As Buddy and I were returning, strolling down our street, I spotted Sybil sitting on the steps to her front porch. I waved.

She glanced up, jumped to her feet and hurried inside, without returning my wave. Had Sherie called her from inside the house? I hadn't heard anything.

I shrugged and let us into our house. Bear's crate was still empty. I started for the pocket door between our kitchen and the training center, then caught myself. This was taking some getting used to, not being able to move around on my own property as needed.

But for Carla's safety, that's the way it needed to be. I texted her.

Do you have Bear?

Yes, came the answer. A couple of seconds went by, as the three little dots danced on my phone's screen.

I wanted to see if Dolly would stay on task with another dog as a distraction.

How'd she do?

Okay.

Want to test her with Buddy?

Nothing for a couple of seconds, then, *Maybe later?*

Okay.

A light tapping on my front door. So light I wasn't sure if I'd imagined it.

I went to the door and peeked out again. Sybil stood on the sidewalk in front of the house.

I opened the door. "What's up, Syb?"

She ducked her head. "Are you busy right now?"

"Nope."

"Can we talk for a little bit?"

"Sure." I looked over my shoulder. Buddy had stretched out on his bed under the window. I signaled him to stay and went outside.

Sybil moved over to her porch steps. I settled on the edge of the training center's porch.

"Mama's mad at me," she said.

"Why?"

"'Cause I snubbed you. She said I had to apologize."

I gave a slight shrug. "No big deal."

"Actually, it kinda is. Or rather the reason behind it... it's a big deal." She took a deep breath. "I was blaming you, but Mama pointed out that it's not your fault."

A lump of dread was growing in my stomach. "What isn't my fault?"

"That psychiatric sanitarium complained about me. Said they didn't want me back there. I didn't really care since I didn't like it there anyway." She paused, sucked in another breath. Her eyes were shiny.

"Then, this morning, the nursing agency fired me."

CHAPTER SEVEN

"Oh no!" I almost broke my mother's cardinal rule and blurted out a swear word.

"They were already unhappy with me," Sybil said, "because up until recently I wouldn't go anywhere near where I might get Covid, because of Mama... and Edna and the other seniors in town. I didn't want to be the one who brought it to Mayfair."

I got that. Will too had worried about being the index case in town and infecting our older neighbors and friends.

"But there were plenty of other assignments. And once the old folks were all vaccinated, I told them I'd go anywhere."

"So why did they fire you?"

She let out a small sigh. "I couldn't get a totally straight answer on that, but... I got the impression it's related to that place. My supervisor let something slip about me helping a patient escape. Then she pretended she'd said something else."

"Russ didn't escape. They discharged him." Or at least, that's what he'd told me. Had he left against medical advice? Should he have still been in there?

But he was fine. Even after somebody destroyed his plane, he didn't seem depressed.

I wanted to reassure her that helping Russ had been the right thing to do. That he truly wasn't depressed anymore.

But the news would be spreading soon enough about the plane crash and his supposed death. I didn't want to cheer her up only to see her punched in the gut later, when she heard about that.

She was still talking. I tuned back in. "…other patients too."

"I'm sorry, what about other patients?"

"The more I've thought about it, the more I think there were at least a half dozen patients who were fine, who didn't need to be there anymore." She shook her head. "But that's crazy, that they'd keep people hospitalized when they weren't ill anymore."

"Not really. Remember what happened to Susanna."

Susanna Mayfair's father, convinced by a doctor that she was incurably depressed, had institutionalized her, and then told the family she was dead. No doubt, he was trying to spare them continued grief. But he'd died shortly thereafter, and for three decades, no one knew that Susanna was still alive, in the hands of unscrupulous caretakers.

Sybil was staring at me, her eyes shiny again. "I hate it when people who are supposed to be healers take advantage…" she trailed off and looked away.

"Tell me about the patients at the sanitarium, the ones you think didn't need to be there anymore."

She took a deep breath, visibly pulling herself together. "They were lethargic, but I think that was a side effect of the meds they were on. As it got closer to time for their next dose, they'd get more energized. Kind of come out of their stupor. That's when they were most likely to ask the nurses when they were getting released."

It was the same thing Russ had said.

"Can you keep a secret?" I asked, mostly rhetorically. I knew she would. "That sanitarium is being investigated."

Sybil sat up straighter on the steps. "Good." Shoulders squared, she gave a sharp nod. "Tell them I'll testify."

I started to say that shouldn't be necessary, but stopped. If Russ's guy at the VA found true fraud, there could be criminal charges, and maybe civil suits as well.

"Okay, I'll tell them that."

"I'll bet it was that Ratchette woman who complained about me. Dr. Johnson's a sweetheart."

Guilt tightened my chest. "Nurse Ratchette must've seen through our ploy with the necklace and realized we helped get Russ released."

Sybil gave me a blank look. "*Nurse* Ratchette?"

"You know, like in *One Flew Over the Cuckoo's Nest*, only that nurse's name was spelled differently."

Sybil still looked confused.

"It was a movie, based on a book. Set in a mental hospital."

Still a blank stare.

"It starred Jack Nicholson. I can't remember who played the evil nurse."

"Jack who?"

Suddenly, I felt really old. "Jack Nicholson. From *The Shining*… Uh, the Joker in the Batman movie."

Recognition blossomed. "Oh yeah, I've seen that."

The Wells's inside front door opened. Sherie stepped up to the screen door, but didn't come out. "Everything okay?"

Sybil glanced back over her shoulder. "Just fine, Mama."

I pushed myself to a stand, the urge to give her a hug so strong, I had a lot of trouble resisting. "Good chat, Sybil. I'll keep you posted."

"About what?" Sherie asked.

"A job lead, maybe," Sybil fibbed, then turned to me and winked.

"I'm gonna go find that Cuckoo Nest movie on Netflix, she whispered.

Once back inside, I called Jo Ann Hamilton, expecting to get her voicemail. But she answered.

"Hey Jo Ann, this is Marcia. I have a couple of questions about Russ Fortham."

"Oh," she answered in that infuriating way therapists have of saying nothing substantial so you have to do all the talking.

"Remember, I do have a waiver. Did he leave the hospital against medical advice?"

"No, of course not. They sent me a discharge report. It didn't say anything about him leaving AMA."

"Have you ever felt that Russ was paranoid?"

A pause for a moment. "No, I've never seen any signs of that."

Something else occurred to me. "The new medication that he's on, does it have psychoactive side effects?" Perhaps the drug was making him see conspiracies everywhere.

"Um, no, not that I know of."

"What trauma caused his PTSD? I'm not being nosy," I quickly added. "I need to know to tailor his training." Which was true, but not the reason I was asking. I was wondering if the nature of the trauma he'd suffered in combat made him more susceptible to paranoia in certain situations.

Jo Ann had gone quiet. "You don't know then?" she said in a low voice.

I opened my mouth, about to say know what? But Ms. Snark snapped inside my head, *That he's dead, you idiot.*

I had no idea what to say. I'd painted myself into the proverbial corner.

Try the truth. My inner mom this time.

"Can you keep a secret?"

Duh, she's a therapist, Ms. Snark pointed out.

Jo Ann chuckled softly. "I've been known to keep a few."

"But this one might have legal implications." It had dawned on me that we—Russ, Carla and I—could be accused of withholding evidence in a crime. I wasn't sure. It was kind of a murky situation.

And I wasn't sure if I should involve Jo Ann as well. But I hated to have her think her client was dead when he wasn't.

And the authorities would figure it out eventually anyway, when they checked dental records or DNA.

Jo Ann let out a soft sigh. A nonverbal prompt, I suspected.

"Russ is alive," I said.

"What? You're kidding?"

"Nope. It was his plane but he wasn't the pilot."

Silence for a half beat as she digested my news. "Thank God!"

"Amen." I found myself making the sign of the cross, something we Episcopalians learn as children, but I hadn't done it in years.

"Who was the pilot?" Jo Ann asked.

"We don't know for sure. He thinks it was this guy who worked at the airport, who was keeping his plane maintained while he was away."

"Russ must feel awful." Jo Ann sounded a little choked up herself.

"He does, but I think he's more focused on staying alive at the moment. He believes the plane might have been intentionally sabotaged. *And* he's set an investigation in motion into that sanitarium because he thinks they're keeping VA patients longer than necessary, to get more money."

"Ah, thus the question about whether he might be paranoid. Yes, his trauma history may be related. He was flying over Taliban-held territory in Afghanistan when his plane had engine problems. He had to bail. He used his parachute to fashion clothes so he could blend in, rubbed dirt on his skin. He must have looked the part of an innocent farmer because he made it out of hostile territory alive. But it took him ten days and he had some close calls. He had to be hypervigilant and suspicious then. So yes, I would not be surprised if he might be selectively paranoid now, under certain circumstances."

I nodded, even though Jo Ann couldn't see me. "He may be right about the sanitarium."

Her sigh this time was more pronounced. "That wouldn't be a total shocker. Medicare and the Veterans' Administration are two of the most frequently defrauded agencies. Big bureaucracies, big budgets, and ailments and injuries can easily be reported as worse than they are, or can even be completely made up."

"He's got someone on the inside at the VA who's checking into it. Regarding the plane crash, he wants me and another person who was with us this morning…" Dang, had it only been this morning? Felt like a week ago. "He wants us to keep quiet about him still being alive, until he figures out what's going on."

"And I suppose you're right in the middle of the figuring-it-out part," Jo Ann said with a soft chuckle.

"No, not really. I only agreed to get some background checks done for him."

Another beat of silence. "Just be careful, Marcia. I'd hate to see anything happen to either one of you, and if Russ is right, whoever's behind the scam is willing to kill to protect themselves."

"We're more focused on the people at the airport at this point. Until today, only three people even knew about the investigation."

Unless Russ's guy at the VA blabbed to somebody, Ms. Snark observed internally.

And I had told Will, but he didn't even know Russ's name, nor would he tell anyone.

"Still, be careful," Jo Ann said.

"I will, and I'll keep you posted."

"Please do." She disconnected.

I went to the study and checked my email on my laptop. Nothing from Elise yet on Charlie Butler or Dr. Johnson—I'd be surprised if there was. She was fast but not that fast.

But there was an email from Russ. He'd listed three names, one of them a woman, with a short summary of whatever conflict he'd had with each.

This is all I can think of right now. I'll let you know if anybody else comes to mind.

Can I ask a big favor? Can you talk to my contact at the VA and find out what's happening with the investigation into that sanitarium? I can't call him, since I'm supposed to be dead.

I called Russ's cell phone.

He answered in the middle of the second ring. "Marcia?" His voice sounded a little off.

Harummph, Ms. Snark said internally. *He almost got blown up this morning. You'd be a little off too.*

True.

First, I 'fessed up to having told Jo Ann Hamilton that he was still alive.

"How do you even know her?" he asked.

"Oh, um, she is, was my counselor as well. And we have a waiver. It was in the paperwork that Mattie Jones went over with you."

"I guess so. I mean, sure, you need to know what makes me tick. But I never really thought about how you'd be talking to my counselor about me."

It *was* awkward, to say the least. And normally I never say anything to the client about talking to their counselor, but this was not a normal situation.

"I just needed some background on the PTSD symptoms. But she thought you were dead, and I couldn't bring myself to let her continue to believe that."

His secret was turning out to be a hard one to keep.

"I understand. So, can you talk to Wes for me?"

I wasn't crazy about the idea, but I said, "I guess I can get an update for you."

"And see if you can find out who he's talked to about it so far, and whether or not he mentioned my name to them."

"I'm not sure how to approach that, but I'll try to think of some-thing."

He gave me the man's full name and phone number. "I'm sorry to have to ask this of you, Marcia. I didn't really think about how hard it would be to…well, to do pretty much anything when you're supposed to be a corpse." He let out a weak chuckle.

"I wish I knew somebody at the airfield I could trust not to blab about my alive status. I'd love to know how the NTSB investigation into the crash is going."

"NTSB, that's…?"

"National Transportation Safety Board. They investigate all plane crashes. A small plane like mine, it might not be a priority, but when there's been a fatality…" he trailed off.

An uncomfortable pause.

"Okay," I said. "I'll get to work on these names you sent, decide which to order background checks on first."

"Run them all. I can afford it. I need to figure this out pretty quick.

Eventually, they'll catch on that it wasn't me in that cockpit." We signed off.

I wandered out into the living room as I called his VA contact. I'd assumed we would just talk on the phone. But when I said I was a friend of Russell Fortham's and was following up on the investigation into the Leesburg Sanitarium, he suggested we meet in person.

I glanced at the mantel clock. It was after four. "It's a little late to meet today. And I'm self-isolating—until my second vaccine is totally effective."

"No problem. There are some picnic tables out behind the VA building, for employees to use if they want to eat outside. We could meet there and keep our distance from each other."

"That sounds good. Say eleven a.m."

He chuckled. "I'll sure be glad when we don't have to jump through all these hoops in order to have a chat with someone."

"Me too." He gave me the street address for the VA building and told me where to find the visitor parking. We disconnected.

I plopped myself down on a stool at the breakfast bar.

Maybe it was a good thing that I would be meeting Russ's contact face to face. Hopefully, I'd be able to tell whether or not he was lying if he claimed he hadn't told anyone about the investigation into the hospital.

If he hadn't and he seemed to be telling the truth, then we'd know to focus on the folks at the airport.

Wait a minute, not *we*. I was not going to get sucked any farther into this mess.

I'd talk to this Wes guy at the VA and report back to Russ, and order these other background checks. Then I'd be done with it.

CHAPTER EIGHT

A text from Carla. *You want to test Dolly with Buddy now?*

Sure. Meet you out back.

Buddy and I went down our yard and through the gate into the training yard. Carla and Dolly were already there.

I looked down at Buddy and twirled my finger in the air. He ran over and romped around them, acting like someone's out-of-control pet eager to play.

Dolly turned her head toward him, but Carla quickly held out her palm to reinforce that she was on duty. Dolly touched it with her nose.

I clapped my hands. Buddy instantly broke off his annoying-dog act and trotted back to me.

"That's pretty good," I called out. "We'll expose her to Edna's dogs eventually. They're the true test." Edna Mayfair's Springer Spaniels, Bennie and Bo, were almost seven now, but they still acted like over-grown puppies.

Carla waved me over to the deck. She settled on the steps to the back porch, and I took one of the chairs at the bistro table.

"I've been working with Dolly to bark on command," she said, "as prep for the *clear-the-room* task. And I think I know how to tackle the next step."

Since we tailored the tasks each dog learned to the needs of their particular veteran, we sometimes had to create new training techniques. The key is to start with something the dog already knows or does naturally and shape behavior from there.

"One of us inside a room," Carla said. "The other one, outside, points to the door and says 'clear room.' Then the inside person calls her to them, tells her to sit, and rewards her. After a while, we drop the other commands to see if she'll do the whole routine in response to just 'clear room.'"

I grinned. "I see you're getting the hang of this think-on-your-feet style training."

"More like by-the-seat-of-your-pants training, but yeah, I'm getting the hang of it."

"The bark-no bark component will be more challenging," I said. We planned to teach the dog to sit quietly if she knew the person in the room, but to bark once for a stranger.

Carla's face sobered. "I've been reading about the controversy around using service dogs to clear rooms."

I groaned internally. Usually when there was a controversy, Carla and I came down on opposite sides.

"Some say that giving the veteran that crutch means they never deal with their anxiety."

I shrugged. "We could say that about a lot of the tasks the dogs do for their owners."

"True."

OMG, she agreed with us, Ms. Snark quipped inside my head.

"Look," I said, "the people who say that don't understand how anxiety works. It tends to be self-perpetuating. Once it becomes attached to something, the mere thought of encountering that something makes you anxious, whether there's anything to fear or not."

She nodded. "Like I used to get anxious whenever I coughed."

I gave her a quizzical look.

"I'd immediately worry that my cancer was back. Then I started avoiding situations that might make me cough, like dusty rooms."

"Exactly. The anxiety can grow and generalize to other things."

"But eventually," she said, in that caustic, I'm-about-to-be-difficult tone of hers, "I stopped being so uptight about it."

"True, time can sometimes reduce the anxiety." I carefully kept my own voice even. "But it doesn't always. And I'll bet you used some soothing self-talk to calm yourself down."

She snorted. "Not sure I'd call it soothing. I'd tell myself to get a grip, it's just a cough."

I burst out laughing and blurted out, "Carla, that is so you."

Surprisingly, she laughed with me.

Dang, I think we're starting to like this woman, Ms. Snark commented internally.

I didn't disagree.

"The veteran who's getting Dolly," I said, "is practically housebound now, because he's so anxious at the very thought of going into buildings." The Marine had been ambushed while clearing a bombed-out house in Syria that should have been empty. "Even in his own home, he can't make himself go into the bedrooms anymore. He's sleeping in his living room."

Carla's eyes had gone wide. "Oh, that's horrible."

"Dolly will give him a way to talk himself through those doorways. 'It's okay,' he can tell himself, 'Dolly would let me know if there was an enemy in there.' The association between going into a room and the fear will weaken–"

"And the anxiety will fade over time," Carla said.

"Exactly."

"Which is precisely what a 'crutch,'" she made air quotes, "*should* do. Help you function until you heal."

Yup, definitely liking this woman.

Will came home in a great mood.

As had become our routine, he texted to say he was out front, but tonight he added a smiley face blowing a kiss.

His text was my signal to clear out of the bedroom so he could do his decontamination entry.

We'd bought a large plastic hamper and set it under the overhang on the deck, next to the slider leading to our bedroom. When Will came home from his police duties—during which he couldn't always maintain social distancing nor guarantee that the perps would be gracious about wearing masks—he came around through the side gate, stripped on the deck, put his clothes in that hamper and made a beeline for the shower.

I'm in the study, I texted back.

When the slider snicked open, Ms. Snark yelled out, "Streaker in the house."

I couldn't help chuckling. *Thank heavens for our tall privacy fence.*

After he'd showered and donned fresh clothes, I found out that his good mood was because he'd closed a big case. That had been the thing he was in the middle of when he'd texted me.

I opened my mouth to tell him about the plane crash, and that my client, who was presumed dead, wasn't.

"I might even get a commendation for this one," he beamed as he opened a bottle of our favorite wine, "which will look good on my resume as a P.I."

I shut my mouth again as he poured the wine.

He raised his glass in a toast. "To better times ahead."

I lifted my glass. "To excellent police work."

He grinned and then ducked his head.

I couldn't bring myself to tell him about Russ and deflate his mood.

Indeed, how did one even introduce such a topic? *Uh, dear, would I be breaking any laws if I failed to tell the authorities that a dead person isn't really dead?*

I resolved to tell him over breakfast.

So we had a pleasant evening and went to bed early. He was gently snoring within minutes.

I, on the other hand, stared at the ceiling for a good hour before I dozed off.

~

Despite the careful instructions, I was wandering around the vicinity of the VA building, searching for the elusive visitors' parking area.

And my brain wouldn't stop ruminating about keeping secrets from Will.

I'd truly intended to tell him this morning, but he'd gotten an early phone call. Yet another new case, I'd gathered while still in a sleepy fog. By the time I'd gotten myself fully awake and shuffled into the kitchen, the only sign of him was a note propped on the counter. Two words. *Love you.*

Warmth and guilt had vied for dominance in my chest.

I swung around a row of cars and spotted a sign with another two words. *Visitor Parking.*

Finally! I hastily parked, retrieved Buddy from the backseat and hurried around the building.

My "contact" was there, at an over-large picnic table, polishing off something that had chocolate icing on it. A plastic wrapper lay next to his discarded mask.

I stopped fifteen feet away and dug in my purse for the puppy-dog mask that Edna had made for me. Not all that professional but all I had on me. I donned it and walked toward the table.

Meanwhile, Wesley Sullivan had stood up and was brushing crumbs off the front of his pale blue dress shirt and orange and blue Florida Gators tie.

His girth said college football player now slowly going to fat. He could ill afford the cupcakes he had just devoured.

But who was I to judge? My sweet tooth led me astray on a regular basis.

His medium brown hair was short and ragged, like a buzz cut that had grown out some.

"My barber went out of business." He ran his hand through his hair, which I'd apparently been staring at too long. "Haven't found a new one yet. Royal pain."

Even more so for his former barber, Ms. Snark commented internally in a distinctly unfriendly voice.

"I'm Wes." He gestured toward the far end of the table.

I sat down gingerly on the end of the bench opposite his and signaled for Buddy to lie down at my feet.

"So, you want to know how Russ's little investigation is going?" he said.

"*Little* investigation?" Ms. Snark blurted out before I could stop her.

Wes gave a slight shrug. "I've talked to several of Dr. Johnson's VA patients, and they all rave about him. None thought they'd been kept longer than necessary."

He shrugged again. "Well, there was one gentleman who said he was. But on checking his records, I found out that he had an adverse reaction to the first medication he was put on, and they had to switch him to something else. That's what took a little longer than was expected."

"These records," I said, "they're provided by the sanitarium?"

"Well, yes. But Dr. Johnson has a good reputation. He's not likely to put something in a patient's chart that isn't true."

Ms. Snark snorted inside my head, but I managed to maintain a neutral expression. "Who in your organization handles the referrals to that hospital?"

Was it my imagination or did his cheeks pale a bit?

Wait! I shouldn't be able to see his cheeks.

He'd never put his mask on.

I gestured toward the paper disposable mask on the table.

"Oh, sorry." He picked it up and dangled it from one ear. "I figured since we're outside."

Fortunately, he couldn't see my gritted teeth behind my own mask. I didn't say anything.

He took the hint and put the mask on properly. "Um, that's what I'll be looking into next, who referred Russ there. Don't worry. Just because he's gone, doesn't mean I'm going to drop the ball."

"You heard that he's gone?"

"Yes." He lowered his gaze to the table. "Such a loss." He shook his head slightly.

"Have you told anyone else about Russ asking you to check out that hospital?"

His head jerked up. "No. Why do you ask?"

Okay, that seemed sincere enough.

My turn to shrug. "No particular reason. But I think he wouldn't want the world to know that he was in the hospital, even though he's gone. I mean, I think we should protect his reputation."

"Of course." He nodded. "I should go see his mother. Offer my condolences."

"Uh, she's in seclusion right now," I said quickly. "Not seeing any-one."

Last thing we needed was this guy going to the Fortham's house and maybe catching sight of Russ. Not to mention the stress on his mom of having to fake her grief.

Ah, the tangled web we weave, intoned an internal chorus of Ms. Snark and inner Mom, *when first we practice to deceive.*

After my less-than-fruitful talk with Wesley Sullivan, I decided to swing by the airfield before heading home. It wasn't much out of the way, and maybe I could get something out of Sonny about how the NTSB investi-gation was going.

Okay, I'd said I wasn't going to get involved, but I wanted something more to report to Russ than Wes's lukewarm reassurance that he wouldn't "drop the ball."

Sonny was the only one in the lobby area of the airport building. He gave me a mournful look and came out from behind the counter, as if to give me a hug.

Buddy stepped between us. It wasn't an aggressive move, but one he'd been trained to make in order to give his veteran ample personal space.

But Sonny thought better of the hug and withdrew. "He bite?"

"Hasn't bitten anyone yet." Not the level of reassurance I would normally give, but in Sonny's case, I wasn't sure I wanted him *too* reassured.

"How ya holdin' up?" he asked.

I tried to look sad. "Okay, I guess. I still can't believe he's gone."

Because he's not, Ms. Snark chortled internally, making it hard for me to maintain the sad face.

"I was in the area and thought I'd stop by to see what the investigators had to say about the crash." It occurred to me that I'd never heard from the sheriff's office, nor had Carla. Had Sonny failed to pass on my phone number to them, or did they feel they already had enough witnesses to what happened?

"It'll be a while before the NTSB issues their report," Sonny was saying. "But I can tell ya what they found and what I think it means."

"What?"

"They found remnants of fuel on some pieces of the tanks. It was jet fuel."

I shook my head slightly. "So?"

"A lot of small planes, especially the older ones, run on Avgas—aviation fuel. It's real different. Small plane engines won't run right at all on jet fuel, but it would take a little bit for it to mess up the engines."

Still slightly confused, I said, "So the plane would likely take off but then would have engine trouble?"

He nodded, and I discreetly breathed out a slow sigh. No one tried to kill Russ. This Charlie guy put the wrong fuel in the plane. A tragic mistake.

But now Sonny was shaking his head. "The inspectors may rule it pilot error, and maybe Russ did get mixed up after bein' away for so long..."

"But?" I prompted.

He leaned forward, his forearms resting on the counter top.

I resisted the urge to step back from his unmasked face.

My body language must have conveyed my discomfort, however. Sonny straightened and took a step back.

"I hate to have to tell you this," he said in a gentle voice. "Did ya know where Russ really was?"

I didn't respond.

"He weren't on no trip. He was in the looney bin, for depression. I think he deliberately crashed, to kill himself in a way that would spare his mama some pain, if she thought it was an accident."

Without thinking, I shook my head, then realized that was okay. Sonny would interpret the gesture as denial.

"Don't know how else to explain it," he said. "Charlie keeps a log of the maintenance he does on the plane. It says he topped off the tanks the night before. But I found a good-sized damp area in the dirt, off to the side of the apron where Russ's plane is normally parked. I think Russ drained the tanks and put jet fuel in them instead."

"Could Charlie have put the wrong fuel in by mistake?"

Say, if he was drunk. But I couldn't think of a way to bring that up. I didn't even know the man, so how would I know his history with alcohol?

Sonny shook his head again. "Nope, no experienced pilot would get them mixed up. Even if Charlie fell off the wagon—he used to have some trouble with the booze—I don't see him makin' that mistake."

It dawned on me that it would be natural to ask to speak to Charlie. "Is he around?"

"Ain't seen hide nor hair of him since yesterday mornin'. I'm a little worried the crash might have sent him on a bender. Especially if he thinks it was his fault. I stopped by his place on my way in. Locked up tight, nobody home."

He sighed. "If he hasn't shown up by this afternoon, I'm gonna go lookin' for him in the local bars."

Now I didn't have to fake a sad expression. My throat was aching, my heart sore for poor Charlie. "Well, I hope he turns up and is okay."

"Thanks. Hey, can I get your number? I'll call you when we get the official report."

Was this a ploy to have an excuse to call me? Had he forgotten I was married?

Maybe he didn't care.

Maybe that's part of your appeal, Ms. Snark commented.

"I gave you my number yesterday," I said.

"Yeah, but I gave that paper to the sheriff's deputy."

I dug in my purse for my business cards, trying to flash my rings around as much as possible. I found a card and put it on the edge of the counter, then stepped back.

"Thanks, Sonny."

"You take care," he called out as I walked toward the door.

I waved back over my shoulder. "You too. Stay safe."

The mantra of 2020, still echoing in 2021.

This is crazy, I told myself as I drove home. I was definitely done with investigating. I'd been exposed to two guys who were around other people regularly and were pretty casual about mask-wearing.

I'd deal with the background checks for Russ, but that was it.

I pulled up in front of our house, cut the engine, and picked up my phone to call Russ.

First, I filled him in on what I'd learned from Wes and Sonny, while unbuckling Buddy from his safety strap and taking him inside. Again, Bear was gone from her crate.

Buddy immediately went to the slider to the backyard and whined softly, signaling he needed to go out.

"They still don't know it was Charlie in the plane then?" Russ said in my ear.

My other ear picked up the sound of voices, or at least a voice, too low to make out words, coming from the training center. But when I opened the slider, I could definitely hear Carla out in the training yard, giving one of the dogs verbal commands.

Maybe she'd left a radio on inside.

"No," I said as I stepped out onto the deck. Buddy romped down the yard and immediately watered a bush. "My guess is they won't figure it out until the M.E. starts the autopsy, which may be low priority since they think they know what happened."

I took a deep breath, bracing to tell Russ that I wasn't going to be his feet and ears anymore. But before I could say anything, Buddy started barking ferociously and raced across the grass to the gates between the yards.

He was joined by another dog's yaps, coming from the training yard. Dolly.

"Russ, I'll have to call you back." I disconnected and ran for the gates.

I fumbled for a moment with the latch, then threw the gates open. Movement in my peripheral vision, but mainly my eyes were focused on Carla.

She lay in a heap on the grass, Dolly standing over her, barking.

I ran toward Carla, but my head was swiveling around, trying to locate whatever caused that motion. Finally, I spotted the source.

A man was halfway up the back fence.

A fresh surge of adrenaline zinged through my veins. "Buddy, grab leg!"

I crouched down, felt Carla's neck, and sank onto my butt when I found a pulse.

The slam of a screen door behind me. I jerked my head toward the training center.

Russ Fortham was running across the yard, Bear on his heels.

CHAPTER NINE

Russ slid to his knees beside Carla's head and reached for her.

"Don't move her!" It came out harsher than I'd intended.

Russ froze for a beat, then gently brushed hair away from her face. "Carla?" he whispered.

"She's alive but I don't know how badly she's hurt." I looked around.

Bear had taken up the *cover* position beside Russ, and Buddy was trotting toward me, the man on the fence long gone. But my dog had something in his mouth.

"Good boy. Drop it."

He did and I stared down at a small, ragged triangle of denim.

Russ was on his phone, talking to the 911 dispatcher. I caught the words "attacker may still be nearby."

My stomach roiled. I gingerly picked up the piece of cloth by one corner and carried it over to the bistro table. I'd get an envelope for the scrap in a minute.

Coughing behind me. I turned. Carla was clutching her neck and trying to sit up.

"Easy now," Russ said, rubbing her back.

I ran over to them and knelt a few feet away, suddenly aware that none of us had masks on. "What happened?"

"Not sure," she croaked out. "I was working with Dolly, and then she barked at something behind me. I started to turn and…" She coughed for a few seconds.

"I'll get you some water, sweetheart." Russ took off for the house.

Sweetheart?

Bear started to follow, but I called her back and told her to lie down.

Carla stared up at me, wide-eyed, her cheeks pale. "There were hands around my neck." Her voice shook. "They came out of nowhere. I fought but…" She tried to clear her throat but coughed instead.

"Were they men's hands?" I asked.

"I…I'm not sure."

Russ returned, jostling a glass of water. He stooped down and held it for Carla.

She drank slowly, gagging a little.

"I saw a man," I said. "Or at least, I think it was a man—climbing the back fence. Buddy got a piece of his jeans."

"What'd he look like?" Russ's tone said he would dismember the guy if he could find him.

"Tall, thin. Gray hoodie, hood up. I just got a glimpse of him, them— it could've been a woman."

The sirens I'd been hearing in the distance were closing fast. They shrieked to a stop out in front of the house.

I stood up and jogged toward the training center, thinking it would be faster for the paramedics to come through there.

I was almost to the back door, when a male voice yelled, "Stop. Don't move!"

I whirled around. A uniformed sheriff's deputy stood in the open gateway between the yards. His hand was on his holster.

I gulped.

From behind him came a familiar voice. "At ease, deputy. That's my wife."

We all sat at respectable distances from each other on our deck—Russ, Will, Carla and myself. The paramedics had checked Carla over, but she'd refused to go to the hospital. Her voice was hoarse, but otherwise she seemed to be recovering from almost having the life squeezed out of her.

Will had taken some photos of the red marks on her neck. They'd likely be nasty bruises by tomorrow.

Now he had a small notepad in front of him on the picnic table. I wondered why he didn't take notes on his phone, but he seemed to prefer the old-fashioned way.

He cleared his throat. "Let me make sure I have this straight."

I expected him to ask me again to describe Carla's assailant, but instead he turned to Russ. "You're the guy who's supposed to be dead in that plane crash?"

Russ nodded.

"And you think this employee of the airfield, Charles Butler, was the real victim?"

Russ nodded again.

Will turned to me. His baby blues were icy. "This is the crash you witnessed yesterday? You and Carla." The unspoken words hung in the air between us, *And you didn't tell me last night that the guy was still alive?*

I swallowed and nodded.

"You knew he was staying in our guest suite?" His voice was hard.

"No, I thought Carla had taken him home."

"I started to," Carla rasped out, "but then we were talking and we realized it would be hard for Russ to hide at his mother's–"

Russ jumped in. "The houses in Mom's retirement community are right on top of each other."

Will turned his icy stare on Carla. She swallowed hard. "Um, I suggested he stay in Marcia's office."

Office was a bit of a misnomer. The back room of the training center was crammed with old records, but there was a small daybed in there.

"So, what happens now?" Russ said.

Will stared at him for a long beat. "I call my boss."

After the first minute or so, the conversation became one-sided. Will said uh-huh and yeah a few times. Finally, he said, "Okay," and disconnected.

He remained silent for a couple of beats, staring at each of us in turn. Finally, he spoke to Russ. "My captain's checking with the sheriff, but for now, it's okay for you to stay here. We're going to try to keep the fact that you're still alive under wraps until we have a better grasp of the situation."

Will glanced at me. "The autopsy of the corpse will be moved up, to confirm it's Charles Butler."

"Once it's been done," I said, "it'll be hard to keep it out of the news, won't it?"

Will nodded. "Any ideas about who the attacker might be?"

"Tall and thin describes Dr. Johnson at the sanitarium," Russ said.

Will gave another sharp nod. "I'll have a little chat with him."

"They're letting you take the case?" I asked, surprised.

"Joe Brown is lead, but the captain's okay with me assisting."

I attempted to imitate his crisp nods, but I felt like a bobble head.

Will told Carla and Russ that they could go. They walked to the open gate between the yards. Just before they disappeared beyond it, Russ reached for Carla's hand, and surprisingly she let him take it.

Love trumps social distancing, Ms. Snark observed.

I smiled. Despite all the craziness and danger, I was glad they'd connected. Somehow, they seemed like a good match. Russ's easygoing nature would help him tolerate Carla's intensity.

And maybe her intensity was part of the attraction. After all, this man used to fly jets into combat zones.

Will turned to me. "I'm going to go talk with this Johnson." His voice was clipped. "Stay out of trouble."

"Um, Sonny at the airfield was assuming that Russ committed suicide. That could be an opening gambit for you, maybe?"

He stared at me for a moment, then gave another crisp nod.

He headed for the side gate. Was that to avoid contaminating the house, or to avoid me?

A kernel of anger had been growing in my chest, but I was trying to figure out if it was justified. Was I being defensive, or did I have reason to be annoyed?

Whichever, I was not comfortable leaving things as they were. I went through the house to cut Will off. I caught up with him at his truck.

"Hey look, I'm sorry I didn't get a chance to tell you about Russ last night–"

"Why not? We were home the entire evening." His tone was sharp.

"And you were so happy, I didn't want to ruin the mood with all this." I waved a hand vaguely in the air.

He didn't say anything, giving me his blank "cop face."

"I was going to tell you this morning, but…"

His face softened some. "I was gone before you got up." His forehead furrowed.

I braced for…whatever…

"And I never even asked you about the crash," he said in a low voice, "self-absorbed jerk that I am. That had to be pretty scary–"

I put a finger against his lips. "It was, and you're not."

"Not what?"

"A self-absorbed jerk, at least not most of the time."

And we know about self-absorbed jerks, Ms. Snark commented internally, referring to my ex.

Will wrapped his arms around me, laid his cheek against the top of my head. "Still, I'm sorry."

Warmth spread through me. One of the many reasons I loved this man—he was willing to say those magic words.

"I really do need to get going." He pulled back some and kissed my forehead. "I'll bring home Chinese, okay?"

"Sounds good."

Will was late getting home, and I was ravenous. We ate the Chinese carryout in silence for a few minutes.

"So," I said, when my stomach was partially appeased, "what did Dr. Johnson have to say for himself?"

"Not much. He gave me the usual runaround about confidentiality."

"Did you point out that the person is dead? Or at least, he's supposed to be dead."

"Yes, and he pointed out that confidentiality does not die with the patient."

"So he gave you nothing," I said.

"No, he eventually allowed that Fortham might still have been depressed when he was discharged, against medical advice."

"AMA?" My mouth fell open. "He said Russ was discharged AMA?" Will nodded.

"That's not what the hospital's report to Jo Ann Hamilton said."

"Jo Ann?" His eyebrows rose. "What's she got to do with this?"

"She's Russ's counselor, and I have a waiver to talk to her."

Will gave a slight nod and went back to his food.

"Did you think Johnson was telling the truth?"

He put down his chopsticks. "No, I thought he was lying through his teeth, even before you told me about the report. But it could be just to protect his hospital from a lawsuit, in case the NTSB finds proof of suicide."

"Does he have an alibi for earlier today?"

"Yes, he was at the sanitarium all day, and his admin verified that."

"Middle-aged woman with a bad attitude?"

"Yes, and how do you know that?"

"Um, I met her the first time I went there, trying to see Russ." Had I told Will about that? I couldn't remember.

"*Before* you and Sybil went spying?"

I had a bad feeling that I hadn't told him about that first visit. "Well, I ran into the woman then too, but I'd gone over the day before, trying to get in to see Russ. His mom was worried, and even Jo Ann thought it strange that they'd kept him for so long." I hated the defensiveness in my voice.

Will closed his eyes, took a deep breath and let it out slowly. Then he opened his baby blues and stared at me. "So, you've been involved in this up to your eyebrows from the very beginning?"

I took my own slow, deep breath. "I was only trying to find out what was going on with my client." Anger was building in my chest, but I opted to ignore it.

I went back to scooping up noodles—with a fork, having never mastered chopsticks. Heck, I've never even made it to novice level with the dang things.

Will was still staring at me.

I put down my fork. "Look, until yesterday and the crash, I wasn't 'involved' in anything." I made air quotes. "I was *doing my job*. You don't give me a blow-by-blow of everything you do at work."

Will deflated some, his shoulders sagging. "You're right. You didn't know at the time that you were poking a hornet's nest."

I had opened my mouth to offer further defense of my actions. I shut it again. *Did he just say I was right?*

Will scrubbed a hand over his face. "It's not that I'm trying to tell you what to do, but–"

I raised one eyebrow at him.

"Okay, sometimes I guess I do that, but it's because..." His baby blues were now cloudy. "I don't want anything to happen to you."

Was that a slight hitch in his voice?

I swallowed hard. "I'd already decided, before the attack on Carla, that I wasn't going to do any more active investigating. I'm not willing to be out in public that much yet, not until more people have been vaccinated or my two weeks is up."

He nodded, gave me a small smile, and pushed himself to a stand. "I'm gonna go to bed early. Big day tomorrow, now that I have yet another case."

I rose and he came around the table and gave me a hug. "I'll get the dishes," I said against his shoulder as I hugged him back.

He kissed my forehead, then headed for our bedroom, on the other side of the study.

Clearing the table was easier, without Bear's big cage in the way. Russ had taken it back into the training center earlier. But I missed the big dog.

I went to the study to check my email.

There was a preliminary report from Elise on Charles Butler. I got a little excited, until I read it. There wasn't much to get excited about.

Charlie was sixty-five, twice divorced, three grown kids from whom he was estranged. He did indeed have a history of drinking heavily but had been sober for almost three years.

Elise said she would work next on Dr. Johnson and the names from Russ's list.

I emailed her back and asked her to run a background check on Russ as well.

It was something Will had mentioned a couple of times, that he always checked into the background of the victim to see if anything about them connected to any of his suspects, maybe in ways that even the victim or their family might not realize.

Still not one-hundred percent convinced that there was some grand conspiracy going on here, I added a note for Elise to watch for anything that might indicate Russ was prone to paranoia.

But I paused before hitting *Send*. The attack on Carla couldn't be a coincidence. Violence like that didn't happen in Mayfair. But why would anyone attack *Carla*?

Russ had suggested the attacker might have been Dr. Johnson, but that didn't make much sense.

My head was starting to spin. I added Mrs. Ratchette to the email, asking Elise to run a background check on her as well. On an impulse, I also added Wesley Sullivan. If we were going to trust him to investigate within the Veterans' Administration, I'd like to know more about him.

And at this point, the investigation was more a fishing expedition. Might as well cast as wide a net as possible.

Ah, so you are still involved *in the investigation*, Ms. Snark pointed out.

My phone rang. I snatched it up from my desk and hit mute, so it wouldn't wake Will.

Then I looked at the caller ID. *Wesley Sullivan*. Had I conjured him up?

I answered and, once the pleasantries were dispensed with, he said, "I've been thinking about what you asked me this morning. I did mention to a couple of people at the VA about my unofficial investigation, but not who instigated it. I only said it was someone who'd recently been discharged from that hospital."

And you just happened to forget that earlier? Ms. Snark snapped inside, but I managed to keep her from saying it out loud.

"Is Russ the only one who's been discharged lately?"

"No. There were two other veterans discharged from there in the last week."

"Can you give me their names?"

"Um, no, because of confidentiality."

Duh, of course.

"Can you check on them tomorrow, make sure no one has tried to harm them?"

"Why?"

Oops, I'd stepped in some doo-doo. "Um, I'm only making sure that Russ's crash wasn't intentional."

"Rumor I heard this afternoon said it was, that he crashed his plane as a form of suicide. Apparently, Dr. Johnson shouldn't have let him leave the hospital after all."

He sounded angry. Did he blame me for his friend's death, because I'd pushed to get Russ discharged?

"Look, Wes, I've spent some time with Russ recently, training him to use his dog." Well, technically, there'd been more investigating than training going on. "I don't believe he was suicidal. The medication Dr. Johnson had prescribed was working, and he was excited about getting his service dog."

A pregnant pause. "So you think someone *killed* him? I mean, the crash could've been accidental."

"I stopped by Russ's airfield," I said, "after I talked to you this morning. The manager there doesn't think it was an accident, although he's assuming Russ was the cause of the malfunction that brought the plane down. He's probably the one who started the suicide rumor."

If Sonny had blabbed that theory to me, no doubt he'd blabbed it to anyone else who would listen.

Another pause. "Okay, I'm going to get to the bottom of this." Wes's tone was emphatic.

I warmed some toward him. Russ had implied that they weren't really friends, more acquaintances brought together by being in the same fraternity.

"I mean, Russ and I weren't close," Wes said, as if he'd read my mind. "But he was a brother, and we look out for each other. I'm gonna get to the bottom of this," he repeated.

"Can you give me the names of the coworkers you told about the investigation?"

"Um, I don't feel comfortable doing that, not until I talk to them again, see who they might have told. I'll let you know what I find out."

"Okay, and Wes…"

"Yes?"

"Be careful."

"Yeah, right…okay." He sounded surprised, as if it hadn't occurred to him that he might be at risk. "I will be," he added in a more sober tone.

We signed off, and I sat back in my desk chair.

Some of the pieces were beginning to fit together. Somebody Wes had told, or someone they had told, was involved in whatever was going on at the sanitarium.

And that someone had gone after Russ to derail the investigation. My sticking my nose in things had caused them to come after me as well. But they'd gotten poor Charlie and Carla instead.

From the back, she could be mistaken for me, at least by someone who didn't know either of us all that well. Her hair was shorter than mine, but she'd had it up in a ponytail today—the way I most often wore mine. And she was in my backyard, training a dog.

I headed to bed, feeling a bit better. Elise would run the background checks, and Wes was going to investigate behind the scenes at the VA. And Will and Joe Brown would track down the guy who'd attacked Carla.

I felt a twinge of guilt as I washed my face in the master bathroom. I'd implied to Will that I had no intention of pursuing an investigation.

But the decision I'd told him about had been made before the attack on Carla. Someone had come into my backyard, and attacked my assistant, thinking it was me.

I stared into the mirror, about to brush my teeth, and watched my face pucker up.

I'm not going to cry.
I put down my toothbrush and gripped the side of the vanity, trying to sort out what was going on inside. My chest felt like it might explode from the jumble of feelings, all of them bad.

I flashed to the day I'd miscarried and a sob broke loose. I swallowed hard.

Then an older memory popped up, from several years ago when someone had planted an alligator in my living room.

That's it! My property, my sanctuary had been violated. Foolishly, I'd always thought of my training yard as secure, with its six-foot privacy fence separating me and my canine charges from the world.

But apparently six feet was nothing for a reasonably fit man to scale. A cold chill ran through me. We really did need to get to the bottom of whatever was going on. I wanted this investigation done. And these feelings gone!

CHAPTER TEN

I didn't sleep well. Shortly after dawn, I gave up and threw on clothes. It was my morning to deal with the horses anyway. Hopefully, the fresh air would wake me up.

I grabbed two apples from the fridge, one for me and one for my horse, and called to Buddy to follow me.

I was surprised to find Susanna Mayfair at the stable, since it wasn't her morning. She and I took turns tending the animals who resided at the Mayfair Riding Stable—my black Paso Fino mare Niña, her miniature palomino Queenie, and three horses and one pony belonging to various other residents of the town.

Susanna was in with Queenie. She pulled out a denim mask with tiny horses on it, as I walked down the aisle to the stalls.

I donned my doggy-covered mask. "Good morning, Susie."

Her eyes brightened and their crow's feet crinkled at the nickname, originally bestowed upon her by her Aunt Edna. But now it was commonly used around town, ever since the gentleman who'd fallen head over heels for her had started calling her "my Susie."

"So, what brings you to the barn this early?" I asked.

Her face fell and she quickly turned away. "Just wanted some quality time with Queenie."

I didn't believe that for a New York minute. "Your aunt in a bad mood?"

It was an educated guess. None of us were as cheery as usual, but the isolation brought on by the pandemic had hit my octogenarian friend Edna the hardest. She'd poured her heart and soul into turning Mayfair into a tourist attraction, and she'd been making some headway, when everything was shut down.

And because she was in her eighties, and Susanna and her husband were in their sixties, Edna's motel had stayed closed until recently.

The Mayfairs had money. They weren't going to starve. But Edna didn't know what to do with herself with no work to be done.

Susanna had hesitated, but now she was nodding. "Worse than usual," she said. "Ever since that sheriff's deputy came callin' late yesterday. He told her he was assigned to Mayfair now and would be 'patrolling,'" she made air quotes, "and 'providing a police presence.'" More air quotes.

This was news to me. A police presence, in Mayfair?

"Aunt Edna's been going on and on ever since, about how it'll give the impression that Mayfair's not a safe town." Susie rolled her eyes. "I couldn't take it anymore so I left poor Dexter to do the nodding and mmhming."

I smiled at her use of *mmhm* as a verb. Dexter, Susanna's son, had certainly had lots of practice listening to his great aunt's occasional rants through the years, since she'd raised him.

Then it hit me why the deputy was in town. Guilt twisted my stomach. It wasn't my fault really. I hadn't invited Russ to stay with us, Carla had. And how could I have known a few questions would lead to someone attacking her, thinking she was me?

My rationalizing did nothing to ease the vise around my chest. Once again I'd brought danger to quiet, peaceful Mayfair. The last time that had happened, a crazy woman had burned down Edna's motel.

"Anyway," Susie said, brightening some. "You want some help with the stalls?"

"Sure. Thanks." I headed for the feed and tack room, still trying to shake the guilt feelings.

Once the chores were done, I took Niña out for a quick romp around the fields behind our house and Sherie's. Buddy ran along beside us.

We enjoyed the pleasant, early morning air. It was the tail end of one of our long, beautiful Florida springs. Soon it would be hot even in the mornings—just less hot than the afternoons. And the bugs would be out full force. We'd still ride, but it wouldn't be this delightful.

I turned us back toward the barn, my mood much improved.

I patted Niña's black neck as we stopped at the side of the road. I glanced down at Buddy. His head was up, gazing at me, tongue lolling out to one side, looking for all the world like he was smiling.

We were about to cross the road to the barn when a sheriff's department cruiser rolled to a stop in front of us. The window whirred down and a familiar face grinned up at me.

"Hey, Marcia, how's it going?"

"Johnny! How'd you get stuck with this duty?"

"I asked for it." Deputy John Redmond's brown eyes sparkled in his broad face. "I'm thinking about moving here."

Hmm, maybe to be nearer a certain diner owner, Ms. Snark observed internally.

I hid a smile. He and Jess had been "an item," as my mother would say, for over a year now.

John stuck his hand out the window, holding out a business card. "My cell number's on the back if you need anything."

Since I couldn't readily reach it from my horse's back, I said, "Buddy, get card."

He trotted over and took the small piece of cardboard gently in his teeth.

"Well, I'll be…" Johnny waved and drove away.

We crossed the road to the barn. I dismounted and took the slightly soggy card from my dog. "Thanks, boy."

At the house, Carla was working with Russ and Bear. Buddy and I slipped quietly through the gate.

Technically, I still had to observe Carla as my trainee, but she was doing fine. Dolly would be the last dog we worked with together.

Carla turned, and I spotted the black and blue marks on her neck. I winced. Thank heavens, Buddy and I had shown up when we did.

I shuddered as I remembered that the guy had been after *me.*

She called for a break, and Russ headed for the training center.

Carla came my way, Bear in tow. "They're doing really well," she called out, then stopped suddenly, hugging herself—at the same spot where she'd been attacked yesterday.

Bear whipped in front of her and jumped up, wrapping her front legs around Carla's waist. She staggered a little but stayed on her feet.

Russ turned and bolted back across the yard. "What's wrong?"

"Bear's doing her job," I said. "Remember I told you there was another situation where she would jump up? This is it. But I'll let Carla explain."

I backed away and acted like I was inspecting the magnolia tree's new buds. A man talking about anxiety attacks and flashbacks to *one* woman would be embarrassing enough.

I observed out of the corner of my eye. Carla had signaled Bear to get down. Now she was talking to Russ in a low voice.

His cheeks pinked but he nodded. Then he crouched down and rubbed Bear's head. "You're full of tricks, aren't you, girl?"

I made a note to compliment Carla later on how she'd handled that. She was definitely becoming more sensitive to the emotions of our clients.

Or she's just more sensitive to this particular client, Ms. Snark added her skeptical viewpoint.

I ignored her, even though she was probably right.

I heard that. She snickered inside my head.

The rest of the day went by without drama. Carla and Russ continued training together with Bear, and continued to observe—both the training and their budding romance.

Around four, Elise sent initial reports on two of the three people on Russ's list. No red flags in them. No run-ins with the law except for a few traffic tickets. One had been involved in a lawsuit, which was finally settled out of court. No details regarding what it was about. He flew charter flights for a small company in Gainesville.

The other—the woman—was a waitress. Her husband was a small plane enthusiast. And they had relocated to California two months ago, which gave her a pretty good alibi, unless she'd come back for a visit recently.

Sorry this is taking longer than expected, Elise had written in her cover email. *I've been under the weather some lately—not Covid! But now I'm kind of slammed, trying to get caught up. I won't charge the rush fee but I will get to the others as fast as possible.*

I sighed. I'd never given her such a long list of people to check out before. I'd have to be patient.

On Thursday morning, I left Carla and Russ to their own devices and did some work with Dolly. We'd barely started when my phone began playing *Somewhere Over the Rainbow.*

Will usually texted first. Slightly alarmed, I gestured for Dolly to lie down, and I answered the call.

"Hey, I wanted to give you a heads up." His voice was sober. "The M.E. finished the autopsy on the plane's pilot."

"Oh yeah?"

"He confirmed the body was Charles Butler."

My chest tightened. I swallowed the lump in my throat. "Anything else interesting?"

"No alcohol in his system."

I wasn't sure how to feel about that. On the one hand, I was glad Charlie hadn't fallen off the wagon. But if he had, that could have given an alternate explanation for the wrong fuel, other than sabotage.

Will cleared his throat. "And keep this to yourself…"

I'd assumed the whole conversation was confidential, so what could be even more so?

"The NTSB investigator gave us an unofficial initial report. He found a piece of one of the fuel tanks that had a small, round hole through it. Way too neat to have been caused by the crash."

That slowly sank in. "A back-up plan, in case the wrong fuel didn't clog the engines enough to bring the plane down."

"Yup, it was definitely sabotage," Will said.

A warm glow grew in my chest, even as my throat closed again at the thought of poor Charlie. I loved it when Will treated me this way, like a partner in a case.

We signed off and I looked down at Dolly, lying patiently at my feet. "Best we avoid the lovebirds today," I told her. I was afraid I'd let some of Will's news slip out, especially if either of them asked if I'd heard anything.

I did *not* want to blow Will's trust.

My guess was Carla and Russ wouldn't miss me. Indeed, they might not even notice that I wasn't around.

I was back to being on my own most of the time, with Will working long hours, and Carla and Russ absorbed in their little world of training and romance.

I'd temporarily taken over working with Dolly, but you can only train so many hours a day. I filled the rest of my time with long walks, naps, reading, and Sophie's self-defense videos.

Thursday evening, Will informed me that he'd been taken off the case. His captain had gotten wind that the attack on Carla had likely been meant for me. That constituted a conflict of interest, so now Joe Brown was solely in charge of the investigation into that attack and the plane crash. But he was keeping Will in the loop as a professional courtesy.

On Friday, Becky and I finally caught up with each other, after playing telephone tag for days. I ducked her questions about my life— too much of what was going on was confidential. If I mentioned any of it, I knew I'd blurt it all out. I diverted her focus back to her family. Her tales of my godchildren's antics cheered me up considerably.

Maybe having a kid would be a good thing. *Dear Lord, just don't give me twins!*

I was enjoying an afternoon nap on our living-room sofa when a cold nose poked my arm.

I opened one eye. Buddy's face was a mere inch from mine. "What's up, boy?"

He ran to the slider to the backyard and let out a sharp bark.

My heart went into overdrive. I jolted to a sitting position. He almost never barked like that. Most of his territorialism had been trained out of him years ago.

But Will had taught him some of the tactics used by the department's K-9 unit. And right now, Buddy was in full *protect* mode, his fur standing up along his neck and back.

I jumped up and ran to the slider, expecting to confront a garotte-wielding attacker.

Instead, a parade of law enforcement marched across our back lawn. Two uniformed deputies and, in front, Detective Joe Brown.

Will came into sight, bringing up the rear.

Signaling for Buddy to stay, I hurried outside and followed them to the gate between the yards. I froze in the open gateway.

Joe Brown was reading Russ his rights while a deputy cuffed him.

CHAPTER ELEVEN

I stayed out of the way, well aware that I'd better not try to intervene. But I managed to catch Will's eye and tilted my head in an imitation of Buddy's *what's-up* look.

He came over to the gate.

"Why is Brown arresting Russ?" I hissed in a low voice.

"Negligent homicide. I'll explain in a minute," he whispered back.

"I thought you were off the case."

"I tagged along…" He trailed off, but I could fill in the rest. To make sure I didn't interfere and get myself arrested.

Or he could've been worried that you'd get hurt, inner Mom pointed out.

We stepped aside as Will's former partner led the way, the deputies escorting their prisoner between them back through the gate.

Russ gave me a pleading look as they passed us.

I responded with a slight nod.

We watched them march across our backyard. "Brown's theory of the case," Will said in a low voice, "is that Russ sabotaged his plane to commit suicide, but in a way that would be less painful for his mom. But Charles Butler took the plane up, because Russ failed to inform him that he was coming to the airfield that day and planning to fly it."

"Russ then is responsible for his death?" My tone was incredulous. "Can they really arrest him for that?"

Will nodded. "Whether the State Attorney's Office will actually prosecute is another story."

"What are we going to do?" Carla's voice was a borderline wail and she was staring at me.

Her presence, standing well back from the others, had registered on the periphery of my brain earlier, but I hadn't heard her approach us.

"You," Will pointed to me and then to her, "aren't going to do anything. This is a police matter and–"

"We could be arrested if we interfere," I impatiently finished his sentence. "So, what are *you* going to do about it?"

At least Will had the good grace to look chagrined. "Unfortunately, there isn't anything I can do. It's not my case and Joe feels he has enough evidence to make the arrest. A gas can with Fortham's prints on it was found in the grass near where his plane is usually parked. It had some jet fuel still in it."

I was a little surprised that he was telling us what evidence Joe had. Was it a sign of how frustrated he was with this case? Or a sign of how frustrated he was with the job in general?

Out loud, I said, "What does that prove? It could be Russ's can but someone else, wearing gloves, used it. Or they planted it there to incriminate Russ. A gas can would be an inefficient way to fill the fuel tank. It would take dozens of trips, from wherever the fuel is in that airport."

We had wandered to the deck and now sat, Will and I a respectable distance from Carla.

"Joe's got that Dr. Johnson at the sanitarium, too," Will said, "claiming that Russ was still depressed and left the hospital against medical advice."

My chest and stomach tight, I said, "That's not what the report sent to his counselor said. I double-checked with her on that."

Will shook his head. "Johnson will probably claim that the report to Jo Ann was incorrect."

"That sounds like you believe Russ is innocent." My insides relaxed some.

Will pursed his lips, then blew out air. "I'm not sure what I believe. But one good thing, if there is someone behind all this, they've got no reason to try to kill him now, or you."

"Because he'll be discredited," Carla said, her voice bitter, "as a suicidal crackpot." Had she been dismissed by authorities as a crackpot when she'd tried to report her ex-husband's abuse?

Will gave her a grim nod.

I ground my teeth. "Wait, how's Brown explaining the attack on Carla, which was meant for me?"

Will's already tense face tightened even more. "He's decided it's unrelated, just some addict planning to break into the house and ran into Carla in the yard."

"He doesn't know this town," I said hotly, as Carla demanded, "Then why'd that guy sneak up on me?"

"Yeah," I said, "it's not like he was halfway across the yard and she spotted him, so he had to disable her to get away. She never even knew he was there."

"Right," Carla said.

Will turned to her. "Detective Brown's alternate theory is that Russ is the one who snuck up on you, to strengthen his claim that someone was out to get him and to stop Marcia from investigating."

My mouth fell open. Carla looked aghast.

"That's not even possible," I said. "The guy was barely over the fence when Russ came out of the house. Unless he's got Star Trek transporter technology, he couldn't have been the attacker."

"Tell that to Joe Brown," Will said.

"I will." I stood up.

He jumped to his feet. "Where are you going?"

"To tell Joe Brown what I think of his theories."

Will grabbed my wrist. "He'll only go back to the drug addict angle."

"But we can get dozens of people from Mayfair to testify that there are no druggies in this town."

"And is a jury in Ocala going to believe that?" Will said.

I deflated. "No, probably not." The county seat, Ocala was a medium-sized city, but it had more than its share of big city problems with a crime rate twice the national average.

Which was one of the reasons I'd moved south from there to Mayfair, shortly after relocating to Florida.

Will slid his hand down to mine and squeezed it. "I need to get back to work. You two," his voice had turned plaintive, "please just stay home and train dogs."

I bristled, tried to pull my hand loose. He held on.

"Will Haines, if you're not going to do anything, then I am. I'm not going to let Russ be railroaded for something he didn't do."

He squeezed my hand again. "Sweetheart, he'll get a lawyer," he said in a gentle voice, "who'll have him out on bond by this evening. He can do his own investigating now, or hire a licensed P.I."

Carla perked up. "He'll be out tonight?"

"Most likely," Will said. "But he's not coming back here. He doesn't need to hide out anymore."

Carla's face fell slightly. "But he'll be out?"

Will nodded. He pecked me on the cheek. "Gotta go," he whispered and headed for the side gate.

"He'll be out," Carla said again softly, her eyes out of focus, kind of dreamy.

But such was not to be the case.

I needed to burn off some angry energy and figured some time spent with a self-defense video might do the trick.

The one I cued up was my least favorite, since Sophie tended to have a tinge of snide under her Irish brogue in it, and the workout was a bit boring. But the content fit my mood today. There was a lot of kicking involved.

So, ladies, ya believe that yer fat because ya've got those big thighs and hips?

Sophie was on her side on a mat, raising her upper leg up and down in a warm-up exercise.

Well lemme tell you that those big thighs are powerful.

I laid on my side on the rug and warmed up as well.

Mr. James Watts, a Scottish fella whom ya might not be surprised to hear discovered the watts in electricity, that were named after him. Well, he was the one that came up with the idea of horsepower. He was thinkin' of those big draft horses when he decided that one horsepower was equivalent to one of those big bruisers galloping along.

I'd looked up horsepower and James Watts online. The only parts she'd gotten completely right were that Watts did discover the electrical unit that bore his name and he had coined the term *horsepower.*

I switched sides as Sophie continued spreading misinformation and mixing metaphors.

Now, the average automobile engine has about two hundred horsepower. And yer thighs, they're like one of them engines. Ya've got some of them two hundred big horses behind each kick. They're like the pistons in the engine, yer legs are.

Sophie shot out her top leg. *Now be sure not to hyper-extend yer knees, my lovelies. But put all of that horsepower in yer hips and thighs —which you think of as bein' so full of fat when they're also full of muscle—put all that behind each kick.*

And kick and kick…

I rewound and repeated the five-minute, leg-lifts-and-kicking segment to extend my workout, then let the rest of the video play out.

Now, here's the part where ya need to use yer imaginations, ladies. Imagine there's a bruiser of a man, who means to do ya harm, standin' over ya.

My imaginary man today looked suspiciously like Joe Brown. Not exactly a bruiser, but definitely the man I would most like to kick at the moment.

Now kick him in the knees. Sophie kicked out, and so did I.
Ya heard me right, ladies. In the knees. They're right there in front of ya. And if ya give 'em a good, strong kick…

She kicked out hard and so did I.

He'll go down every time, most likely screamin' in pain. Then you scurry backward.

Sophie demonstrated scrambling away on her elbows and feet. I scrambled backward across the rug.

Now, if ya need to kick him agin, ya only need to flip over on yer side. But most likely, he won't be gettin' up right away, and ya can holler for the Garda or get up and run away yer own self.

I stood and clicked the video off, and my mind immediately circled back to thinking about Russ in jail. Feeling hollow inside and a little queasy, I went to the kitchen to get a light snack, hoping it would settle my stomach.

Late that afternoon, I checked my email and found a report from Elise on Russ Fortham. Nothing in the report was all that interesting but the email it was attached to said, *Call me when you get this.*

Elise picked up halfway through the second ring. "Marcia?" She sounded out of breath.

"Are you okay?"

"Yeah, um, I was on my exercise bike." Her voice sounded odd. "Lemme grab a towel."

A long pause. Then, sounding slightly less winded, "Did you read the report on Russell Fortham?"

"Yes," I said, intrigued. Elise rarely communicated via anything but email.

"I didn't want to commit this to writing," she said. "But I found some things that could possibly indicate paranoia. One, he filed for divorce, ten years ago, on the grounds of adultery, but he couldn't prove it. And his wife claimed in court..." Elise stopped, loudly sucked in air. "She said he was always accusing her of cheating on him, that she couldn't take the jealousy and paranoia—her word—anymore, so she countersued on grounds of incompatibility."

The most common grounds given these days. It covered a multitude of sins.

"I dug into his employment records as well," Elise said. "In his early twenties, he filed for unemployment. He claimed he lost his job because he accused two other employees of stealing from the company, a construction firm. He said he saw the first guy stealing supplies, but no proof, so management let it go. Then he accused a second guy of the same thing, but the supplies were found in the back of Fortham's own pickup truck. He swore the two guys set him up, but he was the one who got canned."

I sat back in my desk chair and scrubbed a hand over my face. Now I didn't know what to think.

"Okay, thanks." I paused, a little worried, but also not sure how this woman I'd never met in person would take it if I came across as too nosy.

"I'll get started on the other background checks now," Elise was saying.

"Great. Uh, you said you'd been under the weather. Are you okay now?"

"Oh yes, right as rain." Her tone was cheerful.

Maybe a bit too cheerful?

Don't be a nosy Parker, my inner Mom admonished.

"Okay. Sorry to add so much work to your pile."

"No problem. I'll get caught up soon."

We said our goodbyes and disconnected.

I stared into space for a moment. Was Russ paranoid? Had he imagined the whole sanitarium fraud scheme?

But what about the sabotaged plane? And the attack on Carla, which was probably meant for me?

And Sybil was inclined to agree with Russ that patients were being sedated and kept longer than necessary at the sanitarium. But could she be succumbing to the power of suggestion? Then again, if all that wasn't happening, if there was nothing to cover up... why was she fired?

I was still waffling the next day. What if I kept investigating and pissed off Will only to have the whole thing turn out to be Russ's paranoid fantasy? Not only would I feel like a fool but I could do harm to my marriage.

I shook my head and then did what any all-American girl would do. I called my best friend.

"Hey, you," Becky answered, in her usual cheerful voice. "How ya doing?"

I pictured her in my mind's eye—dark curls around her fair, heart-shaped face and a big smile.

"I'm okay, but I've got something going on with a client that I need to sort out."

"The twins are down for a nap, so sort away."

Without naming names or giving too many details, I told her about "the client" whom I couldn't quite decide was on the up-and-up.

"One of these days," I concluded with a sigh, "I'll figure out the formula for whether or not to trust people."

She laughed. "Marcia, there is no magic formula. You go with the information you have at the time and then trust your gut."

I chewed on that for a moment. "That's always been the problem. I don't trust myself to be a good judge of character."

The sound of air being blown out. "Because of your ex-husband."

"Well, yeah," I said. "That was a pretty big mistake."

"And how old were you when you made it?"

"Twenty-five, and… Okay, that was a decade ago, but–"

"No buts–"

She was starting to annoy me. "This coming from the woman who was also gun shy for years."

Another sigh. "Yes, but when I met Andy, I knew he was different." A beat of silence. "Now, back to your client. What do you *know* about him? And what is your gut instinct about that knowledge?"

"He's pretty easygoing." I paused, thought for a second. "But he's got a strong sense of duty, so he'll take up a fight if he feels it's important. I think he's honest. At least, I've never known him to lie." Withhold the truth maybe, like the fact that he was still alive.

"And your instincts say?"

"That he is what he seems to be, but none of those traits would negate that he might be paranoid too, and might see enemies where none exist."

"But someone tampered with that plane," Becky said, "and he's now in jail for it."

My stomach tightened, then I smiled at the phone. I'd said only that someone had tampered with a vehicle which had caused another person's death. She'd made the connection to the plane crash that had been all over the news in this part of Florida. But I could trust her to be discreet.

"So there's a real situation here," she concluded. "He's not just being paranoid."

"But what about the info Elise found on him?"

"In my opinion, it's pretty flimsy evidence. The stuff with his wife might only be he said/she said. Maybe he's the jealous type, or maybe she *was* having an affair. And being jealous in relationships doesn't necessarily mean he's paranoid in general. As for the work situation in his youth, you said he had a strong sense of duty. Well, I'd say that goes hand in hand with a strong sense of justice. And hmm, who else do I know who has to right a wrong when she sees it?"

I chuckled. "Okay, I get it. Those two situations don't make for a very strong history of paranoia. Okay, enough about the case. Tell me about my darling godchildren."

We chatted about the twins for a bit—Winston and Jasmine, or Winnie and Jazzie to their Aunt Mar-Mar. As we signed off, I said, "Thanks for the free therapy."

"Hey, that's what best friends are for."

Two hours later, while Carla and I were working with Dolly, my phone vibrated in my pocket. I surreptitiously checked the caller ID, in case it was Russ.

It wasn't, but the ID said *Barton and Stone*. My gut said it wasn't a scammer or telemarketer.

And Becky was just reminding us earlier to trust our gut, Ms. Snark pointed out.

I stepped away and answered the call.

"Ms. Banks-Haines?" A female voice.

"Yes?"

"Hold for Mr. Barton."

Did people really still do this? Have their secretaries place calls for them, leaving the other person chilling...

"Ms. Banks-Haines, my name is John Barton." A stiff male voice. "I'm Russell Fortham's attorney."

Really glad I'd picked up, I said, "How's he doing?"

A pause. "As well as can be expected. He asked me to tell you what is going on and convey a message."

"Is he out on bail yet?"

"I'm afraid not. His hearing won't be until Monday morning."

Dang. Carla was not going to be happy about that.

"This is most irregular," the lawyer said in a pompous voice, "but he asked specifically that I call you."

Was he born with that stick up his you-know-what? Ms. Snark queried internally, *Or do you think he developed it over time?*

I ignored her.

"His message is, and I quote..." Paper rustling. "'Tell Marcia to call our contact and tell him not to give up.' Does that make sense to you?"

"Yes."

"Ms. Banks-Haines, he told me you'd been helping him. We have a private investigating firm on retainer. We can investigate this case far easier than you can. You're an amateur."

Who's he calling an amateur? Ms. Snark snapped.

I'd begun to bristle but Ms. Snark's offended tone made me want to laugh.

This was what Will had been talking about—the moment when I could, without guilt, turn the whole thing over to someone else.

But I found myself saying, "Thanks for the info," without committing to backing off. "Tell Russ we're..." I didn't want to promise too much, "we're on his side."

I had wandered over to the training center's small deck while we'd been talking. Disconnecting, I sat down hard on one of the chairs at the bistro table.

If I did continue to investigate, I had no idea where to go from here, other than calling Wes Sullivan with Russ's message.

My phone vibrated on the metal table. Caller ID said *Joe Brown.* I groaned, but I answered it.

"Ms. Banks-Haines, where are you?" His tone was mildly accusatory.

None of your business, Ms. Snark said internally.

"I'm training at the moment," I said into the phone.

"At your house?"

"Yes."

"I rang the bell and no one answered."

Crapola, he's on my front porch!

"I'm in the training center yard, but don't come back here. My assistant is working with one of the dogs. Meet me on the main deck behind our house."

I signaled to Carla, pointed to the phone and mouthed, "I've got to deal with this."

She nodded without breaking stride and continued to put Dolly through her paces.

Buddy and I went through the gates just as Detective Brown stepped up onto the large deck. I hurried over and gestured toward the picnic table. "Would you like some iced tea?"

He shook his head and sat on one of the table's benches. I perched on the side of a chaise lounge about six feet away and donned my mask. Buddy settled at my feet.

"I'd prefer that you leave that off while I'm questioning you."

"And I'd prefer not to catch Covid," Ms. Snark snapped before I could stop her.

"I've already had it."

"Which doesn't mean you can't still be a carrier." We were not off to an auspicious beginning here.

You've never really liked this man, have you? Ms. Snark said internally.

No, not really. Joe Brown was a drab man, his clothes and his demeanor matching his last name. And now he was turning out to be small-minded as well.

He pulled out a small notepad and flipped through it. "You told the officers that Mr. Fortham came out of the house shortly after you found Ms. Cummings."

"Yes, that's correct."

He consulted his pad again. "You found Ms. Cummings. Saw the man going over the fence. Checked her pulse. Quieted her dog. And then saw Fortham coming out of the house. I would assume all that took a few minutes."

Objection! Leading the witness, Ms. Snark called foul inside my head.

I reined in my anger and Ms. Snark. I couldn't let on that Will had already told me Brown's theory of the case, and that I thought the theory stunk to high heaven.

"More like a few seconds. For one thing, there was no need to quiet Dolly. She was barking to alert others that her handler was down and needed assistance." It was something we taught all our dogs but I hadn't realized Carla had already covered it with Dolly.

"Once I arrived," I continued, "the dog stopped barking on her own."

"Why didn't the dog chase after the alleged intruder?"

Alleged intruder? Ms. Snark said internally.

"Could Dolly have possibly known who it was?" Brown added.

I stifled a sigh. "Unlikely, and it wouldn't have mattered. We pick dogs that are not particularly territorial and then train any remaining territorialism out of them. Service dogs can't be reactive to others. They are trained to stay focused on their handlers."

"Hmm, I'm surprised that Mr. Fortham didn't come out when the dog started barking."

"Sometimes barking is part of the task the dog is being trained to do. He wouldn't have thought anything of it."

"So why did *you* come running?"

"My dog," I gestured toward Buddy, "was barking and growling at the gate."

"But I thought the dogs were trained not to, uh…" he looked down at the pad, "be territorial."

"His training was…different."

He nodded, again consulted the pad, which I was beginning to think was more prop than anything else. "Back to the timing. Would you say it was about five minutes between the man going over the fence and Mr. Fortham coming out of the house?"

"No, I would say it was less than one minute." I let a little of Ms. Snark creep into my tone.

A slight nod this time. He pursed his lips.

I pressed my own lips together in a tight line.

"Go through it for me again, please. Step by step."

I slowly pulled in air through my nose and counted to five. Then I went through it all again, ending with, "I saw the man scrambling over the fence and told Buddy to grab his leg. I crouched down to check Carla's pulse, and about then Russ bolted out of the back door."

"Hmm, I wonder why he didn't go after the man? Nothing wrong with his body, after all."

I clamped my teeth together. Somewhere in there was a slur against veterans with psychological issues rather than physical injuries. But now was not the time to fight that battle.

"He was concerned about Carla. And Buddy wasn't able to stop the guy. He was already over the fence."

Another insincere nod.

"Hey," I said, "did Mr. Fortham's jeans have a piece torn out of one leg? Buddy got that much of the intruder. I gave the scrap of denim to one of the deputies."

"Yes, we have it."

That's all he said. I debated whether to pursue the matter, but decided my rein on my temper wasn't going to hold much longer.

However, I would definitely be letting Mr. Stick-Up-His-Wazoo Lawyer know about the chunk of denim Buddy had taken out of the attacker's jeans.

Brown stood. "Thank you. Let me know if you think of any other details that might be helpful."

Grinding my teeth, I watched the detective walk away toward our side gate.

My waffling was gone. Brown had pissed me off enough that I was now more determined than ever to clear Russ's name and get him out of jail.

CHAPTER TWELVE

I'd once bought a book, when I'd been toying with the idea of a career change. Its title was something along the lines of *Private Investigating for Idiots*. I recalled a line in there now. If you aren't sure where to go next in an investigation, go back to the beginning.

Hmm, the beginning was the sanitarium. However, I wasn't quite ready to go there yet. I didn't want to tip my hand with them.

But I could go back to step two, which was the airport.

I checked my email. Elise had finally sent a preliminary report on the last person on Russ's list. James "Sonny" Smith had a rap sheet. He'd stolen a car at age eighteen, which made me wonder if there was a sealed juvenile record somewhere. Then several drunk and disorderlies, and he'd served half of a ten-year sentence for involuntary manslaughter, before being released on parole for good behavior.

I winced. He'd run over a pedestrian while driving drunk.

But his slate was clean for the last ten years, the same amount of time that he'd owned the Pine Hills Airport. His credit was okay. The airport had a mortgage on it, and the payments were always on time.

Sonny might not be at Pine Hills on a Saturday but I didn't want to call to check. Best to keep things casual and not give him time to antici-pate my questions.

Worst case scenario, if he wasn't there, I'd have given my car some exercise. And I'd delay having to tell Carla that Russ was stuck in jail until Monday. That was a definite plus.

I texted her that something had come up I had to take care of, loaded Buddy into the backseat of my car, and headed for the airfield.

Inside the main building, Sonny greeted us from behind his counter with, "You again?" The words were brusque but accompanied by a big grin, so I assumed he was teasing.

"Yup, me again," I said in a light voice, then faltered. I should've thought through how I was going to get things rolling. "Um, I'm trying to help Russ Fortham out, see if I can find out anything else about the plane crash."

Sonny's face closed, although he managed to keep the smile in place. "Okay," was all he said.

"Russ says he didn't sabotage the plane, and he's pretty upset about Charlie Butler."

The smile faded completely. "We're all torn up about Charlie." He ran a long, slender hand down his face. "How can I help?"

"First off, are you positive that the plane was sabotaged? That the crash couldn't have been accidental?"

I was sure it wasn't, but I wanted to see his reaction—see if he knew about the tiny hole in the fuel tank.

He shook his head. "No accident. Follow me." He came around the end of his counter and went out the door leading to the airfield. Then he veered off to his right, toward the long cement-block building with the hangers.

Buddy and I hustled to keep up with his long strides. He led us to the far end of the building. There, on a raised cement slab, were two over-sized pumps, like those in a gas station, only with really long hoses.

He stopped and pointed at them. "Self-serve tanks. See those signs?" One read *Avgas* and the other *Jet Fuel*. "Any private plane operator knows never to put jet fuel in a prop plane. And…"

He walked behind one of the pumps and came back with two small plastic buckets. He took down the nozzles, one at a time, and pumped a small amount of each fuel into a bucket. "See, jet fuel is a different color and smells different. No way any pilot would accidentally put the wrong fuel into a plane. Not even if Charlie was drunk, would he make that mistake."

Which he hadn't been, but I couldn't share that info with Sonny since I wasn't supposed to know about the autopsy results.

I tapped my index finger against my upper lip. "Somebody who wasn't familiar with planes, how hard would it be for them to figure out that was a good way to sabotage a plane?"

Sonny shrugged. "Not all that hard, I'd guess. Any family member of a pilot would've probably heard about the different fuels. And it's likely you can find out about it on the internet, if you searched for ways to sabotage a plane."

I nodded, making a mental note to do just that when I got home, although I'd rephrase it as causes of small plane crashes. The words *sabotage a plane* in my search history might land me on some FBI watch list.

"Look," Sonny said, "I like Russ. We've always gotten along great, but can you really trust what he says? I mean he's been in the looney bin for months. Maybe he has those, you know, multiple personalities, like you see on TV."

I bristled and clenched my teeth. "First of all, I can definitively say that Russ does not have multiple personalities, and secondly there are all different kinds of mental disorders–"

He held up his hand, palm out. "Okay, okay. I'm only saying that what *he says* might not be totally reliable."

I put my hands on my hips. "You've known Russ longer than I have. Ever known him to lie?"

Sonny paused, as if in thought. "Can't say that I have."

"And would you say he's an honorable person?"

"Yeah, I guess." He turned and started walking back toward the main building.

I jogged a couple of steps to catch up. Then took a calming breath. I couldn't afford to alienate this man, at least not yet.

"Russ mentioned a pilot, Arthur Godwin, who might have it in for him." Godwin was at the top of Russ's list.

Sonny nodded. "Russ saw him siphoning fuel from someone else's plane. He told me what he saw, and I banned Godwin from the field."

That jived with Russ's note about Godwin. "Do you think he could've been angry enough to sabotage Russ's plane?"

Sonny thought again for a beat as we walked side by side, Buddy trailing a little behind me. "Sabotage it so it wouldn't run, yes," he finally said. "But no, not in a way that would cause it to crash. I don't think he'd commit murder. And all that happened last February, over a year ago."

Still walking, he scrubbed a long hand over his face again. "Although he did threaten Russ at the time. Said he was going to get him back. And of course, he denied siphoning the gas. I had no proof other than Russ's word for it, so I couldn't do more than ban the guy."

"But you took Russ's word for it because you know he's an honest guy, right?"

He glanced sideways at me. "Why would he make something like that up? He was never a troublemaker."

Yes, I couldn't afford to alienate this guy, but I couldn't resist the temptation to set him straight. "So, here's the deal about mental disorders," I said, working hard to keep my tone even. "With the vast majority of them, the person is still sane. They're in touch with reality, and they are still the same person they've always been. Their character doesn't change just because they become depressed or anxious."

He rubbed the back of his neck. "I've seen Russ kinda down at times, but he's never been the anxious type."

Oops! I quickly backpedaled, "I didn't mean that those are Russ's diagnoses. I was only using them as examples."

He stopped at the door of the main building and stared at me, his eyes narrowing slightly. "How come you know so much about these *mental disorders*?" He exaggerated the last two words.

"Because I have a masters degree in counseling psychology."

Sonny didn't look impressed. Instead, his eyes narrowed further. I got that reaction from some people, as if having an advanced degree made you suspicious, because you weren't "plain folks."

"And I train service dogs," I pointed to Buddy, "for veterans with psychological issues, due to *their* service, protecting *our* country."

Sonny stopped squinting at me, but he didn't seem all that chagrined. He opened the door and waited for Buddy and me to go inside first.

"There was one other person that Russ said he'd had some issues with here." I gave him the woman's name, Samantha Richards. Of course, Sonny was on the list as well, but I wasn't going to tell him that.

He went behind the counter. "Ah, sweet Sammie." He chuckled softly. "She's married but she used to try to flirt with Russ. She got pretty annoyed when he wouldn't flirt back. I pointed out to him that she flirts with everybody and he shouldn't get so bent out of shape about it."

"Could she have known Russ was in a mental hospital before the crash?"

Sonny gave me a startled look. "*I* didn't know that's where he was before the crash!" The implication being that if he didn't know, certainly no one else at the airport knew.

"How stable would you say she is?"

He gazed at the ceiling for a moment, giving that some thought. "She's always seemed pretty level-headed to me."

"I heard she'd moved to California. Any idea why?"

"It didn't have anything to do with me," he said, a little too quickly perhaps.

Odd wording.

"None of my business," he added.

"Has she been back to visit here at the airport, since they moved?"

Sonny was shaking his head before I'd even finished the question.

I think he doth protest too much, Ms. Snark commented internally.

Perhaps, but I couldn't think of any more questions to ask about "Sammie."

"Is there anyone else around here that might have a beef with Russ?"

He started shaking his head again, then stopped. "The Nole...Nolan Talbott."

I raised my eyebrows but didn't say anything.

"He's kinda uppity," Sonny said. "Got ticked off one day, 'cause I told him to wait. Talbott had announced he was six miles out, comin' in for a landin', then Russ came on and said he was low on fuel. When Talbott didn't announce that he would hold, I got on there and told the Nole to let Russ land first."

"There's no air traffic controller here?"

Sonny looked around in an exaggerated way. "Nope, don't see none." He laughed. "Honey, this small an airport, everybody just announces their intentions on Unicom and keeps their eyes open."

I assumed Unicom was some kind of communication system for pilots.

"But I watch out for those kind of situations," Sonny was saying, "at least while I'm here. Don't want nobody gettin' hurt, and I gotta protect the airport's reputation."

"Does Talbott go by the Nole?" Nole made sense for Nolan, but *the* Nole?

"No." Sonny grinned. "I called him that behind his back. He's a Seminoles' fan. I'm a Gator."

There hadn't been anything in Elise's report about Sonny having a college degree. But I wasn't surprised that he'd taken sides in the long-standing rivalry between two of Florida's biggest state universities, Florida State and the University of Florida. Many folks in northern and central Florida who'd never gone to either school were nonetheless Seminoles' or Gators' fans.

"We follow the Gators' basketball team," I said.

He smiled at me. Apparently, I was forgiven for being an educated elitist.

"Is Nolan around today?"

"Nah, he don't have his plane here anymore."

"Do you know where he and Arthur have their planes now?"

"Not off the top of my head. Might have it in their records, though." He walked over to a monitor and keyboard on the counter and tapped some keys. "Art's at Gainesville Regional now. I think he's doing private charters. Talbott's at Williston Airport."

I'd noted that he'd used Art's first name and Talbott's last, even though Art was a fuel thief and Talbott was only a snob. But then, he was also a 'Noles' fan, probably the least forgivable of those three sins in Sonny's eyes.

"Can you think of anybody else who might have it in for Russ?"

He thought for a moment, then slowly shook his head. "He's pretty easygoin', gets along with most everybody."

I nodded. "How about Charlie? Does he have any enemies? Do his kids hate him?"

"Nah, it's more like they barely knew him. He told me he didn't blame them for not wantin' nothin' to do with him. He was always either workin' or at the bar when they were growin' up. And it's not like he had bags of money that they're gonna inherit."

I nodded again. "Thanks for all your help." I sketched him a wave and started for the door to the parking lot.

"Hey, you goin' to his funeral?" Sonny called out as I began to push the glass door open.

I half turned, leaned against the door. "When is it?"

"Not scheduled yet. They haven't released the body. I'll let you know though."

"That would be great. Thanks again."

Before heading for home, I texted Elise and added Nolan Talbott to her list of folks to do background checks on. Then I took the chicken's way out and texted Carla, giving her the bad news from the lawyer that Russ was stuck in jail for the weekend.

I was pulling out of the airport parking lot when she texted back. *I kind of figured that, when I hadn't heard from him.*

Guilt had me wondering if I should invite her over to my deck when I got home and try to console her. I mean, it's not every day that your new love gets arrested.

Nope, she'd hate that. I told the guilt to shut up and lie down.

Dinner that evening started out fine. Will grilled pork chops on the deck, while I microwaved potatoes and made a salad.

We sat down to eat at the picnic table. After a few bites, I said, "Um, in the interest of full disclosure, I'm still looking into Russ's case."

Will stopped mid-chew and hastily swallowed. "You're what?"

"I'm investigating what really happened with the plane crash. I don't believe for a minute that Russ sabotaged his own plane, and I can't let him languish in jail."

"Languish?" Will said, his face totally neutral, which was far more disturbing than an angry expression. He was giving me his "cop face."

I told him that Russ couldn't get a bail hearing until Monday.

"That's a tough break," he said, while slathering butter on his baked potato. "But that doesn't mean you should go poking around in things."

I gritted my teeth. I hated those words *poking around*.

"Nonetheless, I'm going to check into it further."

He put down his knife and fork. "You're interfering in a police investigation."

I snorted. "Brown isn't investigating anymore. He's only trying to prove his theory." I told him about his ex-partner's visit today and his attempts to steer my answers toward lengthening the time from the guy scaling the fence to when Russ came out of the training center.

Will listened but then said, "You're still interfering in police business. You could get hurt...or go to jail."

"I'm not afraid of jail." But my voice quavered slightly, bringing the truthfulness of that statement into question. I'd been interrogated before by the police, far more rigorously than my little chat with Brown today. We're talking dingy rooms with metal tables bolted to the floor. Those experiences were unpleasant enough, but I'd never actually been arrested.

I blew out air and looked down at my half-eaten food. "I know my doing this causes you to worry." And I most definitely knew what it was like to worry about one's spouse's safety. "But I can't abandon Russ."

He shook his head. "You're too fearless for your own good sometimes."

Those words jolted me. I would have never, ever thought of myself as fearless.

Anything but...

And suddenly I was crying, with no idea why.

Will was up and around the table. He knelt next to my chair and wrapped his arms around me. "Marcia, what's wrong?"

I struggled to put words to what was going on inside of me. My thoughts and feelings were a jumble. I pulled away from him some, needing a little space to unravel that jumble.

At arm's length, I stared at him. Much to my surprise, the words, "I'm tired of being afraid," came out of my mouth.

CHAPTER THIRTEEN

An hour later, we were cuddled up on the loveseat in our study, still talking, our half-eaten dinners abandoned.

I'd finally managed to articulate at least some of what was going on —that I'd been afraid for most of my adult life, ever since I'd agreed to marry Ted Goldman. I was afraid I was making a mistake (which I was), afraid the marriage wouldn't work out (which it didn't), afraid he was having an affair (which he was), afraid he'd cheat me in the property settlement (that one, I didn't let happen), afraid I wouldn't make it on my own as a dog trainer, afraid to let myself love Will, and so on.

"Other than when I'm training," I said, "the only other time I'm not afraid is when I'm investigating something on someone else's behalf."

Will shifted a little to look down into my face. "But that's when you're most at risk."

I twisted around to face him. "I'm not talking about fear of physical harm. I feel that when there's an actual threat. This is more a low-grade anxiety about all the things in life that could go wrong." I ducked my head. "Too many things did go wrong when I was married to Ted, and that anxiety has been a more or less constant presence in my life ever since, kinda like background noise. You get used to it being there and don't notice it."

"Makes sense," Will said.

"The psyche usually does, once you figure out where something is coming from. But now what do I do about it? I need to either shift my attitude or make some other tangible change."

Something flashed in Will's eyes. "What kind of tangible change?" His voice was wary.

I put my hands on either side of his face, felt the roughness of stubble under my palms. "Don't worry, you're the best thing that's ever happened in my life."

"Phew, that's a relief." He grinned, then kissed me gently. "So what changes do you have in mind?"

"That's the problem. I don't know." But the seed of an idea was forming in the back of my brain.

We both sat back. His arm snaked around my shoulders again. I put my hand on his thigh.

"Are you afraid when you go to work?" I asked him.

"No. It's like you said. I'm appropriately afraid when I'm in a tight spot, but I don't assume that will happen until it does."

"Exactly." The seed was growing, the idea crystallizing. "I need to do some attitude shifting, and I should probably go back to Jo Ann for some counseling sessions for that." I paused, trying to bring things a bit more into focus.

Then I took a deep breath. "I'm thinking the tangible change may be that I help you with your private investigating."

His eyebrows shot up. "What?"

I swiveled around again in the half-circle of his arm. "Look, hear me out. I've loved those times when we've worked as partners, bouncing ideas off each other. You'd be the P.I. but I'd help from behind the scenes, or maybe do some interviewing, when we know it's safe."

If he thought I was going to be chasing bad guys, he'd never go for it. And indeed, I didn't particularly want to chase the bad guys. I'd be happy to leave that to him. I just wanted to feel the thrill of chasing down clues and putting the pieces together.

I realized in that moment that it was the best fun I'd ever had, except maybe riding a horse—and I couldn't stay on poor Niña's back all day. I resisted the urge to laugh out loud. Will likely already thought I was a little around the bend.

And to be investigating *with* Will, instead of worrying about him being mad if he found out what I was doing... That sounded like heaven.

His expression was thoughtful. "You don't think we'd get on each other's nerves," he asked, "working together like that?"

"No. Do you?"

He stared at me for a couple of beats.

My heart bounced around in my chest, then lodged in my throat. What was going on behind those baby blues?

Suddenly, he grinned. "Nah, and it could be fun."

Excitement bubbled up and I did laugh out loud.

"You'd still train dogs?" he asked.

"Yes, so there'd be times when we'd be doing our own thing, to give us a break from each other."

He nodded. "It might just work, and I have some other news, that affects our P.I. aspirations."

I loved that he'd used the word *our*. "Oh yeah?"

"Got an email from HR, but with all the craziness yesterday I forgot to tell you about it. All the extra hours I've been working lately, it seems I've accumulated way more comp time than is allowed, and the department is required to cash out some of it, so–"

"How much?"

He held up a hand. "There's more. I asked if I could cash out all of it. They said all but twenty hours. We'll have a windfall of almost a month's pay. That should help get things rolling, and I'll do the private stuff part-time for a while, before leaving my job."

He squeezed my shoulders. "We wanna keep the health insurance for now, if we're having a baby."

And with that, my body tensed all over again with the old familiar anxiety. *Did I really want a child? Was I cut out to be a mother?*

Pausing the trying to get pregnant had apparently given me more time to heal emotionally from the miscarriage, and now the questions were back.

I shook my head slightly. Enough angst for one night. I shoved the doubts aside and suggested to Will that we go to bed.

The cryptic nature of Russ's message through his lawyer had left me wary. I was equally cryptic when I'd left a message on Wes Sullivan's voicemail. "Our mutual friend asks that you continue as planned."

I'd worried that he hadn't gotten the message, but Sunday morning, he finally texted back. *Will do.*

I found Arthur Godwin's website, advertising his charter service out of Gainesville Regional Airport. It had only been active for a little over a year.

Perhaps he was a long shot. It had been some time since his run-in with Russ. But as the saying goes, revenge is a dish best served cold. And who knew what restrictions the pandemic had put on his actions? Maybe he'd been sick or quarantined for part of that time. He was fifty-five, not the most vulnerable age group but getting close to it, and he could've been self-isolating because of other health issues or, like Russ had been, to protect vulnerable family members.

Nolan Talbott was an even greater long shot. Most likely, he was more angry with Sonny than with Russ. And having one's elitist sensibilities offended didn't seem like a crime worthy of murder as a response.

While Sonny's legal problems in the past were interesting, I wasn't sure they were relevant. Other than his conviction that being in the "looney bin" meant Russ was unreliable, Sonny hadn't shown any animosity toward him.

I emailed Elise to dig further into both Godwin's and Nolan's backgrounds, specifically to see if they had anger issues or were otherwise unstable. I'd wait for her more complete report on flirtatious Sammie before deciding if she was worth looking at more seriously.

I debated about whether to call Godwin or go see him in person—it was an hour and a half drive. Sighing, I admitted to myself that I really needed to see his face while we talked.

Then I had an idea. I found an email address on the website and sent a message through my phone, introducing myself as the personal assistant of a CEO—making up both his name and the company he supposedly ran—who might want to set up an ongoing contract for all his travel needs. I requested an appointment with Godwin for Monday afternoon.

Satisfied that the investigation was moving along, I texted Carla to see if she was up for a training session. She was. With Russ gone, we'd traded dogs and cages again. Dolly was now with her.

As I walked out back and headed for the gate between the yards, I felt downright peaceful inside. No slight tightness in my chest or stomach, no niggling fear in the back of my mind that Will would be angry about my "poking around" in police business.

Even my worrying about Will's physical safety on the job had eased. Soon he would be out of the sheriff's department, a private investigator who would be unlikely to find himself in physical danger all that often. He'd said that philandering spouses and people faking injuries to defraud insurance companies would probably be our bread and butter, and that neither group tended to get violent.

Carla and I spent an hour and a half working with Dolly, until she was going into the designated room and sitting automatically, for either one of us.

"Now what's the next step?" I asked Carla.

"Do it again later and see if she remembers," she said with a chuckle.

I smiled and nodded. "And then?"

She ran a hand through her hair. "Well, there are two more parts to the task. Coming back out of the room if no one is there, and barking if a stranger is in there. I can work on the coming back out on my own."

I nodded again. "That's the simplest of the two anyway, so it should be next."

"How are we going to expose her to strangers, though, since I can't go out into the world yet?" Her second shot was scheduled for four days from now, the same day that my two weeks would be up and I could assume I was fully immunized.

"I'll recruit neighbors to start off with. Most of them should be willing to help."

"One advantage to social distancing," Carla said. "Dolly hasn't met any of them while we were out on walks."

At eleven-ten Monday morning, my phone rang. *Barton and Stone* popped up on my caller ID. "Hello," I answered, expecting a female voice telling me to hold for Mr. Barton.

Instead, a male voice said, "Ms. Banks-Haines?"

"Yes…Mr. Barton?"

He cleared his throat. "I'm afraid I have some bad news."

His ominous tone made my stomach knot.

"Mr. Fortham won't be getting out on bail," he said.

"Why not?" I screeched.

"The judge set bail at a very reasonable sum. I was about to accept it, and then someone in the back of the courtroom said he was a doctor and he was there to ask the judge to Baker-Act Mr. Fortham and commit him to the Leesburg Sanitarium."

My knot turned to acid and my stomach heaved a little. I swallowed hard.

"I…I've never had this happen before." Barton sounded quite flustered. "Mr. Fortham refused to accept bail. He told the judge he'd stay in jail. I mean, I know he can afford ten thousand dollars, and he'd get it back…" The lawyer trailed off.

"So he's still in there?"

"Yes, and he's on suicide watch now. That doctor kept insisting he's suicidal."

"Dr. Johnson?"

"No, that wasn't his name." Papers rustling. "I'm sorry, Ms. Banks-Haines, I was so thrown that I didn't write down his name."

"That's okay. And call me Marcia. It's easier." I debated for a second how much to tell this guy. "If I'm your P.I., I mean working for you, does client-attorney privilege protect what I tell you about Russ's situation?"

"Well yes, but Ms. Bank–"

"Marcia," I said firmly. "So, I'll be sending you an invoice for our services, for say, ten dollars." I took a deep breath. "There's a very good reason why Russ wants to avoid, at all costs, going back to Leesburg Sanitarium." As succinctly as possible, I filled him in on all that had happened.

When I'd finished, he said, "Ms. Ban... Marcia, that is a fantastic story."

Oh for Pete's sake, Ms. Snark yelled inside my head, *Get that stick out of your–*

Shhh, I've got this.

"It is, Mr. Barton, but fraud happens, as I'm sure you know. And the VA is a common target."

"Ms. Ba...Marcia, I did not mean to imply that I didn't believe you. It's just one heck of a story."

"Yes, it is," I concurred. "Tell me, what does suicide watch mean?"

"It means that Mr. Fortham is in the medical dorm rather than the general population. I stopped in to see him there, after court. It's quite clean. And he doesn't seem discontent with the outcome of the hearing."

I'd been in jails—always as a visitor, mind you—and I doubted that it being "quite clean" was much consolation for Russ. But being hauled off to that sanitarium again was not an option.

"Please tell Russ that we are continuing to investigate and we *will* get to the bottom of this and get him out of there."

"Will do, and Ms., um, Marcia..."

"Yes?"

"Thank you."

"Thank *you*, Mr. Barton." I disconnected.

I found myself humming as I drove toward Gainesville that afternoon.

Guilt twisted in my gut. How could I be so carefree when Russ was in jail?

You're not supposed to take the cases personally, remember? Ms. Snark commented.

Good point. I needed to learn how to detach some from our clients—

Will's and mine, that is. They would always be in some kind of trouble. That's what would bring them to us in the first place. I couldn't let their troubles affect my life and mood.

The tune I'd been humming was one of my mom's favorites, a song from an old Doris Day movie.

I made myself sing it out loud. "*Qué sera, sera.*"

Whatever will be, will be. My mother's voice trilled inside my head.

I didn't hear from inner Mom as much these days, now that my real mom lived in Florida. And when I did, that inner voice wasn't as critical as it had once been.

Mom and I'd had some heart-to-heart talks during the last year, and I'd discovered that she wasn't the rigid, strict parent I'd perceived her to be as a child. Oh, she was strict, but there were reasons behind her rules back then, most of which didn't apply now.

"*Qué sera, sera,*" I sang again, grinning at Buddy in the rearview mirror.

Only he wasn't there. For a moment, I'd forgotten that I'd left him home. If Godwin was the one who'd sabotaged Russ's plane, Buddy's presence might identify me as the woman who was poking around in his case.

His absence put a small dent in my good mood.

I realized I was so chipper because I was just three days from fully vaccinated status, when I could move about in the world with much less fear of Covid.

My phone rang. *Wesley Sullivan* popped up on my dashboard screen.

"Hey, Wes," I answered.

"Hey yourself," he said through my speaker. "I'm still working on things here at the VA. How's Russ holding up?"

"I don't know. Some doc showed up at his bail hearing, ready to Baker-Act him the minute he got bail. So he opted to stay in jail. But now he's on suicide watch."

He mumbled a couple of curse words. "Are you sure Russ *isn't* suicidal?"

"Can't know for sure, since I haven't talked to him lately. But that new medication he was taking, he'd said it was working great. And his lawyer says he's in good spirits."

"Okay. I know Johnson in passing, through the VA. Lemme talk to him and see if I can get him to reevaluate the suicidal–"

"Please don't!" I quickly said. "I mean, I'm not sure we want to show our hand yet. And Russ is probably safer in the medical dorm at the jail than in the general population."

"Okay. But I'm afraid his reputation is going to be shot. Even if we can clear him of all this, he'll still be seen as unstable. All too often, our vets have to deal with that stigma, if they're diagnosed with PTSD and/or depression. And now it will get out that he was hospitalized for several months."

"But if we can show that he was kept there long after he should've been." I thought of something Jo Ann had said, that she was surprised the VA psychiatrist hospitalized him in the first place. "Maybe even that he didn't need to be there in the first place, then we can hopefully restore his reputation."

Silence for a beat. "Hopefully. But you stay out of the VA end of the investigation. Let me handle that. It's too dangerous, since whoever is behind all this may be getting more desperate."

I shook my head at my dashboard screen. Just what I needed, another protective male.

"Don't worry, I can take care of myself. But I will leave that end of things to you. I'm on my way to see someone who used to have their plane at the airport. He and Russ had a run-in last year. It's possible that the plane sabotage isn't even related to the fraud."

"Alleged fraud," he said, then chuckled. "We sound like a cop show. Keep me posted, and I'll let you know about any developments on my end."

I smiled as the screen informed me he had disconnected. It felt good to have an ally.

A frisson of excitement ran through me. Soon it would be Will and me, every day, sharing info on cases and bouncing ideas off of one another.

The more I thought about it, the more our new plan felt right.

Arthur Godwin was not at all how I'd pictured him. I'd imagined a short, balding, middle-aged guy with a paunch.

He was tall and slender with a full head of dark hair, gray sprinkled through it. His eyes were also dark and he was probably handsome, although I couldn't see the lower part of his face. I appreciated that I didn't have to ask him to wear a mask.

I'd switched out my puppy dogs for one of Will's black cloth masks that he wore to work.

I was going for classy and had worn a black dress, with a black cardigan to make it seem more tailored, and a string of pearls I hadn't worn in years. I'd pulled my hair back in a bun, and matching pearl posts adorned my ears. I thought I was a decent facsimile of a rich man's personal assistant.

And Godwin was a decent facsimile of a successful businessman. He wore black jeans and a short-sleeved white dress shirt with a blue and black striped tie, and sat behind a polished oak desk. If I hadn't known his age, I'd have pegged him as at least five years younger, in his late forties.

I'd been ushered to a leather loveseat across the room. It threatened to swallow me up. I did my best to cross my legs in a ladylike manner and tugged my skirt down along my thighs.

"My employer," I said in my best snooty voice, "began using charter services at the beginning of the pandemic rather than flying first class on commercial planes. But recently he hasn't been satisfied with the sanitation practices of his current service."

"I assure you, we thoroughly clean our planes between each flight," Godwin said.

"Good, because quite honestly, my employer is a bit of a germophobe. You have more than one plane then?" I extracted a pad and pen from my black tote bag.

"My partner and I have two. If your Mr....uh..."

"Fleming, Sean Fleming." I'd combined the first and last names of the first actor who'd played James Bond with the spy series' author. What could be classier than that?

"If Mr. Fleming is willing to pay a modest monthly retainer," Godwin said, "we can arrange our schedule so that one of the planes is always at his disposal. There will be a fee, of course, for each flight as well."

He named the fees and I managed not to gasp. I wrote them down on my pad.

"And your planes are jets?" I asked as I tried to figure out how to segue into talking about Russ. I'd planned to say he referred us to Godwin, but it might sound weird if I just brought that up out of the blue.

"One's a small jet and the other a turboprop, but both are quite comfortable," Godwin was saying. And then, bless his heart, he gave me my opening. "How did you hear about our services?"

"Russell Fortham recommended you."

His eyebrows shot up as I suspected they would. "Really?"

"Yes, he and Mr. Fleming are acquainted, and since Mr. Fortham is a pilot, it seemed logical to ask him for a referral."

When Godwin didn't say anything, I added, "He said you used to be at the same airfield."

"Yes," he said slowly, his eyes now wary.

Hmm, maybe this wasn't the best approach. He wouldn't want to say anything bad about the man if he thought Russ was friends with his potential new customer.

"Of course, Mr. Fleming doesn't know Mr. Fortham very well. They met at a party a few weeks ago. That's why Mr. Fleming sent me to check all this out." I waved my hand in what I hoped was an imperious gesture.

Godwin leaned forward, forearms on the desk. "I'm glad they're not good friends," his voice was hard now, "because one of the stipulations of the contract would be that Fortham doesn't get anywhere near my planes."

Apparently, he'd heard that Russ was still alive, but maybe didn't know that he was in jail.

I faked a shocked look. "Why not?"

"Because the man's a liar and a thief."

"Aren't you afraid to say things like that? You could be sued for slander."

"Not slander if it's the truth."

Can we spell PROJECTION? Ms. Snark commented internally.

I silently agreed. And I wasn't at all sure that his assessment was accurate. Slander, libel and defamation of character were murky legal territory, in my mind, at least.

"Oh my." I patted my hair nervously. "It sounds like you two are enemies. I wonder why he recommended you."

"Most likely feeling guilty."

"He did something to you?"

"Yes, but I'd rather not get into it. Besides..." He leaned back in his chair, arms spread wide. "The best revenge is to live well."

I thanked Godwin for his time, took the business card he proffered and made my exit.

In my car, I took a deep breath and processed the interview before starting the engine.

There was definitely anger still over the incident with Russ, so much so that he was willing to jeopardize a lucrative deal. And Godwin had convinced himself he was the innocent party. Was he angry enough, though, to sabotage a plane and kill a man?

I doubted it, as that might jeopardize his good living. But I would have Elise dig some more into the charter business. I sent her a text before heading home.

I wasn't humming now. Godwin's firm belief in his own innocence had planted a seed of doubt again. *What if Godwin really was the injured party—falsely accused—and Russ was the thief and/or liar?*

If that were the case, then Godwin would have even more reason to want revenge.

And, if that were the case, I couldn't trust a thing Russ had told me.

CHAPTER FOURTEEN

I was halfway home when Elise called.

"Got some more info on Arthur Godwin." She sounded a bit breathless.

"Boy, that was fast. Hey, are you okay? You sound like you've been running a marathon."

"Um, yeah, I'm fine." The sound of air being sucked in. "I was already checking out some more things about Godwin when you texted." She cleared her throat. "He isn't listed on the charter service's paperwork as a co-owner. It's a sole proprietorship." Her voice got steadier as she spoke.

"Hmm, interesting. Especially since he referred to 'his partner,' quote, unquote, several times during the interview I just had with him."

"And…" Elise's voice sounded more normal now, "he was accused of stealing gas from an airplane at least once before."

"Oh?" *Sorry, Russ,* I mentally apologized for doubting him. "I found a small claims case filed against him for five-hundred dollars, by a Franklin Jarvis, who claimed Godwin had siphoned one of his plane's fuel tanks dry and was starting on the other one when Jarvis caught him."

"Hmm, I wonder why Sonny didn't mention that."

"He might not have known. The case was settled out of court, and it might have had a non-disclosure agreement as part of the settlement."

"In which case," I said, "neither party could talk about it. Still, I can't imagine that this Jarvis guy wouldn't have complained to Sonny at the time that it happened."

"Maybe he did, but after the settlement, he might've asked Sonny to keep it to himself."

"Okay, that makes sense," I said, "and it also would explain why Sonny took Russ's word over Godwin's when Russ accused him of the same thing."

"And Godwin's keeping his name off of anything official, in case there were rumors that might nix their set-up at Gainesville Regional."

"But why would his partner go along with that?" I asked.

Elise chuckled softly. "The partner is much younger, and guess what his wife's maiden name is."

"Godwin. She's Art's daughter?"

"Yes, and their address is an apartment in northeast Gainesville, an okay part of town but not the wealthiest, whereas Godwin and his wife own a house on a ten-acre property south of Gainesville, assessed for over $400,000."

I whistled softly. "Daddy-in-law has the bucks, but son-in-law has the clean reputation."

"So they go into business together," Elise finished. "Hmm, I wonder if Godwin might see my client as some kind of threat, that he might rat him out to the folks at the Gainesville airport?"

"Could be," Elise said. "On Talbott, I couldn't find much. He's a high-priced lawyer, has led a pretty clean life. No lawsuits, nothing I can find that indicates anger issues. He might have them, but they haven't led to anything that leaves an electronic trail. I'm going to dig a little deeper into both his and Godwin's finances, as much as I can."

"Do you have a phone number for Talbott?" I asked as I pulled off onto the shoulder of the country road I was on. Elise gave me the number and I added him to the contacts on my phone.

She and I signed off, and I called Nolan Talbott.

"Hello?" His voice was tentative—he probably thought I was a tele-marketer.

"Mr. Talbott," I said in my most official sounding voice, "I'm investi-gating the manslaughter case of Russell Fortham. I believe you know him."

"Who?"

"Russell Fortham. You two used to have your planes at the same airport."

"Never heard of him." His voice was now distinctly impatient.

"How about Sonny Smith?"

"That s.o.b. What about him?"

"I take it he did something you didn't like?"

"Yeah, but it isn't worth getting into. And what's he got to do with this Russell guy?"

That seemed rather obvious to me, but I answered him. "Sonny owns the airport where you both had your planes."

"He owns Williston too? I thought that airport belonged to the city."

"No, I'm talking about Pine Hills Airport."

A pause. Then, "Look, lady, I don't know what you're trying to sell here, but I'm on my way to an important business meeting–"

Anger tightened my chest. I cut him off before he could hang up on me. "Russell Fortham was the pilot whom Sonny allowed to land ahead of you," some of my annoyance had slipped into my voice. I decided that was okay, "…that day that *isn't worth getting into*. He was running out of fuel."

"Yeah, that was Sonny's story, but he was always playing favorites, making me wait to land or take-off."

"So your beef is with him, not Fortham?"

"Lady, I never even knew the other pilot's name. We use our planes' registration numbers, not our names." And with that he disconnected.

Well duh, Ms. Snark commented.

"Yes," I said out loud, "but aren't those numbers on the outside of the planes somewhere?" And Pine Hills wasn't a very big airport. Talbott could've easily figured out who Sonny's alleged favorites were.

As I was about to put the car back in gear, my phone pinged. Will's name flashed onto my dashboard screen, along with the text, *Call me when you can.*

My stomach immediately tensed with the old anxiety. The anxiety that had *not* been present all day today as I worked on the investigation.

Crapola, I've developed a phobia of talking to my husband.

I made a face and instructed my Bluetooth to call him.

"Hey there," Will said.

"Hey yourself." I smiled at the screen, the anxiety dissipating.

"I just heard that Russ turned down bail. What's with that?"

I told him about the developments at the bail hearing.

"Was it Johnson from the sanitarium?"

"No, the lawyer, Mr. Barton, said not, but he couldn't remember the doc's name. Apparently, he's not used to clients wanting to *stay* in jail and it shook him up a bit."

"Wish I'd seen that," Will said with a chuckle. "John Barton rattled."

"You know him?"

"Yup. Slickest defense lawyer in the county, and for once I'm glad he's on the case."

Relief washed through me. We might manage to get Russ out of this mess yet.

"So, what have you been up to?" Will asked.

Everything tensed up inside again. But I made myself answer honestly. "I've been checking out two guys that Russ had run-ins with at the airport. The one guy claims he didn't even remember his name. The other is still holding a grudge, for sure."

"A big enough grudge to sabotage a plane?"

"That's the million-dollar question."

"*How* have you been checking them out?" Will asked.

Gulp, Ms. Snark said internally and snickered. She and I might be in agreement more often lately, but she still enjoyed my moments of discomfort way too much.

Gripping the steering wheel, I said, "I called the one guy and went to see the other, but I pretended to be someone else with both of them."

Well, with Talbott, I'd mainly avoided giving him my name.

"But they both have your cell phone number now."

"Umm," I said, stalling.

At the same moment, Will said, "We need to get some burner phones."

"Burner phones?"

"Disposables that can't be traced."

I know what burner phones are. I'm just surprised..." I trailed off.

Will sighed. "Surprised that I'm not scolding you," he said in a gentle voice.

"Well, yeah."

"Marcia, I'm *training* you."

My insides relaxed so fast I slid down in the driver's seat some. I was glad I wasn't driving while having this conversation.

Will was still talking. "I've been thinking. If we're going to make a success of our new P.I. agency, it would be helpful to have two operatives ready to hit the ground running when we start it."

"Operatives, as in I get my P.I. license too?" My voice ended on a bit of a squeak.

"Well, I have to get mine first, and then you have to train under me for a certain number of hours. I need to research all that."

"We're really gonna do this, huh?"

"Yes, we're really gonna do this." A pause. "Unless you've changed your mind."

"No," I quickly said. "I'm so excited, I'm giddy."

Will laughed. "Just checking, because you've been known to change your mind before." His tone was teasing.

I chuckled along with him.

"Where's your giddy self off to next?" he asked.

"I don't know. I'm kind of out of leads until I talk to Russ again, get his take on the responses I got from these two guys."

"I can get you on his visitor's list. But you should wait until Thursday, when your two weeks from your last vaccine are up."

I wasn't sure I was willing to wait that long—I was eager to see for myself that Russ was okay—but for now... "Thanks for getting me on his list."

"See you at home later. Love you."

"Love you too." I disconnected and smiled at the dashboard screen. Five years ago, when Will and I were dating, I hadn't been able to say those words without stuttering. That's how distrustful I had been, not of him, but of romance in general, and of my own feelings and judgment.

"You've come a long way, baby," I said out loud.

Ms. Snark chuckled. *Even though you still talk to yourself.*

Another thought sobered my mood. I wasn't going to change my mind about the P.I. agency, but I might about having a baby.

My stomach tensed. I wasn't at all sure how Will would react to that.

You'll work it out together, my inner Mom said.

Dang, some of the old anxiety was back, although on a scale of one to ten, it was about a four. Whereas before, it had hovered between five and six most of the time, skyrocketing to ten or beyond at times.

"It's progress," I muttered as I put the car in gear.

The next couple of days were a mixed bag of mixed bags. Will and I excitedly made plans for our new P.I. agency, but I had no success catching up with Wesley Sullivan. He wasn't answering my voicemail messages or texts. I was worried that he'd asked the wrong question of the wrong person and something bad had happened to him.

It was taking longer than expected to get my name on Russ's visitor list. Will said it was because the jail personnel were shorthanded, but how long does it take to type a name into the computer?

Carla had managed to talk to Russ on the phone. He'd told her he was fine, but she'd said he sounded depressed.

Well duh, Ms. Snark had commented internally. *He's in jail.*

Of course, the situation with Russ had Carla in a horrible mood, but Dolly was responding well to her training. It was definitely time to recruit some strangers.

Finally I got a text from Wes on Tuesday evening. *Not coming up with much here. How are things on your end?*

A little stalled right now. But should have more on the airport leads soon.

Good. Keep me posted.

You too.

On Wednesday morning, I had my first ever virtual counseling session. A few minutes in, Jo Ann said, "You've never mentioned free-floating anxiety before. Can you identify when it started?"

I nodded at my laptop screen. "I've been thinking about that. It's been around most of my adult life. But not all the time, just most of the time. It's not there when I'm training dogs, or when I'm investigating something, or when I'm riding my horse."

"You feel confident doing those things…"

"Hmm, yes and no. I can't say that I'm confident as an investigator yet, but because I'm a novice, I can forgive myself if I make mistakes."

"Fear of failure then?" JoAnn asked gently.

I shook my head. "My folks raised me to see failure as an opportunity to learn something. I mean, I feel bad when I fail, but it's not that hard to shake the feeling eventually."

"Is it more a social anxiety?"

See, this is what I like about counseling. You can keep saying "No, that's not quite it," again and again, and the other person stays right with you, giving you time to sort it out. Even Becky wasn't that patient.

Jo Ann cleared her throat softly, which brought me back to task— probably her intention. She might be patient, but the clock was ticking.

"Again, yes and no. I'm fine meeting new people and I like parties. Well, except the ones I had to go to with Ted. But I think the anxiety has something to do with disapproval." I flashed back to Will's words from yesterday, asking if I thought he was scolding me. "It's like I'm a kid, waiting for someone to berate me about something."

"Let your mind drift some," Jo Ann said, "and ask yourself when you first felt that way."

An immediate flash of squirming in a pew. I sat up straighter in my desk chair. "It's why I hated going to church. The old ladies would glare at me if I got restless or made *any* noise, and during the social hour after-wards, at least one of them would fuss at me about something."

Jo Ann was nodding.

"My mom told me last year that she was so strict about cussing and such because of 'the old biddies.'" I made air quotes. "Her words. She didn't want to give them any more ammunition… And I just got another piece. I felt like the old biddies were judging my parents as well, especially my father. I felt like I was letting him down. Not that my parents ever said anything like that."

"So, this fear of disapproval–"

I held up a finger. "Not all disapproval, no. I didn't feel it when I started working with Carla, and initially she disapproved of pretty much everything I did. That annoyed me but it didn't make me anxious."

"Because, as her trainer, you're above her in the pecking order," Jo Ann pointed out.

"Yeah. It's more about judgment."

"By someone you care about, in Will's case… Or perhaps someone you perceive to be above you in the pecking order?"

I nodded. "Those parties with Ted were excruciating. I was a simple pastor's kid. I wasn't cut out to hobnob with high society. And afterwards, Ted would lecture me on all the things I did wrong, like laughing too loud."

"Sounds like social hour after church all over again."

"Yes, and speaking of confidence, I didn't have enough of it back then to realize Ted and his friends were no better than I was."

Jo Ann leaned forward, her face and shoulders filling my laptop screen. "Have we ever talked about the difference between guilt and shame?"

I shook my head. "I don't think so."

"Guilt is when we feel bad about doing something wrong." She sat back again. "Shame is feeling bad about *ourselves* for doing something wrong."

I shrugged, not really seeing that much difference.

"Guilt motivates us to do better," Jo Ann continued. "Shame is immobilizing. We only want to crawl in a hole somewhere."

I nodded slowly. "Yup, that's how I felt around the old biddies, and around Ted most of the time. Like a child being shamed."

I grinned at my laptop. "Dang, Jo Ann, you're really good at this counseling thing."

She chuckled, then leaned forward again. "Next session, we tackle if you really want a child or not."

I grimaced as she ended the session.

Later that morning, I was leaving the house to pick up my last curb-side grocery order, when my phone pinged.

A text message from Wes. *Not coming up with much on my end.*

What's not much? I replied.

Nothing, I'm afraid.

"This is ridiculous," I said out loud. Wes was not a trained investigator... well, I wasn't either, yet, but I had more experience at it than he did.

I needed to talk to Russ so I knew which way to go next.

I texted Will. *Did you get me on Russ's visitor list?*

Yes. Talk later.

I didn't take the terseness of his message personally. It meant he was in the middle of something.

Buddy looked up at me from his spot under the window. "Sorry, boy. You still can't go with me." Dogs were even less welcome at a jail than they were in a grocery store.

At first, the deputy behind the glass window politely told me to go away. Then he told me less politely.

I was informed that yes, I was on the visitors' list, but my visit should have been approved in advance by someone farther up the food chain than he was. He didn't put it that way, of course.

I dropped my husband's name, and the deputy, with a sigh, made a couple of phone calls.

After a forty-five minute wait, my ID and vaccine card were checked. I was told to empty my pockets and put everything in the little moving bin, like banks and pharmacies use at drive-thru windows. I knew the drill so I'd left my purse locked in my trunk. After passing through a sally-port, one metal-and-glass door clanking shut behind me, before the one in front opened, I was escorted by a different deputy through a labyrinth of corridors.

He showed me into a small room. "Sit on the far side of that glass barrier. Don't try to touch or give anything to the prisoner. After the prisoner leaves, stay in your seat until I come for you."

The barrier was in the middle of a metal table, which sat below a small, barred window.

I nodded and did as I was told. The metal chair was cold, the glass barrier thick. Perhaps it had been added because of Covid.

But the set-up was less intimidating than some jail visitation rooms I'd been in. Always on the visitors' side, mind you.

The cement-block walls were painted a depressing gray but they were spotless. I wondered if the main visitation area was as sanitary.

The door opened and Russ shuffled in. He looked horrible. The wide white and orange horizontal stripes of the jail uniform made his shoulders appear to be even broader, but the rest of him seemed to have shrunk some inside the loose-fitting jumpsuit. The orange reflecting onto his cheeks above his mask gave him a jaundiced look.

A different deputy followed him in, gestured toward the empty chair. Russ sat. "Don't try to touch each other," the deputy said and left.

"Hey, Marcia." Russ's voice was raspy, lackluster.

"Hey. Um, I hate to have to say this, but you don't look too good. Are you okay?"

He nodded. "Hanging in. They're weaning me off my anti-depressant."

"Why?" I said too loudly.

"Johnson told the doc here that the new med might have caused 'suicidal ideation.'" He lifted handcuffed hands to make air quotes.

"And have you had suicidal ideation?"

"Not in months, not even when I was being held in that hospital. I told Johnson that again and again," he said, a desperate edge to his voice. He looked away. "And not here, *yet*."

The *yet* sent a flutter of anxiety from my chest down into my stomach. But I had no idea how to comfort him. The normal platitudes—this too shall pass, look on the bright side, etc.—all seemed ludicrous in this gray room with bars on the window.

The best I could offer was action. I leaned forward. "I've done some checking on the people at the airport, and a guy, Talbott, who wasn't on your list. Sonny mentioned him." I told him about my conversations with Talbott and Godwin.

"Talbott's right. He likely wouldn't know to put my face or name with the tail number of my plane. And he was mostly mad at Sonny. I walked right past where he was bawling Sonny out, and Talbott didn't even glance my way."

"How about Godwin? We did some more checking and he's not listed on any of the paperwork for the charter company or with Gainesville Regional Airport. He's hiding his past transgressions. Is there any way he might think you're about to out him as a fuel thief?"

Russ shook his head slowly. He was looking a little better as we talked.

"I've never had any contact with anyone official there, except for the tower and ground control. I've landed there a few times, picking up friends or family who flew in on commercial flights."

"When's the last time that happened?"

"Six months ago. My mom wasn't doing so good, and my brother came to visit, you know, just in case."

"Could Godwin have seen you at the airport?"

"Quite possibly, if he happened to be there at the time. I went into the terminal to meet my brother. When I took him back to Gainesville at the end of the week, I only dropped him off. But if Godwin saw my plane, he'd probably recognize it."

"Did your brother come stay with her while you were in the hospital?" It was none of my business, but hey, I'm nosy.

Russ shook his head. "She'd rallied a good bit by then, and he's got a family, small kids. Hey, could you do me a favor?"

"Sure."

"Check on her for me. The neighbors look in on her, pick up things for her. But I'd feel better if you touched base. She doesn't like to be a bother, but if you insisted…"

"I'll call her once I'm out of here. I'm on my way to the grocery store anyway."

His relief was palpable.

"Russ, are you sure there's nobody else who might have it in for you?"

He shook his head. "Trust me, I've had way too much time to think the last few days. I can't imagine anyone else who'd have any kind of grudge against me, especially one that would make them want to kill me."

"Why did you have Sonny Smith on your list?" His comment after Sonny's name had been rather vague—*possible jealousy*.

"It was kind of an impulse to add him. But you said anybody that could conceivably have a beef with me. He and I had words a couple of times over Sammie. Uh, Samantha Richards. She was always flirting with me, which made me uncomfortable because she's married. But then Sonny seemed miffed that I was snubbing her. He pointed out that she flirts with everybody and that I should be nicer to her."

That jived with what Sonny had told me.

"So I flirted back a bit with her, and Sonny seemed to be mad about that…" Russ trailed off.

Interesting. Sonny *hadn't* told me that part. "Do you think Sonny and Samantha were doing more than flirting?"

Russ thought for a moment. "Could be, but if he was going to take out his competition, you'd think he'd go after her husband, not me."

Not necessarily, Ms. Snark commented internally, *if he likes his women married so they don't want commitment.*

And jealousy isn't the most rational of emotions, I added.

"I'm glad you talked to him," Russ said. "He's pretty much the hub in the wheel of that airport."

"So he knows pretty much anything that goes on there?"

"If it happens during the day. He leaves between five and six and everything's self-service after that. I mean, we pretty much just self-announce on Unicom, even during the day."

Thanks to Sonny's explanation of what had gone down with Talbott, I kinda knew what he was talking about. "Have you ever seen anything fishy going on after hours there?"

He shook his head. "Not much goes on at night at all. The runways aren't well lit. A few folks take off or land in the early evening, if it's still light out, but otherwise…"

"Why doesn't Sonny invest in better lighting?"

Russ shrugged. "Like a lot of small, private airports, Pine Hills runs on a shoestring. Besides–" He stopped, cleared his throat. "I'm not sure how to describe this. It's like the airport is Sonny's toy. He loves watching the planes and kibitzing with the pilots. I'm not sure that he *wants* much to happen when he's not there."

I smiled a little. Somehow that jived with my sense of Sonny. "How about this Samantha? Did you know she recently moved to California?"

"No, but I can't say that's shocking news. If I were her husband, I'd want to get her away from all that testosterone at the airfield."

The metal door rattled.

I leaned farther forward. "Hey, promise me something?"

"Sure."

The door swung open, and a guard stepped into the room.

"Promise me," I said in a low, rushed voice, "that no matter how bad it gets, you won't hurt yourself. I *will* get you out of here."

He gave me a solemn look. "I promise."

The fact that he didn't argue, didn't claim again that he wasn't suicidal, scared me more than anything else had.

The guard took him away, and within seconds, my original escort came for me.

The clang of the metal door, slamming behind us as we left the room, reverberated through my body. The knot in my stomach, which had been there throughout the visit, grew into a brick of dread.

Dear God, I fervently prayed, *let me be able to keep my promise.*

CHAPTER FIFTEEN

I was tempted to go straight to Leesburg Sanitarium and give Dr. Johnson a piece of my mind.

What was the man thinking? Russ was struggling with being in jail and being accused of killing a man, and the doc takes him *off* his antidepressant?

But I took a deep breath and drove toward the grocery store. If I was going to be a professional detective, I needed to stop taking investigations personally and "running off half-cocked," as my mother would say.

And Will would agree with her, Ms. Snark chimed in.

"I'm not going to do it, okay?" I answered her out loud.

I called Mrs. Fortham. She sounded fine and said she was good with groceries at the moment. After a couple of rounds of "I'm going there anyway" and "I don't want to be a bother" and "No, really, it's no bother," she did admit that she had a prescription waiting to be picked up at the Publix pharmacy in Belleview.

I got it for her, along with my groceries.

At her house, I stayed on the porch with my mask on, to be on the safe side. She had an advanced case of COPD. She carried around one of those portable oxygen gizmos, hanging from a strap over one of her stooped, slender shoulders.

"I don't understand why Russell is in the hospital again," she said in a wavery voice. "Do you know what's going on?"

I was speechless for a moment, a very unusual state for me. Apparently, Russ had lied to her. Was being in the hospital less humiliating than jail? Or maybe he was trying to minimize her worrying.

"Uh, I think there was a minor problem with his medications. They needed to adjust them." Not that a minor adjustment would require hospitalization, but she seemed to buy it.

Walking back to my car, I wondered which would make me more anxious as a mother, having a child in a mental hospital or in jail? I shuddered slightly, hoping I'd never have to deal with either scenario.

At the car, it dawned on me that I hadn't crossed my fingers to negate participating in the lie.

Really, Marcia, my inner Mom said. *Do you think that's still necessary? We all tell white lies, even me.*

I digested that on the drive home.

When I pulled up to the curb in front of my house, Sybil was sitting on her front steps, her eyes closed, a slight smile on her face—enjoying the spring weather, I assumed.

I carried two bags of groceries to my porch, set them down and took a step toward her. "Guess what, Syb! Tomorrow is the first day of the rest of my life."

She broke out a grin. "You're clear then?"

"Yup, as of tomorrow, it will be two weeks since my second shot."

"Woot!" She jumped up. "Hey, let me help you with your groceries."

Keeping our distance from each other, we carried the other bags from the car.

Sybil stood in the open doorway of the front door as I put perishables away. "Wanna hear something funny? That conversation we were having about 'Nurse Ratchette.'" She made air quotes. "I remembered something today that makes that closer to reality than we thought. The first time I was at the sanitarium, I walked into a patient's room and she was in there. She had the charge nurse's little cart with her laptop, and she was typing something into the patient's record. I stopped cold and stared at her, because I'd assumed she was strictly administration. She smiled at me and said she was a registered nurse, and she sometimes checked charts, to keep the nurses on their toes. Then she held a finger to her lips, implying I should keep it a secret that I'd seen her."

Sybil shook her head. "I should've been more suspicious at the time, since she wasn't just checking the chart, she was typing something into it. And she was way too friendly. I think that's the only time I saw her smile. But I was new there and didn't realize that was out of character for her."

I left the rest of the groceries for later and got out a pitcher of iced tea and two glasses. "Sorry I don't have any sweet tea." I nudged one glass of tea and the sugar bowl along the length of the breakfast bar, and stepped back.

"That's okay, I don't need the extra calories." She patted her hip, which was at least two sizes smaller than mine.

I stifled a twinge of envy and waited for her to put some sugar in her glass, then step back to the doorway. I doctored my own iced tea. "Do you remember anything else that was off about that place? Now that we suspect they're fraudulently keeping patients longer than they should."

If Wes wasn't finding anything on the VA end, that meant it was time to focus more on the sanitarium itself.

Looking thoughtful, she took a sip of tea. "You know, one time I escorted a patient to Dr. Johnson's office for a therapy session. As I was leaving, I saw him tap a blue folder on his desk and he said something along the lines of, 'I see in your chart that you're still feeling tired.'"

After a pause, I asked, "Why's that odd? Do you think that was one of the patients they were sedating to keep them there longer?"

"Maybe, but what was odd was that he had a paper version of the chart. All those records are kept electronically. All he had to do was call up the patient's chart on his computer."

She took another sip of tea. "Ya know, I got kind of friendly with one of the daytime charge nurses. I could make a call and see if I can find out more about the second paper chart."

"That would be great, if it's not going to get you in trouble, that is."

She shook her head. "Nope. I know just how to play it." She downed the rest of her tea and put the glass on the end of the breakfast bar. "I'll let you know what I find out." She waved and left.

I spent the afternoon helping Carla with Dolly—and I was definitely helping now more than training Carla. We repeated the first part of the *clear room* task several times. Then I helped with the *cover* task by being the person approaching from behind.

Friendly, people-oriented dogs like Dolly naturally react to someone approaching. The trick was to consistently get a certain level of reaction. When she twitched her ears forward and swished her tail but stayed seated, she got a treat. If she got overly enthusiastic and stood up, no treat.

Being Dolly, she quickly caught on.

But still we had to repeat the process *ad nauseum*. Finally, Dolly yawned and looked longingly toward where Buddy was napping under the magnolia tree.

Carla chuckled. "I think she's asking if we're done for the day?"

At dinner, Will seemed a little peeved that I'd jumped the gun by a day and gone to the jail. That is, until I told him about the thick glass partition in the spotless visitation room.

I filled him in on what I'd found out. "If Godwin saw him when he was at the Gainesville airport, he may think Russ is a threat, that he might tell the airport authorities on him."

"This guy merits another interview," Will said.

"Yeah, but I can't go there now as a private eye, after having pretended to be some rich guy's assistant."

Will grinned. "Yet, another reason why it's handy to have two of us."

My heart swelled in my chest as I returned the grin.

"I think I'll take off a half day tomorrow," Will said, "and use up some of that comp time I can't cash in to pay Mr. Godwin a visit."

~

My doorbell rang at eleven-fifty the next morning. I peeked out the picture window in the living room.

Sybil stood on our porch, a big covered pot and foil-wrapped objects at her feet.

"Say wha'?" I opened the door, and she grabbed me in a big hug.

"Lordy, that felt good," she said, when we let go of each other.

"I brought lunch to celebrate." She stooped down, picked up the two foil-wrapped items and handed them to me.

One felt like a plate of something and the other was long and skinny and warm to the touch. I put them on the breakfast bar and turned back to her.

She'd hefted the pot up in front of her. "Mama made a pot of her famous chicken soup for our dinner last night, and I told her I would be putting the leftovers to good use."

At the words *chicken soup*, Buddy stood up from his bed under the window. Tail wagging, he trotted over.

Sybil laughed. "Oh, you mercenary dog, you. You'd sell your soul for some of Mama's chicken soup, wouldn't you?"

His tail wagged harder and he nudged his head against her thigh.

We both laughed. "I think that's a yes," I said.

Excitement bubbled in my chest. I threw my arms out and twirled around the kitchen. "Isn't this great? You can come into my house now. We're back to normal."

She grinned. "Getting there."

I got out dishes and flatware.

Meanwhile, Sybil put a few bites of chicken and noodles in Buddy's dish, being careful to pick out the pieces of onion, which are not good for dogs.

While we slurped down the yummy soup, with home-baked bread and butter, Sybil gave me the results of her talk with her nurse friend.

"I played the I'm-still-new-at this nursing-thing card, so please help me understand why there were two charts. Apparently, Dr. Johnson keeps his therapy notes separate. He does a summary of the patient's progress for the main chart. But he wants to see the nurses' notations before each session, so every morning Mrs. Ratchette prints out any additions to the charts for those patients he's seeing that day."

I nodded. That kind of made sense. Or at least keeping the therapy notes separate did. But why did he need a paper update of the nurses' notes when he could just call them up on the computer? Was he a technophobe?

"And guess what—my friend Cindy isn't at the sanitarium anymore either. I thought she was a regular employee, since she was the charge nurse during several of my shifts. But she's a traveling nurse too. She told me that *all* the nurses there are temporary."

"Whoa, that's not suspicious, much."

"I thought so." Sybil's face brightened. "On a lighter note, look what I brought for dessert. Tada!" She pulled the foil cover off the plate, revealing three fudge brownies. "We might even leave one for Will," she said with a wink.

Lunch with Sybil definitely brightened my day. But after she left, I found myself pacing the floor. Somehow, I couldn't shake the feeling that the separate patient charts were significant.

And I was increasingly worried about them weaning Russ off of his antidepressant. Were they replacing it with something else?

Based on the way he'd seemed yesterday, I'd say no, or at least, not yet.

I checked my email and found a report on Dr. Johnson from Elise. In her cover email, she said it had been hard to narrow down which Robert Johnson to investigate—it was such a common name. But she'd finally found the one with a connection to the Leesburg Sanitarium.

He was squeaky clean, with excellent credit and not even an unpaid parking ticket. And no indication that he was living beyond his means.

Ms. Snark snorted internally. *He's a blinkin' Boy Scout.*

I ignored her and read on. Elise had included a press release from a few years ago. It went into the background of the sanitarium, which had been on shaky ground, only operating at half capacity, until the Pennington Group bought it. They'd fired all of the staff and brought in Johnson as the new administrator.

I never would've pegged him for a shrewd businessman, but apparently he'd turned the place around in short order. Filled all its beds and had it running in the black, mostly because he'd been able to negotiate a contract with the VA to take some of their veterans who needed long-term hospitalization.

I texted Will. *Call me when you can, when you can talk privately.* Then I paced the floor some more.

He called ten minutes later.

"I need to talk to Dr. Johnson at that sanitarium," I said without preamble, a bit surprised by the urgency in my own voice.

A half beat of silence. "My day's been good. How's *your* day been so far?"

"What? Are you…you can't talk freely right now?"

"No, that's not it." He sighed. "I was being sarcastic. *Why* do you need to talk to Johnson?"

"Okay, you can't do that anymore," I blurted out. I sat down hard on one of the breakfast bar stools.

"What do you mean? Do what?"

I shook my head. I didn't *know* what I meant.

But apparently Ms. Snark did. *Talk to us like we're a child*, she said internally.

I clamped my lips tight to keep the words from escaping.

Still not trusting myself to open my mouth, I sucked in a deep breath through my nose. My instincts said to table the issue of the dynamics in our relationship. Now was not the time and over the phone was not the best approach.

"This is serious," I said. "I forgot to tell you something about my visit with Russ. On Johnson's orders, they're weaning him off his antidepressant, and he wasn't in very good shape yesterday. I need to talk to Johnson and see if and when they're going to put him on something else. Otherwise, I'm afraid he *will* end up becoming suicidal eventually."

"You don't think he is now?"

"No. He specifically said he isn't, but then he added the word *yet.*"

"And you believe him?"

"Yes, I do. Both messages."

"Good enough for me."

My heart warmed in my chest, and I almost forgave him his earlier sarcasm. Almost.

"But can't you just call Johnson?" he asked.

"Um, I think I'd be more successful in person." Especially since I had every intention of doing more than talking, but I wasn't ready to tell Will about my half-baked plan.

"It's not safe for you to go there on your own."

"I know," I said, perhaps a little more emphatically than necessary. "That's *why* I texted you."

Either Will didn't notice my irritated tone, or he chose to ignore it. "I'm finishing up some paperwork, and then I was going to take off to see Godwin. But I can do that later. Meet me a block from the sanitarium in an hour."

"Got it." I disconnected and sat at the breakfast bar, staring into space for a moment. It felt like something significant had just happened.

I shook my head. I'd have to think about that later. Right now, I needed to focus on the investigation, and what I hoped I'd find out by visiting Johnson's office.

I parked behind Will's pickup truck, a block down from the sanitarium's entrance. As I got out of my car, my phone rang.

It was Will. I answered. "Why are you calling me when I'm walking toward your truck?"

"Because we're going to use our cell phones as a poor-man's wire."

As I reached the passenger side of his truck, he lowered the window.

He looked downright scrumptious in his pale blue dress shirt, the sleeves rolled up and the collar unbuttoned. He mimicked putting his phone in his shirt pocket.

Fortunately, I was wearing a camp shirt that had pockets. I slipped my phone into one of them. It stuck out the top some and looked a bit weird, I thought. Women don't normally carry their phones there. But if I put it in my jeans pocket, that would defeat the purpose of the open line. Muffled voices would be all Will would hear.

Be careful," he said.

I nodded and headed for the entrance.

And encountered my first obstacle—the gates were closed and locked.

CHAPTER SIXTEEN

There was a buzzer and intercom speaker on one gate post. I hit the buzzer, praying that someone other than Mrs. Ratchette would answer.

No such luck. "Yes, can I help you?" Her tone was brisk but not completely unfriendly.

"I need to speak to Dr. Johnson, please." I tried to sound as professional as possible.

"And you are?"

"Mrs. Banks-Haines." I hoped by leaving my unusual first name out of the mix, maybe she wouldn't realize who I was.

Again, no such luck. "Dr. Johnson is a busy man. And why are you even here? Mr. Fortham was discharged days ago."

"It's a confidential matter," I said in a tight voice. "I'm not at liberty to discuss it with you, only with Mr. Fortham's doctor."

"He's not his doctor anymore, since the man managed to get himself thrown in jail."

"The matter I need to discuss is related to that."

A pause. "You need to make an appointment."

I was trying to come up with a way to counter that when I noticed people were wandering about the grounds—some wore light blue scrubs, others street clothes.

"Why are the gates locked?" Ms. Snark blurted out. "They weren't before."

"All our staff and patients have now been vaccinated, so they can socialize with each other. But we must screen people coming in, make sure no one brings in the virus."

So the wanderers on the lawn were patients. Some stood in small clumps, talking. I was happy for them, that they could now enjoy some social contact. But being locked out was frustrating my plans.

"I've had both shots, the last one two weeks ago."

"Nonetheless, you need to make an appointment. Dr. Johnson is much too busy to see you today."

Movement on the porch of the main building caught my eye. It was the much-too-busy Dr. Johnson. He sketched a wave at some nearby patients. A couple of them waved back.

"Dr. Johnson," I called out.

Mrs. Ratchette actually laughed at me. "He can't hear you in his office," she said in a derisive tone

Apparently, she didn't know that her boss had wanderlust.

Johnson was scanning the lawn, trying to find the patient who'd called his name. Finally, he glanced toward the gates, where I was waving my arms in the air. He raised his hand in a friendly wave back.

A buzzer sounded and the gates swung inward. I realized he had a remote control in his hand.

I ran for the porch. As I approached, Mrs. Ratchette came out the front door.

She's gonna try to intercept us, Ms. Snark said.

The gates swung shut behind me. "Ms. Banks-Haines, what brings you here?" Johnson called out.

"Marcia, please." I jogged up the steps and ducked around Ratchette. "I need to talk to you about Russell Fortham."

Ratchette was spluttering behind me. "I told you that you need to make an appointment."

"No problem," Johnson said. "I have a few minutes now." He lowered his head slightly and dropped his voice. "You have been vaccinated?"

I nodded, and he gestured toward a set of French doors sitting open at the other end of the porch. "Then come on in."

I followed him to the French doors, while Ratchette stomped back through the main door of the building.

Leaving the doors open, Johnson gestured for me to take a chair in front of a large polished oak desk. The top of it was chaos, papers scattered everywhere, a few blue folders among them. He quickly gathered those up and flipped them over so the patients' names weren't showing.

He settled into his desk chair. "So, what can I do for you on this beautiful day?"

"You can tell the jail staff to put Russ Fortham back on his antidepressant." It came out harsher than I'd intended.

He blinked twice. "I'm afraid I don't have the authority to do that."

"But you told them to take him off of it, that it might be making him suicidal."

He was shaking his head. "No, I talked to a nurse practitioner over there." He paused, eyeing me, perhaps deciding how much he should or could tell me.

"Look," I said, "I visited Russ at the jail yesterday. He told me everything. And you have the waiver he signed in your files."

Johnson gave a slight nod. "I told the nurse practitioner that this particular drug, although very effective, can have the side effect of making some people manic and sometimes suicidal."

"As I understand depression, only people with bipolar disorder can be thrown over into mania by an antidepressant."

He gave me a superior smirk. "And how is it that you have come to *understand* depression?" The inference being that I was only an uneducated dog trainer.

Pressure was building in my chest. I took a deep breath and tamped down the anger. "I have a master's degree in counseling psychology and I've taught at the college level." I let a little of Ms. Snark bleed through in my tone. Which was a mistake. "But I decided I prefer dogs to people," she said.

Sheez, give you an inch, you take a mile, I scolded her internally.

Johnson didn't seem impressed, which didn't surprise me. As Jo Ann had reminded me, psychiatrists are the top of the heap in the hierarchy of the mental health field.

"Is Russ Fortham bipolar?" I asked in a firm voice.

"You know I can't answer that."

"Ah, but you can. There's a waiver, remember?"

He didn't respond.

"Why did you keep Russ in here for so long? He said he was feeling much better after the first six weeks."

Johnson sighed. "Speaking in general terms, first we have to wean patients from whatever they were on before. And as I said, the antidepressant we most often use has an excellent track record, but it also takes a long time to take effect. We start folks on it as soon as we can, but it's not unusual for our patients to remain lethargic and borderline suicidal for twelve to sixteen weeks, before they truly experience the full benefits of the drug."

"But Russ told you he felt better, that he needed to get home to help his mother, didn't he?"

"Of course. Patients almost always tell me that they're all better and can go home, but I know from their charts that they're still symptomatic." He touched the edge of the pile of blue folders. "The nurses see them day in and day out and they report on their lethargy and despondence."

I carefully kept my voice calm and even. "Do you all ever sedate depressed patients?"

He looked startled. "Of course not. That would be counterproductive."

"I would think so." I faked a cough.

His face tensed. "I thought you said you'd been vaccinated."

"I have been…" Cough, cough. I waved a hand in the air. "This is allergies." Cough, cough. "Old buildings…" I waved a hand to encompass the room. "Could I get a…" cough, "…glass of water?"

"Sure." He jumped up and headed for the wooden door that I assumed opened into the central hallway.

As soon as he was through it, I ducked behind the desk, nabbed the top blue folder and opened it on the floor. I used my phone to take snapshots of the first few pages of notes on the right and the list of medications on the left.

I quickly put it back and returned to my seat. I was diligently coughing away when he came in with a glass and a bottle of water.

I took the bottle, waved off the glass—I wouldn't put it past Mrs. Ratchette to put poison on the rim. I sipped the water, still intermittently coughing slightly.

"Sorry about that," I said in a voice now legitimately hoarse from all the fake coughing.

I sat back in my chair. "Here's the deal, Doctor. When I saw Russ yesterday, he didn't look good. They're taking him off the antidepressant you had him on but they haven't put him on anything else. He swears he's not suicidal, and that he hasn't been for weeks, and I believe him. But I'm also afraid that he will become so if he has to stay in jail, without his antidepressant."

I paused, took a deep breath. "You did good work with him, and now that is being undone."

He held up his hands in a helpless gesture. "There isn't anything I can do at this point."

"Aren't you concerned about your patient?"

"Yes, but that's just the thing. He's not my patient anymore. He's under the care of the jail's psychiatrist."

"But you could consult with him, give him your input."

He shrugged. "I doubt he'd do anything on my say-so, and he's probably re-evaluated Russ by now."

Somehow I doubted that, but I made a mental note to have Will check on it.

"Could you at least try?" I asked, feeling a little desperate. "You know, one doctor to another, peers. He should–"

"But I'm not that kind of doctor."

"What?"

"I'm a PhD psychologist, not a psychiatrist."

"Wha'?" I repeated stupidly, my mouth hanging open.

"I'm the administrator here and I do therapy with the patients, but we have a contract with a psychiatrist who comes in twice a week and prescribes all our meds."

"Does he actually meet with the patients?"

"Of course, although not everyone in every week. He checks the charts and makes a point of seeing anyone who isn't responding as expected to the meds."

I was still trying to wrap my brain around this shift in reality. Thanks to that dang hierarchy in the field, Johnson did not have ultimate authority over what happened with Russ's meds, even though he and Jo Ann knew the man's mental state better than any psychiatrist who'd spent fifteen minutes with him.

Dr. Johnson was right. He couldn't do anything for Russ.

As he escorted me to the door, I was not looking forward to dealing with Mrs. Ratchette. That thought jogged my memory.

"Doctor, wait." I held out a hand to stop him from opening the door. "Did you know that Mrs. Ratchette writes in patients' charts?"

"No. Of course she doesn't." He shook his head.

"I know one of the nurses who used to work here. She said she walked in on her typing something in a chart one day. Mrs. Ratchette said she was an RN and liked to check up on the nurses occasionally."

He shook his head more vehemently. "Your friend must have been mistaken. Mrs. Ratchette isn't a nurse, and why would she write in the charts?"

I faked a casual shrug. "I thought it was rather odd."

"I'm quite sure it was all a misunderstanding. Perhaps she was joking when she said that, and she most definitely wouldn't write in charts."

I nodded. "I'm sure that's what happened. My friend must have misunderstood."

"Thank you for coming to see me, Ms. Banks-Haines." Dr. Johnson turned the doorknob but didn't open it right away. "I will do my best to convince the psychiatrist at the jail to start Mr. Fortham on a new med as soon as possible. And I'll try to get over there to visit him in the next day or two."

"Thank you, Doctor." I considered warning him that his visit needed to be set up in advance, but I decided I didn't care if his time was wasted.

He opened the door for me, then followed me out into the over-wide hallway.

Mrs. Ratchette was on her desk phone. "Gotta go, Jimmy." She hung up.

"How's your son doing these days, Mrs. R?" Johnson asked her.

"He's fine, Doctor. Thanks for asking." She turned to me as I walked by her desk, a big smile plastered on her face. "Have a good day, Ms. Banks-Haines."

As I walked toward the front door, I felt her gaze on my back. I tried not to visibly shudder, recalling how Sybil had said the woman rarely smiled.

The one she'd just flashed me was as phony as a three-dollar bill. It had not reached her eyes.

They had been hard and icy.

CHAPTER SEVENTEEN

Once I'd been buzzed through the gates, I hustled to Will's truck and climbed into the passenger seat. "Did you get all that?"

He shook his head. "Only up 'til your coughing fit and he went to get you some water."

Dang! I must've accidentally disconnected him when I was taking pictures of that file.

Will was staring at me. "Marcia, what did you do?"

Trust us, you don't want to know, Ms. Snark said inside my head.

"Nothing. I think I'm allergic to something in that old house." I coughed to prove my point.

He narrowed his eyes at me and guilt tightened my chest. I wanted to tell him, but he was still a police officer, and what I had done might be illegal…was probably illegal…

Okay, it was illegal.

Best he didn't know, at least not until I'd checked something with Sybil.

I did fill him in on the rest of the conversation with Johnson, however, including that he wasn't the right kind of doctor. He couldn't do much about Russ's current situation.

"What did you think about all that regarding the meds?" he asked.

"Do you think he was telling the truth about them taking so long to kick in and causing mania and suicidal thoughts?"

"That last part… Yeah, some drugs can do that, but, with rare exceptions, they'll only make someone manic if the person is bipolar. But the first part—I've never heard of a psychoactive med that takes twelve weeks or longer to kick in. Usually, it's six to eight weeks. But I'll have to ask Jo Ann about all that."

"So Russ is bipolar and that's why the drugs made him manic?"

I shook my head. "It's a circular argument, and it's all based on the assumption that Russ is or has been suicidal recently. Russ was down, he was put on a new med, which eventually lifted his mood—he was downright cheerful even, after finally getting out of the hospital."

And falling for Carla, Ms. Snark added internally. *Love will make anybody a little manic.*

"But if he then becomes suicidal again, the cheerfulness must be mania, and both it and the suicidal tendencies were caused by the new med. And if he's manic than he must've been bipolar all along, not just depressed because of his PTSD."

I shouldn't be revealing so much about Russ's mental health, but Will knows that the veterans I work with have PTSD.

He was shaking his head. "I'm confused."

"No wonder. There's a heck of a lot of assuming and justifying going on without a whole lot of facts."

"Do you think Johnson was behind sabotaging Russ's plane?" Will asked.

I shook my head slowly. "I don't see it. Although I guess he could have hired someone to do it."

"So others are in on the fraud here as well, and they're the ones doing the covering up?"

"Oh, I think Nurse Ratchette is definitely in on it."

"*Nurse* Ratchette?"

"It's a joke between Sybil and me. I'm not sure…" I trailed off. I'd been about to say that I wasn't sure Johnson was in on the fraud. Maybe he believed that this wonder drug they used really took that long to kick in.

But I wanted to check with Sybil about some things first, before I went there.

"What?" Will said.

I shook my head again. "Lost my train of thought." I opened the truck door and jumped out. "See you later at home."

He nodded, then waited until I was in my car and had pulled away from the curb, before pulling out behind me.

We were halfway to I-75, where Will would peel off to head for Gainesville, when a white SUV passed his truck in a no-passing zone. I watched in my rearview mirror, wondering if Will would haul out his portable cop light and pull the guy over.

No swirling lights back there. I chuckled softly. *He doesn't want to waste time on writing a traffic ticket.*

The SUV was now tailgating me. I was just past the next curve when the jerk crossed the center line.

Seriously, you're going to do it again?

Only he didn't move past me. Once he was fully in the other lane, his front fender bumped against my back one.

What the...? I struggled a bit with the wheel to stabilize my car. Thankfully, he hadn't hit me very hard.

My heart pounded and my stomach roiled—an overreaction to his miscalculation. I doubted he'd hit me hard enough to even leave much of a dent. But I'd had people try to run me off the road before, so I figured I was having a mild flashback.

I took my foot off the gas, searching for a good spot to pull over and check our cars, and exchange insurance info, if necessary.

It registered that he hadn't gone on by. I glanced in both my mirrors. He wasn't behind me either.

Where'd he go? Heart accelerating again, I twisted my head around to look back over my shoulder.

He was hovering in the other lane, in my mirrors' blind spot. We were now on a straightaway. I tapped my brake, expecting him to zip past.

I checked the rearview mirror. Will's truck was rounding the bend of the curve.

Then the jerk's fender bounced off of mine again.

Adrenaline blasted through my system. The back end of my car fish-tailed. One tire went off onto the soft shoulder. I hit the brakes, which was probably the wrong thing to do.

My car went into a skid and jolted farther off the road. Fighting the steering wheel, I prayed I wouldn't flip over.

The loud wail of a siren. Now there were lights strobing from the top of Will's roof behind me.

The white SUV blasted past. The window glass was heavily tinted, but I got a shadowy glimpse of the side of the driver's head.

I finally wrestled my car to a stop, then sat there shaking, and questioning what I'd seen.

It had looked like the driver was wearing some kind of helmet.

CHAPTER EIGHTEEN

I wiggled my toes and flexed my fingers. Physically, I was okay. My air bag hadn't even deployed.

Mentally, I was pretty shaken. I took a deep breath and started to let it out slowly.

Knuckles rapped on my window. I jumped and jerked my head around, my heart trying to catapult out of my body.

Will's scared face close to the glass. "You okay?" he yelled.

Fear suddenly morphed into anger, red-hot pressure in my chest. I jabbed the button to lower my window. "Get that jack–" I caught myself.

My mom had thoroughly ingrained in me the no-cussing rule, but all the words that came to mind right now were ones that would break that rule.

Will was still standing there, staring at me with worried eyes.

"Get him," I growled.

"Yes, ma'am." He took off back to his truck and a few seconds later, it flashed by me, lights whirling, siren screaming.

By the time he returned, empty-handed, I had checked my car over. The tires were okay. There was a large dent in my back fender and a scrape in the paint. It wasn't too bad, but any bodywork was expensive and I was wary of filing an insurance claim for yet another hit-and-run fender bender.

This being run off the road was *really* getting old.

You realize if you become a P.I., it will no doubt happen again. My inner mom, not scolding, more her practical voice.

"You're probably right," I muttered under my breath.

"What'd you say?"

I startled slightly. Will had stepped up beside me and was also staring at the dent.

I shook my head. "He got away, I take it. Did you get his plate number?"

He nodded but his brow was furrowed. "I called it in already. Tag was stolen. Belongs to a new red Porsche."

I let out a nervous laugh. "That was no red Porsche." My knees had gone wobbly. The adrenaline was draining out of my system.

"Do we have to wait for deputies to show up?" There was a slight whine in my voice.

Will looked at me, studying my face, then he shook his head. He gently grasped my elbow and led me to my open driver's door. "Sit here for a minute, while I get some pictures."

He snapped photos of the car, the skid marks, and the ruts my tires had dug into the soft shoulder. He put out some flares and made a phone call.

He was on there for several minutes, glancing at me occasionally, before pocketing his phone and walking my way. "Since this may be related to Joe's case. They're sending out the crime scene techs. Come on. A deputy will bring your car home."

I gratefully climbed into his truck.

Will dropped me at home, saying he wanted to interview the red Porsche's owner. "You gonna be okay?" His eyes were gentle, worried.

I wasn't sure how to answer that. On the one hand, I was still feeling a little shaky and would've loved to spend some down time with him.

On the other hand, with him out of the house for a while, it would be easier to talk to Sybil without raising questions.

So I sucked it up and nodded, stepped out of the truck, and waved as he drove away.

The inner door of the Wells' house was sitting open to catch the breeze. I tapped lightly on the frame of the screen door.

Sybil appeared behind the screen and I motioned for her to come outside. "I need to show you something," I said in a low voice.

"Who is it, Syb?" Sherie called out from the depths of the house.

I quickly shook my head. Normally, I love getting Sherie's practical advice, but in this case, I was bending confidentiality rules all over the place. Best not to involve her.

"Just something for me," Sybil called over her shoulder and stepped out onto the porch.

I gestured to the training center's front steps. We sat side by side and I got out my phone. I showed the photo of the first page of the patient's file to her.

"I tried not to look at the patient's name, but do you recognize it?"

She took the phone, squinted at the screen. "Yes, he was there when I worked there the last time."

"Scroll through the nurses' notes and see if they look right."

She did so, the furrow in her otherwise smooth brown forehead deepening as she read. Then she flipped her finger across the screen scrolling back to the beginning. She poked at the screen. "That's what I thought. He'd already been hospitalized for a month when I was there, and he told me he was feeling much better. He's one of the ones I suspect they were sedating. He would be pretty upbeat in the afternoons, and then become lethargic after the evening meds were distributed."

She stopped, took a deep breath. "And he's still there a month later, and according to these notes, still depressed, although 'showing some improvement.'" She made an air quote with her free hand.

"Check the last photo. It's his meds."

"Hmm, no mention of the sedative that many of the patients were on. Maybe they stopped giving it to him."

"Maybe," I said, "but I doubt it. Here's my theory. I'm thinking that

Dr. Johnson isn't in on the fraud." I leaned over, flipped to a page of nurse's notes and pointed to a spot. "See here where 'Still somewhat lethargic and despondent' is at the end of the nurse's comments."

Sybil nodded.

"I think Ratchette adds things like that to the notes, prints them out for Johnson's file on that patient, and then deletes the additions. And she may be giving him a fake medications list."

Sybil tilted her head, her expression skeptical.

"I just had a half-hour meeting with Johnson. He seemed to genuinely believe that the antidepressant they're using, although a good one once it kicks in, is really slow to take effect. And he was quite taken aback when I suggested that Rachette was writing in the charts. According to him, she's not a nurse. He swore she'd never do anything like that."

"But of course he would say that, if she's his accomplice. Hang on." She handed me my phone and jumped up. "I'll be right back."

She returned with her laptop, sat and opened it. Tapping a few keys, she called up a website, then turned the computer toward me. "It's the modern version of a PDR. You know what that is?"

"Sure. Physician's Desk Reference." The huge book was printed each year with information on thousands of medications. "All a doc needs to prescribe safely, at his fingertips."

Pulling the laptop straight on her lap again, she gave me a small smile. "Only now it's at his or her fingertips via a keyboard. They stopped printing hard copies in 2017. Now it's called the Prescribers' Digital Reference."

She took my phone in one hand and pecked keys on the computer with the other. "Harumph," she said, sounding exactly like her mother. She turned the laptop again so I could see the screen. "Here's the antidepressant Johnson is so fond of. Look at the time frame for it to become effective."

I shaded my eyes against the sun, now starting to set beyond the barn across the road from us. As I suspected, the drug claimed to become fully effective at four to six weeks.

"That's pretty standard for most antidepressants." Sybil shook her head. "You'd think Johnson would know that. Any psychiatrist would. I don't buy that he isn't in on the fraud."

I stared at her. "You didn't know? He's not a psychiatrist. He's a psychologist."

Her mouth dropped open. "Say what?"

"Yup. He told me that himself today. Meds are prescribed by some part-time shrink, who no doubt takes the word of the nurses for how the patients are doing."

"But he'd be looking at the real charts. You'd think seeing some patients progressing so slowly would set off alarm bells for him."

"Maybe Ratchette's figured out a way to fool him too. Did you ever meet him?" I asked.

"Only once, briefly. His name is Woods…or Woodrow. Something like that." She scrolled through my photos again. "I thought he was the on-call doctor, for when Johnson wasn't there."

She stopped scrolling and turned the phone toward me. "Look."

It was the medications list. "What? I don't see anything?" I said after a moment.

"That's because it's not there. The bottom of the page is totally blank. That's where the physician's signature should be."

I took the phone from her and stared at it. "What does that mean?"

"The computer system they use, only the doctor can change the meds list. A box pops up requiring him or her to sign with a stylus, whenever a change is made."

"So somebody printed out the list, covered part of the page and then photocopied it?"

"Somebody, as in Nurse Ratchette," Sybil said, her voice bitter. I couldn't blame her since it was likely the woman had gotten her fired.

"And the photocopy goes in Johnson's file," I said, "so he doesn't see that the patient is on a sedative. I specifically asked him about sedating depressed patients and he seemed a little shocked that I'd even ask that."

"Maybe more evidence that he's not in on the fraud," Sybil said. "But you know who else should be picking up on what's going on? The VA case worker."

"Hmmm." I made the noncommittal sound as I dug around in my

brain for an elusive memory about case workers. "I think Russ's counselor said something about a case worker."

And he or she might be able to help me get him out of jail.

Back in my house, I called Jo Ann Hamilton, and got voicemail. I left a message to call me asap regarding Russ's case worker. Then I called our VA contact. Again, my call went to voicemail.

"Hey Wes, call me when you can. I've got another angle we might try. Case workers."

I settled in the study to do some online research. By the time Will got home, I knew a lot more about Dr. Johnson's favorite antidepressant, but neither Jo Ann nor Wes had called me back.

Will had brought a pizza home for dinner. After plopping the box on the breakfast bar counter, he examined our wine rack.

"So, how'd it go with the Porsche owner?" I asked, half expecting him to tell me it was police business.

But he didn't. "He hadn't even noticed that his tags had been switched," he said, still perusing our wine selection. "He also owns a pickup truck, which he uses for work. Doesn't drive the Porsche that much."

Will turned, a bottle of red in his hand. "He said it was a present to himself, for his fiftieth birthday."

I rolled my eyes.

He chuckled. "He's kind of a walking, talking stereotype of a midlife crisis, complete with a toupee."

Will fished the corkscrew out of a drawer. "The tags that are now on his Porsche were also stolen." He applied the corkscrew, popped the cork.

I went to a cabinet and fetched two wineglasses.

"They belong to an eighty-seven-year-old widow. When I went to her house, the driveway was full of cars. She died a week ago. Heart attack. Today was her funeral."

My throat tightened slightly as I carried the glasses to the breakfast bar.

Will began pouring ruby red liquid into them. "Her car had a fake temporary tag. They're easy to make these days, with templates online. No prints on any of the plates."

"They'd been wiped clean?" I grabbed some paper plates and napkins.

"Yeah." He started pouring the second glass. "This wasn't some kid on a lark. This guy made sure the tag couldn't be traced back to him."

We sat on the stools at the breakfast bar. Will flipped the pizza box open, and we each took a slice. We ate in companionable silence for a moment.

"I've got some new info," I said.

He raised his eyebrows as he took another bite of pizza.

Hmm, how to get around the whole taking-illegal-photos-of-a-confidential-file thing? I too bit off more sausage, cheese, crust and tomato sauce, buying time.

I chewed slowly. It was really good pizza.

Will swigged some wine. "Are you going to tell me or am I supposed to guess?"

I swallowed. "I have reason to believe that Dr. Johnson isn't in on the fraud at the sanitarium. The part of the conversation that got cut off this afternoon, I was asking him about some things Sybil told me." I filled him in on her witnessing Mrs. Ratchette writing in a patient's chart.

I took a sip of wine. "Johnson said she isn't a nurse and Sybil must've been mistaken–"

Will tensed. "You didn't give him Sybil's name, did you?"

"No, of course not. I said a friend who used to work there. Anyway, he seemed genuine. I believe that *he* truly believes Ratchette would never do such a thing."

Will nodded and ate more pizza.

"Sybil also told me that Johnson keeps separate files from the official charts, with his therapy notes. Ratchette makes him photocopies of the nurses' notes." I paused, sipped more wine for courage. "I have reason to believe those photocopies are doctored."

He raised his eyebrows again. "Oh? What leads you to believe that?"

"You don't want to know."

He chewed on more pizza, washed it down with wine. "Okay."

That's it? Okay? Ms. Snark said internally.

Don't look a gift horse in the mouth, inner Mom told her.

Ignoring their voices, I gulped the rest of my wine. I wouldn't get a better opening than this.

"Earlier today, when I said I needed to talk to Johnson."

"Yes?" Will said absentmindedly. His eyes were on my glass as he refilled it.

"You asked why…" I took another sip. There was something to this liquid courage thing. The slight alcohol buzz helped me throw caution to the wind. "Your tone seemed sarcastic."

He snorted softly. "Well, you have been known to go off half-cocked. Remember that Navy guy who hired you to play detective? He–"

I held up my hand in a stop gesture. "That was three years ago. I've learned a few things since then."

Will let out a slight chuckle. "Well, you've gotta admit…"

Pressure was building in my chest.

"…he had you–"

"Stop!" Heat flushed my cheeks.

He looked as startled as I felt. I took a deep breath.

"If we are going to work together as private investigators," I said, in as even a tone as I could muster, "you can't be condescending like that."

"I" statements, Jo Ann reminded me internally.

Will all you people get out of my head!

"*I* need to feel," I said out loud, "that you respect me as an equal, that we're partners."

Will glanced away. "You do have a tendency to assume your clients are all innocence and light."

I bristled, but caught myself before I responded defensively.

Again going for an even tone, I said, "I've grown a bit in that area as well. I've had quite a few second thoughts about Russ, that he might really be suicidal, and/or paranoid. But I don't believe for a New York minute that he sabotaged his own plane. That's just ludicrous."

Will actually nodded. "And the attacks on Carla and now on you say that someone out there doesn't want this whole thing investigated."

I could let things go at this point. The tension had eased. We were back on common ground…

But I shook my head slightly. "If we're going to make this working-together thing work, you can't do that again."

Will swiveled toward me on his stool, held up his hands, palms out. "What do you want from me?" His tone was half belligerent, half forlorn.

My stomach tensed. "Not that much." I grabbed one of his hands and held it between both of mine.

He tried to pull loose. I held on. He hadn't tugged all that hard, which told me he didn't want to fight any more than I did.

"I need you to not use that tone again, or at least try really hard not to go there again."

He stared at me for a beat. Then he said, "I will try not to do it again. Okay?"

I nodded. "Thank you."

I squeezed his hand, let it go, and we turned back to our plates.

"What if I forget and screw up?" he said after a moment.

"Don't worry, I'll remind you."

He turned toward me, his expression odd, part annoyed, part… scared?

Duh," Ms. Snark said internally, *he has his own demons from a failed marriage, remember?*

I put my hand over my heart, as if swearing an oath. "And I will try really hard to make the reminder gentle, not naggy."

We ate lukewarm pizza, still delicious, and sipped wine for a few minutes.

Now he was staring into space, with that expression that says someone is miles away. I assumed he was thinking about work.

"You know," he said in a low voice, not looking my way, "there's six years between us. We've never really talked about that."

"It's not that big of an age difference," I said.

"No, not now, but when we first met. You were in your early thirties and I was seeing forty on the horizon. I thought of you as much younger than me back then." He turned to face me. "You're right. I need to adjust my thinking."

My heart warmed in my chest. This was the main reason I loved this man. He was far more astute about human dynamics than most men, heck, than most people. And he was willing to put his perspective aside and look at something from a different angle.

That trait probably came from years of being a detective.

Or perhaps that trait is what makes him a good detective, inner Mom said. *So tell him.*

Tell him what? Oh…

I slid off my stool and wrapped my arms around his shoulders. "I love you, Will Haines."

He chuckled. "I love you too." And he kissed me.

I woke up the next morning feeling better than I had in months. I was fully vaccinated, and things were great between Will and me. *And* we were about to embark on this new adventure together, as private investigators.

Then I remembered poor Russ in jail and my mood deflated some.

I sat up on the side of the bed and grabbed my cell phone. I'd put it on *do not disturb* when things had become amorous last night.

No call or text from Wes, but Jo Ann had returned my call, at ten-fifteen last night. I listened to the voicemail message.

"Marcia, sorry I couldn't call earlier." She sounded exhausted. "And sorry for calling this late. I had a suicidal client I spent the evening getting into the hospital. Russ does have a case worker. She was assigned when he was hospitalized. Last time I talked to her was after he got out. I'm not sure she even knows that he's in jail. Her name is Gloria Vargas, and her number is…wait a sec…" A pause and she rattled off a phone number.

In robe and slippers, I went into our study to get a pad and pencil. Replaying the voicemail, I jotted down the number. I glanced at the clock on the wall. Nine-thirty. Dang, I'd never intended to sleep so late. I'd forgotten to set my alarm.

In the bedroom, I threw on clothes. My phone rang out in the study. Still in my slippers, I raced to grab it before the call went to voicemail, hoping it was Wes.

It wasn't.

It was Sybil, sounding breathless. "Marcia, I hate to bother y'all with this," there was much more Southern in her voice than usual, "but we're stranded out on the main road, near the turn off for town. Some jerk tried to pass us on a curve and miscalculated. He shoved us off into the ditch and then took off."

My heart sped up. "A white SUV?" I ran through the living room.

"Yeah, how'd you know? Well, I guess there are a lot of white SUVs in Florida." She let out a nervous laugh.

A brick of dread had formed in my stomach. I signaled Buddy to follow and threw open the front door.

"Mama swears she's okay and can walk but I'd feel better if you came and got us, if it's not too much hassle."

I reached my car, realized I didn't have my car keys. *Crapola!*

"Wait, here's a white SUV coming back this way," Sybil said.

My heart rate skyrocketed. No time to go back for keys.

I ran to the edge of the horses' pasture and vaulted over the fence, landing on a stone. It cut painfully into my slippered foot.

"Maybe it's him," Sybil innocently prattled on in my ear. "Guess he's not a total–"

Buddy had slipped under the fence. Limping slightly, I took off a-cross the field.

"Sybil!" I shouted. "Lock the doors and keep the windows up. He's the same guy who ran me off the road yesterday. It's related to that sanitarium."

I wasn't sure what I was going to do once I got there, but three women and a dog were better odds than two women, one of them a senior citizen.

"What's the guy doing?" I huffed into the phone as I dodged a pile of manure.

"He's pulled on past and parked on the shoulder behind us." Her voice was low, scared.

Buddy stopped to water a tall weed. I yelled, "Buddy, keep up!" Then felt bad when I realized he hadn't been out yet this morning.

Sorry, boy. I kept running.

"Tell Sherie, pretend you're knocked out. I'm almost there." I glanced over my shoulder. Buddy was racing toward me, but I didn't wait.

I'd reached the other side of the pasture and ducked between the fence railings. Angling across the street, I ran toward the main road, the shoulder's gravel, sharp under my slippered soles.

I spotted Sybil's silver sedan, canted at an angle in a ditch, back end sticking slightly out into the road.

My heart skipped a beat. They were just past the curve. Someone coming around it would hit them.

I had a stitch in my side but forced myself to keep running. Buddy caught up.

Then I saw the man, standing by Sybil's front grill. Tall and thin, jeans, a long-sleeved dark tee. A motorcycle helmet with the visor down.

He was staring into the interior of the car.

I watched in horror as he lifted a baseball bat high in the air.

CHAPTER NINETEEN

"Buddy, grab arm!"

A black blur streaked past. My dog jumped from a few feet away and sank his teeth into the guy's arm.

His momentum knocked them both over. The bat went flying.

"Buddy, hold!" Into the phone, I yelled. "Get out. Now! Run toward me, toward town."

Sybil jumped out of the car, reached back in to help her mother slide across.

Buddy was standing on the man's chest. The guy was writhing, arms flailing, trying to get him off.

Sherie was out of the car and they were racing in my direction. I was afraid the guy was going to hurt Buddy in his struggle to get away.

"Off, Buddy. Protect!"

The big dog jumped away from the man, but stood between him and us, barking ferociously. The guy scrambled to his feet and took off for his SUV. Buddy kept barking.

Sherie and Sybil had reached me. Afraid he might make a U-turn and come back after us, I grabbed Sherie's upper arm. With her daughter on the other side, we practically lifted her off her feet, our younger legs pumping hard.

"Buddy, come," I called over my shoulder.

He whirled around and raced after us.

We reached the turnoff for Mayfair. I dared to glance back. No sign of the white SUV.

I slowed us down, loosened my grip on Sherie's arm. But we all kept jogging toward the motel.

I called Will and miraculously he picked up. I succinctly filled him in. "Be there in twenty," was all he said before disconnecting.

Once safely on the motel's Victorian porch, Sherie grabbed me and Sybil and clutched us against her in a bear hug. "Thank you, Lord Jesus," she whispered in our ears.

Amen! My mother's voice inside my head.

I said it out loud, "Amen."

We pulled apart. Sherie rubbed her arm.

"Sorry," I said.

"No problem. Well worth the bruise." She tried to grin at me but it was a little crooked.

"What was he going to do with that baseball bat?" Sybil said in a shaky voice.

"Probably bash in the windshield," I said, "to make the accident appear to be worse than it was."

Sherie shot me a sharp look.

But she needn't have worried. I wasn't about to tell Sybil the rest of my speculations, that he would have checked for pulses, and finding them still alive, used the bat on them.

I glanced around, searching for Buddy. He'd stayed on the ground near the bottom of the porch steps. He whined softly.

This dog wasn't a whiner. He only did so when he needed to go to the bathroom or was worried about me, had sensed my anxiety.

"I'm okay, boy," I reassured him.

I'd misread his whine. He took my words as permission, cocked his leg and peed on the latticework around the porch base.

We all looked at each other. Sherie's eyes were dancing. We cracked up. I silently thanked him for the distraction.

"What the devil is that dog doing?" Edna's voice, scolding, cut through our slightly hysterical laughter.

Sherie turned to her friend. "You're not gonna believe what just happened."

A car squealed around the curve next to the diner, half a block away, sending my heart rate sky high again.

But it was a sheriff's department cruiser. It screeched to a halt and Deputy Johnny Redmond jumped out.

"Y'all okay?" he called out.

"Yes, but a guy–"

Johnny held up a hand. "Will called me. I'm on it."

He was back in the car and had blasted away from the curb before I could close my mouth.

Sitting at the breakfast bar, Will and I compared notes over an early lunch that neither of us particularly wanted. I hadn't had any breakfast, but still I only nibbled on my peanut butter and banana sandwich.

"Since you couldn't see his face," Will said, "that brings us no closer to identifying this guy, but Buddy got a chunk of his shirt–"

I snorted softly. "He's collecting the guy's wardrobe, one fragment at a time." I was trying for a joke but it fell flat.

Will gave me a small smile. "There's blood on it."

I winced. I'd been dreading the day when Buddy bit down too hard and drew blood. That could get a dog put down.

Will reached across the breakfast bar and squeezed my hand. "Don't worry. He won't be able to do much about a dog bite when he's facing three attempted murder charges."

"Four, if you count Carla."

"Are you sure it was the same guy?"

"Am I sure, yes. Can I testify that it was, no. But it was the same build, and how likely is it that more than one person is out to get me?"

Will smirked.

"Don't you dare say what you're thinking."

He chuckled softly. "The good news is we can get DNA from that blood. The bad news is it will take at least a few weeks to get those results back."

"I thought you all had one of those new gizmos at the sheriff's department, that can test DNA quickly."

"We do, but we'd need a bigger sample than a tiny smear on a little piece of cloth. We had to send it to the state lab."

My stomach grumbled. I took a bite of my sandwich and chewed, the blend of sweetness from the banana and saltiness from the peanut butter a delight on my tongue.

The tightness in my chest, that had been there all morning, loosened some. I ate with more enthusiasm for a few minutes.

"So why do you think this guy keeps coming after us? Well, mostly me, I guess. It seems kind of reckless."

"It's gotta be someone connected to that hospital. That's the only thing that explains him going after both you and Sybil. And I suspect he hasn't done his homework."

"What do you mean?" I popped the last bite of my sandwich in my mouth.

"Well, you're thinking he's being reckless because he's gone after you twice now and Sybil once, and almost got caught each of those times. But I don't think he realizes you're married to a cop. I suspect he thinks it was just bad luck that an unmarked police vehicle came along as he was trying to run you off the road."

"And he didn't expect Sybil to call me when he ran them off the road. From his perspective, now that Russ is being blamed for the plane sabotage and his credibility is shot, all he has to do is–"

"Get rid of the women who were poking around at the hospital."

I bristled, but Will was grinning. He was teasing me.

"And make it look like a car accident," I added, as I picked up our sandwich plates and carried them to the sink. I turned and leaned against the granite counter's edge.

Will slid off his stool. "Could the guy have been Johnson?"

"I don't think so. He's not quite that thin. And I don't see him wielding baseball bats to bash people's heads in."

"He could've hired somebody."

"Yeah, I can see him doing that. But again, I'm not sure he's even aware of the fraud."

"Well, I gotta get back to work." Will turned toward the door, then said over his shoulder. "By the way, the Porsche owner is sending me a list of all the places he's been in that car in the last couple of weeks." He sketched me a wave and was out the door.

I was a little surprised he'd told me that, indeed, that he was keeping me so much in the loop when it was officially a police investigation. Maybe it was the captain taking him off the case, or the fact that Joe Brown was handling it poorly... or maybe he was already beginning to disconnect from the job that he knew he'd be leaving in a few months. But something was shifting in him.

As I was loading the sandwich plates into the dishwasher, my phone pinged, announcing a text. It was from Wes.

CWs not the problem. Only 2 of our vets who went to that hospital had the same one.

I assumed CWs were case workers, which reminded me to call Russ's. I punched in the number that Jo Ann had given me.

"Gloria Vargas." A harried, older woman's voice. No Southern accent so most likely a transplant like myself.

"Ms. Vargas, this is Marcia Banks-Haines. I'm calling about Russell Fortham."

A beat of silence. "Yes?" Her voice was wary now.

"I work for the agency that's providing Captain Fortham with a service dog. I have a waiver of confidentiality and I've already spoken to Jo Ann Hamilton, Russ's counselor."

"Yes?" A bit impatient this time.

I'd better cut to the chase. "People keep trying to label him as suicidal, but he's not. I met with him yesterday and he was fine. His mood was normal, under the circumstances."

"Who are you again?"

"I'm a service dog trainer." I matched her terse tone. "But I have an advanced degree in counseling psychology. I know depression when I see it, and the absence of it when it's not there."

"Look, Ms...."

"Banks-Haines."

"I'm quite aware that he's no longer suicidal. He was released from the hospital last week, if memory serves me right. Now, I'm very busy. I have to–"

"Did you know he was in jail?"

"Huh?"

I guess that's a no, Ms. Snark quipped inside my head.

Another beat of silence. "Maybe you should start from the beginning, young lady."

So I did. I filled her in on Russ's suspicions about the hospital and that we had begun a quiet investigation. I didn't mention Wes or Sybil for now. Then I told her about the plane crash, Russ being arrested, and someone from the sanitarium showing up at his bail hearing to Baker-Act him.

"Now, he's in jail, under suicide watch, and they're weaning him off the antidepressant that was actually helping him. I'm not sure they've started him on anything else or even that anyone has done an official psych evaluation recently."

"Are they sure the plane was sabotaged?"

"Yes. Russ thinks someone tried to kill him, because we're investigating."

"Ms. Banks-Haines, this all sounds a little...fantastic."

"Call me Marcia. It's easier. And I'd be inclined to agree with you, except there've been two attempts on my life since we began investigating, and one on someone who was helping me."

She sucked in air. "Was? They weren't..."

"No. They're fine. I meant they were helping me in the past. I'm not about to involve them anymore."

"Okay, let me see what I can arrange to get the captain evaluated."

"Uh, ma'am, I know you're busy, but can you do it soon? I'm not sure Russ's mood won't deteriorate if he has to stay in jail much longer. And he's worried about his mother. You know about her situation?"

"Yes, he told me about her. Tell her we're working on getting him out."

"I will. Thanks so much."

We disconnected and I flopped down on the sofa. "Phew." Buddy came over and nudged my knee. He whined.

"You need to go out?"

He put his paw up on my knee and whined again. *Duh.* He was responding to my emotions, as he'd been taught to do.

I patted his head. "I'm okay, boy, but thanks for asking."

Realizing I hadn't checked my email in a while, I went into the study. Buddy followed and settled in the middle of the rug. I booted up my laptop.

Aha! An email from Elise, with attachments. I bounced a bit in my desk chair. Hopefully, she'd found some thread I could pull on.

In the cover email, Elise apologized again for taking so long to get to all of them. *I stayed up all night to get these done. Let me know if you want me to go deeper on anyone.*

I began with the follow-up reports on Talbott and Godwin. Elise had dug into their finances.

Talbott wasn't quite as well off as he pretended to be—he was somewhat overextended credit-wise—but nothing else stood out in his report.

Godwin was a different story. He was a lot overextended. He'd mortgaged his house to the hilt around the time that he and his son-in-law started their charter service. And Elise had found something else, although I didn't have a clue how she'd dug it up. He'd brought several charter clients with him to the new company. Apparently, he had been cultivating these clients while he was still flying out of Pine Hills Airport. But he hadn't applied for a business license in Marion County, and Elise wasn't sure if flying charter clients around would require some kind of upgrade in his pilot's license. She was still researching that question.

I knew who could answer it, however. But first...

I opened the report labeled *Supplemental-James "Sonny" Smith.* She'd found some additional info on his schooling. He'd left his Catholic high school in the middle of ninth grade. Next to that notation, she'd put *(Got in trouble?)*

He'd finished high school in the public school system. His grades must have been good because he'd gotten into the university—so he was legitimately a Gator. But he'd only lasted a year.

More of the same pattern of misspent youth, but nothing to raise alarms. I called him.

"Hey, doll," he said, when I identified myself. "How's it going?"

"Not bad, all things considered. I've got a question for you."

"Shoot?"

"Does a private pilot need additional training or licensure to fly charter flights?"

"Yeah, he or she would need a commercial pilot's license, as well as instrument training, if they don't already have it. Why do you ask? Dog training losing its appeal?" He chuckled.

"No. Did you know Arthur Godwin was flying charter flights out of your airport, without a commercial license?"

He blurted out a cuss word. "No, I did not know that." His voice was tight. "If I had, I would've booted him out of here much sooner."

"He's gone into business with his son-in-law up at Gainesville Regional. I'm wondering if he was stealing fuel to save money on his charter flights, to invest in that venture."

"Could be. So he's your prime suspect now?"

"He's one of them."

"You got other leads?"

"One or two." We were investigating Godwin because that's what a good detective does—you follow all leads, but the helmet-wearing dude running Sybil off the road didn't fit. That pointed more strongly toward the fraud at the sanitarium. However, I didn't want to remind Sonny that Russ had been in a mental hospital, or the "looney bin" as he'd called it.

After a pause, Sonny said, "Hey, about services for Charlie. They won't be releasing his body for a while yet, but I've organized a memorial service for him. It's at a church near here. They've got a big tent so we can be outdoors."

"Great. When and where?" I grabbed a pencil.

"Sunday evening, at six-thirty. But it's hard to find. GPS always gets it wrong, tries to take you down a road that doesn't connect."

I got that. This part of Florida was riddled with roads that stopped and then started up again blocks or even miles later. Before getting married, Becky had lived on a cul-de-sac in Ocala, but three blocks over was another section of road with the same name. People were always getting lost trying to find her.

"Why don't you meet me here at the airport at six?" Sonny was saying. "I'll lead you over to the church."

"Sounds good." We disconnected.

I opened Elise's report on Wesley Sullivan, feeling a little guilty for having ordered it. One, I was obviously overburdening Elise with so many requests, and two, I was spending Russ's money willy-nilly. Wes was an ally, not a suspect.

My chest tightened with more guilt as I read the report. No criminal record nor anything else that indicated he was anything other than what he seemed to be, a fortyish government bureaucrat.

Tsk, he's never married. My mother's voice inside my head.

Mom, I responded internally, *lots of people don't marry in this day and age.*

But that made me wonder. Did he have a long-term girlfriend, or boyfriend? He could be gay.

Did any of that matter? *No.*

I returned my attention to the report. He'd started at the University of Florida in 1998 and graduated in 2003 with a degree in business.

Elise had noted that two things were unusual. Based on his social media postings, he went on vacations to exotic places twice a year.

That seemed somewhat extravagant for his income, Elise had written, *so I checked a few other things. He has a substantial line of credit against the equity in a duplex he owns.*

"Which is probably how he pays for those vacations," I muttered.

And something else interesting. He bought the duplex twelve years ago and he has the first mortgage almost paid off.

So he's frugal. He no doubt eats a lot of brown-bag lunches at that picnic table behind the VA building.

The last report was for Mrs. Ratchette, née Emily Jane Hughes. I wasn't the least bit surprised that she was not a nurse. She'd attended a community college for a few semesters—mostly business courses, not a nursing program—but she hadn't received a degree.

The next paragraph was a bit of a surprise, however. Her son was not her husband's child. She'd gotten pregnant at age sixteen and had raised the baby on her own until her early twenties, when she'd married William Rachette, who was fifteen years older than her. They'd had no other children, and William had died four years ago, after a series of strokes.

Had she married William because he was willing to take the package deal of mother and child?

Okay, that wasn't fair. They could've been madly in love. He would've been in his mid-thirties, not exactly an old man.

As usual, Elise ended her email by asking if I wanted anything else. I was about to type *no*, but thought better of it.

I sat for a moment, contemplating where we were with the investigation. The doctored files Ratchette gave Johnson implied that he was oblivious to what was going on at his own hospital. But they also indicated that something was definitely going on.

There *was* fraud at the sanitarium and Mrs. Rachette was in it up to her stuck-in-the-air nose, but was that why Russ's plane was sabotaged?

That was certainly possible, probable even.

But we could be looking at two different things here. Godwin could be the saboteur and it had nothing to do with the fraud at the sanitarium.

I texted Will with a short summary of the new info on Godwin and asked him if he could get up to Gainesville today.

Then I emailed Elise, requesting that she dig deeper into Emily Ratchette. And could she find the name of the psychiatrist who did contract work for the Leesburg Sanitarium?

CHAPTER TWENTY

I met Carla and Dolly out back to do some training.

They had been practicing the second part of the *Clear* task—what the dog should do when a room was empty.

Carla demonstrated for me, sending Dolly into the training center's kitchen to "Clear room." A few seconds later, she came back to the doorway and sat.

"Good girl," Carla crooned and gave her a treat. "She's ready for the stranger phase. We just need some strangers."

"Lemme see if Sybil and/or Sherie can help out now." It was the perfect excuse to check on them.

Their front door was closed. I rapped lightly.

A few seconds later, the snick of a deadbolt being turned and the door opened. "Hey, Marcia," Sybil said.

"Hey, Syb. Good to see you're being careful."

She gave me a lopsided smile. "I had to oil the deadbolt. It wouldn't move, it's been so long since we used it."

Ours was that kind of town, or at least it had been. I prayed it would be again soon.

"I'm sorry I brought this down on you all, and the town."

She shook her head. "You're doing the right thing, helping a good person who's in a bad situation. We'll all survive."

Dear Lord, I hope so, I thought but didn't say out loud.

"How's your mom doing?"

Sybil grimaced. "She's a bit sore. She's lying down, which is why I'm standing here in the doorway instead of inviting you in."

I waved a hand in the air. "No problem. Actually, I came over to ask a favor. Could you help us with a training task? It shouldn't take more than about ten minutes."

"Sure. Lemme get my keys. I'll be right over."

I waited for her on my porch, then had her sit down in the living room. Carla was outside with Dolly.

"Okay, the dog we're training is going to come in here. She'll sit down in front of you. When she does, say 'Bark,' in a fairly firm voice. Don't say or do anything else. I'll come in after that."

"Got it," Sybil said.

I went outside, leaving the sliding door open, and Carla gave Dolly the "clear room" command. She bounded into the house and sat in front of Sybil, who told her to bark.

The dog let out one sharp yip.

I did a happy dance in my head, as I quickly entered the room, praised Dolly, and gave her a treat.

"Do you want to do it again?"

"The idea is to get her to distinguish between friends and strangers, so no, unfortunately, you can only be a stranger once."

"How many times do you need to do that," Sybil asked, "until you're sure she's got it?"

Carla groaned from the doorway. "About a thousand."

I chuckled. "We might have to settle for thirty or forty. We'll run out of 'strangers.'"

"I'm sure Mama will help so that's one," Sybil said with a small grin. Then her face sobered. "That is, if she's really okay. I made her promise to go to the hospital if she's not better by tomorrow."

"I'll stop over in the morning, using the need for more strangers as an excuse, and if she isn't fine, we'll gang up on her."

Sybil produced a full-blown grin. "Sounds like a plan."

Will texted that he was headed for Gainesville to talk to Godwin. *How precisely did you find out that he was doing charter flights illegally before moving his operation to G'ville?*

Good question, I texted back. *Let me ask.*

I called Elise.

"Check their website," she said, "and read the accolades, especially the second and fourth ones. That's what made me suspicious. Do you want me to dig even deeper?"

"Hang on a sec." I went to the study, woke up my laptop, clicked on the link I'd bookmarked, and scrolled down to *What Our Customers Say About Us.* The second testimonial said, *I've been a charter client of Art Godwin for several years now. Great service at a reasonable cost.*

Next to it was the smiling face of a handsome, forty-something businessman, the breeze ruffling his hundred-dollar haircut. And in the background was the terra cotta main building of Pine Hills Airport.

Gotcha, Art!

"Nope," I said into my phone. "I think this is just what Will needs. We'll take it from here." I thanked her and disconnected.

I texted the website link to Will.

The Chinese carryout Will had brought home was good. The news he'd brought wasn't.

He hadn't gotten anything useful out of Godwin, although he'd seemed anxious when Will brought up the charter clients he flew in and out of Pine Hills Airport.

"He swears they weren't charters. The passengers were only paying for gas. He claims that's allowed with a private pilot license, to share expenses with passengers."

"Yeah, except that he was stealing the gas from other pilots."

"He did more than swear when I brought that up. He was furious, claims he's never stolen anything in his life."

"Do you believe him?"

"Heck no. He doth protest too much. Kept saying he was the most honest person ever. People who are truly honest don't feel the need to proclaim it repeatedly."

"Where do we go with that angle now?"

Will shrugged. "Good question. I think I'll let him stew for a day or two, and then go at him again."

He lifted a chunk of shrimp with his chopsticks and popped it into his mouth. We ate in silence for a few minutes.

Will broke open a fortune cookie. His gaze on the slip of paper, he said, "I've got more bad news."

For a second, I thought he meant his fortune was bad news.

"The guy who ran you, and Sybil and Sherie, off the road..." He shook his head again. "That's been turned over to the traffic guys. They're treating it as a case of road rage."

I dropped my fork. "Say what?"

"Joe refuses to acknowledge that it might be related to his case, so off to traffic it went."

I fumed for a moment, then said, "That reminds me. Did the Porsche owner give you his list of where he's been with the car lately?"

"No, he blew me off. Said he's been too busy."

"Can't you threaten him with obstruction of justice or something?"

"I could threaten but I couldn't make good on the threat. Better to keep using the honey approach, for now at least. If he doesn't come up with something soon, I'll try a little vinegar."

I had barn duty the next morning, but I had to skip riding Niña. It was pouring.

Of course, the rain stopped as soon as I sat down at my breakfast bar with a bowl of cereal—the apple I'd grabbed earlier hadn't made the cut as a real breakfast.

I was slurping down my raisin bran, when I got a text from Jo Ann Hamilton.

What's happening with Russ? And when are you going to schedule a session to discuss the child issue?

Sighing, I put down my spoon and answered the first question.

Talked to his case worker. She's working on getting him a new eval asap.

I put my phone back down, having no intention of answering the second question. I picked up my spoon.

The phone rang. I glanced at the caller ID. *Jo Ann.*

I let it go to voicemail. That meant we'd waste the first five to ten minutes of the next session analyzing my "resistance," but I just wasn't ready to deal with that issue yet. We'd been over it again and again, *ad nauseum.*

And then the miscarriage, and I'd thought I knew what I wanted. But now…

You'd better figure it out soon. A chorus of voices in my head, Ms. Snark and inner Mom ganging up on me again.

But they were right. My doctor had said to give it a month after my second vaccine before trying to make a baby again. Thirteen days and counting, before I had to make the most important and irreversible decision of my life.

My phone rang again while I was putting my cereal bowl in the dishwasher. I grabbed it off the breakfast bar. It was Becky.

"Hey you," I answered.

"Hey yourself. How's it going?" Her cheerful voice immediately brightened my mood.

"Not bad. Will and I are making some progress in our first unofficial investigation together." I filled her in, still waltzing around anything that would identify Russ, even though she'd already figured out the case was about the plane crash.

I also downplayed the guy running me off the road.

"It's so exciting that you and Will are going to start the P.I. agency together," she said when I'd finished.

"I know. I get giddy every time I think about it. So, how are my godchildren?" My heart warmed at the thought of their sweet little faces, framed with dark curls like their mother's.

"They're driving me crazy at the moment. Two-year molars coming in. Any news on the baby front over there in Mayfair?"

"I've got to wait another two weeks... And I'm having second thoughts." Yes, I said I didn't want to deal with the issue yet with Jo Ann, but that was because she would hold my feet to the fire for at least the length of a counseling session. With Becky, I could change the subject if I wanted to.

"Geez Louise, Marcia," Becky said with exaggerated frustration.

Or at least I thought it was exaggerated. Maybe she really was tired of hearing it. Even best friends have their limits.

So I started with the insight I'd had during my last session with Jo Ann, about feeling like a child waiting to be shamed and the subtle undercurrent of anxiety that had caused for years.

"Wow," she said, "I never would have thought of you as an anxious person."

"Me neither. You know, when something's with you all the time, it seems normal."

"Is it gone now?"

"Most of the time." I thought about Will's patronizing tone the other day. "And when I feel it now, I notice. It's not normal anymore."

A slight pause, then, "I don't think I fully felt like an adult until the twins were born."

"Really?"

"Yeah. There's nothing like multiple fetal feet kicking your bladder to make you feel like a full-blown woman."

I chuckled with her, until my next thought sobered my mood. "How do you deal with the worry, Beck?"

She sighed. "A healthy dose of denial. You tell yourself you're doing everything possible to take good care of them and protect them, and you convince yourself that will be enough."

A fist squeezed my heart as I recalled two Halloweens ago, when doing everything possible to protect her children *hadn't* been enough—

when Winston had been kidnapped. Becky and Andy had been devastated.

We had all been devastated.

"It took months to stop worrying every minute…" her mind had apparently gone in the same direction, "…after we got Winston back."

"Thank the universe we got him back, safe and sound."

"Thank you!" Becky said. "You found him."

I felt a flash of the faith I'd had as a child, before church and God became associated with shaming old biddies. "I think I got a little guidance."

"Hey, something just occurred to me," Becky said. "You've already got the worrying, with Winnie and Jazzie." She used my nicknames for them. "I mean not as much as if you were their parent and taking care of them every day, but–"

"But it would still break my heart if anything happened to them," I finished for her.

"Exactly. So why not have the joys of parenting as well?"

Something shifted inside as her words sunk in. "Hmm, I'll have to chew on that some."

My phone bleeped in my ear, indicating an incoming text. "Hang on."

It was from Carla, asking if I was ready to do some training.

"Gotta go," I said to Becky. "Duty calls."

"Investigating or training?"

"The latter."

I texted Carla to bring Dolly over to our backyard. Then I went next door to the Wells's house.

"How are you feeling?" I asked when Sherie answered my knock.

"A little stiff but better than yesterday."

Sybil's face appeared over her shoulder. "I'd still rather you'd go to the hospital and get checked out."

Sherie half turned. "And I'd rather have a daughter who wasn't a nag." She softened the words with a smile.

"Sherie, would you feel up to helping us—"

"I already told her about it," Sybil said.

"Great. Syb, why don't you come too? And we'll try something else once we've done the first part with your mom."

"Sure." Her dark eyes sparkled with excitement.

You used to be that excited about training, Ms. Snark commented internally but without her usual snide tone.

I blew out a soft sigh. Yet another issue I had to sort out. How much dog training would I be able to fit in—would I *want* to fit in—once I was an investigator?

I led the way to my porch and asked Sybil to stay there for a few minutes. She sat down on the steps.

Inside, I settled Sherie in a chair at our dining table, and we went through the "clear room" routine.

When I heard Dolly bark, I hurried inside. "Good girl." I gave her a treat. "Dolly, this is Sherie."

My neighbor held out her hand for the dog to sniff her fingers.

Instead Dolly put her paw in the outstretched palm.

Sherie grinned. "Well, howdy do, Dolly?"

Carla chuckled from the doorway. "I taught her that. I figured it would ease the tension after she's barked at somebody."

I paused, considering if there was any downside to this.

"Don't worry. She only does it with the right cue." Carla took a step inside. "Dolly, this is Marcia." She pointed at me.

The dog trotted over, sat in front of me, and offered her paw.

I laughed. "I think that's a great addition." And I also thought that Carla was definitely ready to graduate from being a trainer-in-training. With a small jolt, I realized I would miss her.

I sent Carla and the dog out back, then invited Sybil in and gestured for her to sit on the sofa. "Neither of you say or do anything when Dolly comes in." They nodded.

I stepped outside the slider, and Carla said, "Clear room."

The dog ran inside. I peeked around the edge of the door. She sat first in front of Sybil and wagged her tail.

After a beat, I said, "Dolly, clear room." She ran over to Sherie and sat. She cocked her head, then looked at me.

I raced over to her, before she could become confused and perhaps bark. "Good girl. You're such a good girl." I knelt next to her and rubbed behind her ears.

I swear that dog grinned at me.

I spent the rest of the afternoon recruiting neighbors. I got the two Baker girls—Allie, now fourteen, and Sarah, now ten—to come help. They thought it was great fun, and after they had each been the "stranger," I had them both sit in the room. Dolly once again ran to each and sat without barking.

Allie asked if she could train to be a service dog trainer. "If you still want to when you're sixteen, come see me," I told her.

Rachel Bachman was watering her flowers. I recruited her and her gangly, teenage stepson, TT—for Tony Too. Poor kid. Why couldn't they just call him Junior?

Jess Randall and her waitress, Lisa, came over during the lull between lunch and dinner carryout orders.

Unfortunately, Susanna and Edna weren't home. Dexter stood behind the screen door on the back of the motel and informed me that they'd gone to the Walmart in Belleview to buy new towels. "I got one more day." He held up a finger. "Mama said I gotta wait two weeks from my last vaccine before I can be around people."

I could've suggested that he wear a mask and come on over to my house, since I was fully vaccinated. But Dexter was a simple soul, a brick or two short of a full load, thanks to the beatings his late father had given Susanna during her pregnancy. I didn't want to confuse him. "Okay, I'll catch you all later."

I even managed to talk our postmistress, Charlene Woodward, into helping out. She was afraid of dogs, but I pointed out that this was a border collie, one of the sweetest breeds ever, and interacting with Dolly might help her overcome her phobia.

She broke out in a sweat when Dolly entered the room, but she remembered to say "Bark."

Dolly did, and I quickly said, "Dolly, this is Charlene."

The dog lifted her paw. Laughing—a little nervously, but laughing nonetheless—Charlene took the paw and shook it.

By four o'clock, I'd run out of neighbors who were home. I'd make the rounds again this weekend.

But I was content for now. Dolly had performed beautifully, only getting confused a couple of times about who she was supposed to bark at.

The rest of the afternoon and evening were uneventful, which was not necessarily a good thing.

I worked out to not just one but all three of the self-defense videos, then checked my phone for texts and my laptop for emails.

Still no news from Russ's case worker. And nothing more from Elise. She owed me at least one more in-depth report, maybe two. I'd lost track.

If you're gonna be a private eye, Ms. Snark pointed out in her best snide tone, *you need to be more organized.*

I mentally stuck my tongue out at her, but I opened my laptop to create a spreadsheet.

I was halfway through listing each suspect and all we knew about them when Will came home. He'd heard nothing from the Porsche's owner.

"He's got one more day," Will said, "and then it's time for vinegar."

With matching sighs, we put it all aside, grilled steaks, drank wine and talked about color schemes for the nursery.

My phone rang, yanking me from a sound sleep. In the dark, I fumbled on the nightstand for it.

"Wha'?" Will mumbled beside me.

Amazing. He could answer his own cell phone in the middle of the night before the first ring was completed, but the somewhat different ring tone of my phone solicited only a muffled, semi-somnolent response.

I finally located the offending instrument and checked caller ID. *Jo Ann*, my screen read.

My heart pounded. Why was she calling—I glanced at the time on my phone—at four-twenty in the morning?

"Hello," I said softly into the phone.

Grumbling, Will rolled over on his side, away from me.

Seriously, Ms. Snark griped internally. *How often does our phone ring in the middle of the night, compared to his?*

"Marcia, I'm so sorry to call this early." Jo Ann's voice was a bit frantic.

"What's up?" I whispered. I jogged down the hall toward our study.

"I just got a call from the case worker, who got a call from the jail. Russ tried to hang himself in his cell."

I froze halfway down the hall. "No way."

CHAPTER TWENTY-ONE

"I know it's hard to believe," Jo Ann said, "but…" She sounded choked up.

"Is he…?" She'd said "tried." I prayed for lack of success.

My throat had closed, but otherwise, my reaction was still disbelief.

"Mrs. Vargas said he's okay," Jo Ann said. "A little woozy, they told her."

Woozy?

I pivoted slowly, shaking my head. "Do you have details?"

"He was found by the guard, when he did his check on the suicidal inmates."

"Method?" I walked back toward the bedroom.

"His bed sheet, torn into strips and tied together. He was hanging from the bars."

Something hardened inside my chest.

Back in the bedroom, I stared at Will, who'd gone back to sleep. "What exactly does 'hanging from the bars' mean?" I didn't bother to keep my voice down.

"I don't know. That's all she said. What are you thinking?"

I half smiled. She'd picked up on my this-can't-be-right attitude.

"I'm thinking he didn't try to kill himself. He was slightly depressed when I saw him the other day, but he was a long way from suicidal."

And he'd promised me he wouldn't hurt himself.

"I think this was another attempt to either kill him *or* discredit him by proving to the authorities, once and for all, that he is crazy and suicidal."

Will harrumphed in his sleep. I was beginning to look forward to waking him up.

"Jo Ann, I'll call you back when I know more."

"Wait! What are you going to do?"

"Go over to the jail, with my husband."

"Okay, I'm going to call Gloria Vargas back. See if she's willing to meet you there. She has some clout as a VA case worker."

Not as much clout as a sheriff's department detective, I thought.

"Do you want me to come too?" Jo Ann added.

I thought about that for a beat. "Probably not necessary."

"Let me know what happens."

"Will do."

We arrived at the jail at five-fifteen, wearing yesterday's clothes, thrown on in a frenzy.

It took more than a flash of Will's badge to get us into the medical dorm. But after some discussion—during which Will suggested calling the sheriff, and waking him up, to get authorization—we were escorted to a room with several beds lined up against one wall.

At the far end, a glass window separated the room from a guard's cubicle. A young Hispanic deputy watched us intently.

A kid in a white doctor's jacket—he looked about sixteen to me—glanced up from beside a bed occupied by a very large lump under a blanket. His face registered some alarm. "Who are you?"

I guess he wasn't used to civilians in his infirmary in the middle of the night.

"Sheriff's Detective Haines," Will said, "and my partner, Marcia Banks."

My heart warmed inside my chest.

"We have reason to believe," Will continued, "that someone tried to kill Mr. Fortham."

"But he was on suicide watch," the doc said, as if that explained everything.

The guard's eyebrows had gone up. Apparently he could hear what we were saying.

"Is Mr. Fortham awake?" I asked.

"More or less," the doctor said.

We went around to the other side of the bed from the doc, who didn't move.

"We need to talk to him, alone." Will's tone was firm.

The doctor shrugged and walked away.

I crouched beside the lumpy form on the bed and put my hand on a blanket-clad shoulder. "Russ?"

He struggled to roll over, to free himself of the blanket. "Marcia?" he said groggily.

"Yes. Are you okay?"

"I guess."

I noted red marks across his neck. "What happened?"

"I don't know for sure." His voice was raw. "I, um, woke up, in the infirmary, a little while ago." He looked around, as if trying to figure out where he was now. Then his eyes rolled partway back in his head.

I glanced up at Will. "I think he's been drugged."

To Russ I said, "What's the last thing you remember before waking up?"

"I was in my cell. I'd laid down on my cot and was thinking about…" He blushed. "I, um, drifted off. That's all I remember."

How sweet that he'd gone to sleep thinking about Carla. But what had happened after that? Surely he didn't try to hang himself in his sleep.

Russ's eyes were drifting closed. "Sorry," he slurred, "I'm havin' trouble stayin' awake."

The kid in doc's clothing was headed back our way.

"We need some blood drawn," Will said, "to run a tox screen."

The doc bristled. "I can't do that on your say-so."

Will glared at him.

I had been eyeballing the name badge just above the breast pocket of the man's white coat. No MD after his name. Instead there were a bunch of letters that included RN and NP.

"The symptoms you think are caused by some drug," he was saying, "are likely from the brain hypoxia—lack of oxygen to the brain."

I cleared my throat softly and stared at his name badge.

Will followed my line of vision. "Let's start over," he said, in a friendlier tone. "I'm Detective Will Haines, and you are?"

A slight hesitation, then, "Richard Sylvan, nurse practitioner."

"Nice to meet you, Mr. Sylvan," I said, also in a friendly voice. "Is Captain Fortham's oxygen level back to normal?"

"Of course. That's the first thing we took care of. And what's with the 'Captain?'"

"He's a veteran, Air Force," I said.

"Oh." The NP looked slightly chagrined.

"How long was he oxygen deprived?" Will asked.

"No more than a couple of minutes."

I breathed out a soft sigh of relief. Probably no permanent brain damage then. "He doesn't remember anything after going to sleep," I said.

"That's most likely the brain hypoxia as well. It can cause temporary memory loss." The NP had relaxed some.

"So the memory of what happened might come back?" Will said.

The NP nodded.

"How do you know it was only a couple of minutes?" I asked.

"The guard had just done his standard check. He said he had a nagging feeling about the way Fortham was lying on his cot. He had his eyes closed but he seemed tense. So Grimes—that's the guard—he went down to his cell again after five minutes and found him. Fortham had tied the sheet to the bars higher up, and leaned into it until he passed out." The NP used his hands to stretch an imaginary sheet across his own throat.

"Allowing time for rigging the sheet that way, it couldn't have been more than a minute or two that he was without sufficient oxygen."

"Would the hypoxia cause him to be groggy?" I asked, glancing at Russ's now sleeping form.

The NP also turned slightly and looked at Russ. "I don't know. The only other cases of it I've seen were patients with sleep apnea, and they're sleepy all the time."

"Because the apnea is waking them up repeatedly during the night?" I said.

He nodded.

"So there might be something to our suspicions about drugs?" Will said.

The NP let out a humorless chuckle. "The warden will tell you there are no drugs in this facility. But we see the occasional OD here in the infirmary, so some stuff is getting smuggled in." A slight hesitation again, then, "I'll draw a sample and get it to the lab first thing in the morning."

"Thanks," Will said. "We'll be in touch. Where are the suicide watch cells?"

The NP gestured toward a door to the left of the guard's window.

We walked to it and waited for the guard to buzz us through.

He met us on the other side. Will explained that we were investigating the Fortham suicide attempt, again introducing me as his partner.

I hoped that wouldn't come back to bite him, but I was definitely basking in the warmth of the role.

"Sorry, sir, I just came on duty. Grimes left early. Said he felt ill." The guard's eyes were wide. Was he worried about Covid? Surely the jail personnel had been vaccinated by now. Or was he shaken by the attempted suicide?

"Tell me about Grimes," Will said.

I wandered down the row of cells. Most had two cots in them, occupied by sleeping forms. One contained a sleeping inmate and an empty cot covered by a fitted sheet.

The end cell had to be Russ's. It held two empty cots. My heart stuttered at the sight of lengths of sheet, tied together with fat knots, hanging in a large loop from the bars above one of them.

I hastily turned away, wandered back toward Will and the guard, trying not to think about how close Russ had come. If the guard hadn't sensed something was off, if he'd waited until his next normal check-in time, at best, Russ would be brain-damaged.

At worst, he'd be dead.

An elusive thought nagged at the edges of my sleep-deprived brain, but I couldn't quite lasso it and drag it out into the light.

As I stepped up next to Will, he was thanking the guard. "We need to see the cell now."

"It's down here." I pivoted and led the way. I pointed into the last cell.

Will stopped. He scanned the barren space. "Rodriguez."

The guard, who had followed us, said, "Yes, sir?"

"Can you unlock this cell, and then get me, us something to use as a large evidence bag?"

"Sure thing, Detective." He opened the cell door and headed back the way we'd come.

While we waited, Will used his phone to take photos of the cell, and especially of the sheet loop from various angles.

The guard returned with a large, plastic garbage bag. "Will this do?"

"That's fine." Will gestured for him to give it to me. "Lay it out, open on the cot."

I did so and Will gingerly untied the knots attaching the loop to the cell's bars. He laid the sheeting down carefully and brought the sides of the bag up around it.

Jolted again by how close Russ had come to death, I glanced away. The elusive thought galloped past the edge of my consciousness. I reached out to grab it. "The sheets," I blurted out.

"What?" Will said, as he closed the bag's drawstring.

I slipped out of the cell and over to the one next door, where there was an empty cot covered by a fitted sheet. "Bring that here for a minute, would you?"

He hauled the bag around to that cell's door.

"Open it for a sec," I said.

"I don't want to get the sheet contaminated."

"Just open the top enough to see in."

He did so, and I looked at one sheet, then the other, back and forth a couple of times. He followed my line of vision and also looked at both of them.

"They're not the same color," he said.

"And not the same thread count. I'd bet money on it."

"Hey, Rodriguez," he called out.

"Shh, that guy's asleep." I pointed to the other occupied cot.

"Don't worry," Rodriguez said as he jogged up to us. "He's on a sedative that knocks him out cold at night."

Hmm. I wondered how hard it would've been for someone to get their hands on a dose of that guy's sedative, and maybe give it to Russ.

"Do you all get your sheets from one source?" Will was asking.

"Yeah," the guard said. "From a linen supply company."

"And are they always like this one, kind of coarse and off white?"

The guard nodded.

"Can we take this sheet?" Will asked, pointing toward the one on the empty cot.

"Sure. You want another bag?"

"Nope, we only need this for comparison."

Will handed me the plastic garbage bag as the guard unlocked the cell. Will stepped in and yanked the sheet off the cot.

Outside the cell, he traded with me, taking the bag and handing me the balled-up sheet.

Will nodded to the guard. "Thanks a lot, man." He walked away.

I nodded my thanks and ran a few steps to catch up with my "partner." "Aren't you going to declare the cell a crime scene?" I whispered.

He shook his head slightly. "I'm trying to operate under the radar here," he whispered back. "Hopefully, my boss won't find out that I got involved in this until after we know what happened."

"What about Russ? Is he safe here?"

We had reached the corridor outside the medical dorm. Will stopped and turned to me, taking off his mask. He sighed and his rugged face sagged. "He's about as safe as we can make him, short of breaking him out of jail. Once I have more info, I'll call the infirmary and ask them to keep him there, under guard, for at least twenty-four hours."

He started walking and I fell into step next to him. We didn't speak again until we were outside of the jail building.

I took off my mask. "What's the plan?"

"I'm going to call a buddy of mine at the state lab in Jacksonville, see if he's willing to come in on a Saturday to check out the sheet. Then I'm going to make a surprise house call to the guard who went home sick."

"I'm sorry. This was supposed to be your day off."

"No, it's good that I'm off. That way I can–"

"Keep it under the radar. Got it."

"Yeah. Joe's not gonna be happy when he finds out I've been mucking around in his case."

We'd reached the side of his truck, one of the few vehicles in the parking lot. Will put the garbage bag and the other sheet on the cab's narrow backseat. He wrote out a label and stuck it to the black bag with tape from his glove box. "As evidence bags go, it's a little makeshift, but it'll have to do."

A throat cleared behind us.

We whirled around, almost colliding with each other.

A woman stood ten feet away, in a navy skirted suit, curly gray hair framing a frowning face. She was on the upper edge of middle-aged.

"You wouldn't happen to be Marcia Banks-Haines?" she said to me.

I nodded. "And you're Gloria Vargas. Thanks for coming out so early."

Will moved to put his mask back on. She waved a hand at him. "I've been vaccinated."

"We have too," I said. Will and I took turns filling her in. Will mentioned the differences between the sheets, and I threw in our suspicion that Russ had been drugged.

When we'd finished, she said, "Is my client safe?"

Will grimaced. "Honestly, we could keep him safer if he was out of jail, but with them thinking this was another suicide attempt..." He trailed off.

Mrs. Vargas's chin went up. "I'll see what I can do."

She turned and walked briskly toward the jail.

CHAPTER TWENTY-TWO

I fell asleep on the drive home, jolting awake as Will stopped in front of our house.

"Before you go in," he said, "find Johnny Redmond and tell him what happened. Ask him to stick close to our street today. There might be another attempt on you or Sybil."

I shuddered, more because of the risk to Sybil and Sherie.

I glanced at his dashboard clock. Five after seven. "The diner's open so he shouldn't be hard to find."

Will grinned and I hopped out of his truck.

"I might be late. Don't wait dinner."

I nodded and blew him a kiss.

~

That Saturday morning felt like the longest in my life.

For one thing, it had started way too early, with Jo Ann's frantic phone call. I was seriously sleep deprived, which made it hard to concentrate as Carla and I worked with the dogs.

Will texted a few times with brief progress reports. Sometimes excruciatingly brief.

Had good luck at the lab was one of them.

At lunchtime, Buddy and I headed up the road. I was craving one of Jess's grilled cheese sandwiches with tomato bisque.

Johnny Redmond pulled his cruiser up beside us and lowered his window. "You goin' to the diner, Marcia?"

I nodded.

"Tell Jess I said hi." His voice was wistful.

I had a funny feeling he wasn't taking any breaks from his patrolling today. "Will do. Would you like me to get you a sandwich?"

His face brightened some. If he didn't get to visit his lady love, at least he'd get to eat. "Tell her my usual."

I sketched him a salute and he went around the curve in Main Street, toward the main entrance into town.

I looked both ways, far more carefully than I normally would, just in case the helmeted crazy driver had somehow slipped past Johnny's vigilance. Then Buddy and I crossed the road to the diner.

"I hate this," I said to him as we stepped up on the curb. My heart hurt for my town, normally one of the safest places on Earth.

Buddy cocked his head at me.

Through the diner's plate-glass window, I waved at Lisa and pointed off to the side, to indicate we'd be at one of the picnic tables around back. Jess had always had several back there but she'd added more, well spaced under giant live oaks. Only one was currently occupied, by a young couple.

I donned my puppy dog mask and sat at a table some distance from them. Lisa came out and took my order.

A couple of minutes later, a masked Jess came around the corner. She plopped onto the bench across from mine, at the opposite end. Today, her diminutive body was not wrapped in her usual white chef's jacket, although her dark hair was covered with a hairnet.

Her late fiancé had suggested the jacket—to give the diner more class, he'd said. Was her not wearing it a sign that she was truly moving on from Dan's death?

Instead, she wore snug jeans and a blue knit top that showed off her slender figure quite nicely.

Yup, she's dressing for Johnny these days, Ms. Snark chortled.

"I'm fully immunized now," I announced, excitement in my voice. I still wasn't quite used to my new-found freedom.

"So am I, and Lisa." She slipped off her mask.

I did as well and took a deep breath. As I exhaled, a silent prayer of gratitude rose toward the heavens. I'd never take fresh air for granted again.

"You aren't busy today?"

"I'm caught up for now on the orders." Jess tapped her phone, lying on the table. "Lisa will text if she gets more in than she can handle."

"Before I forget, Johnny says hi and he wants his usual. I'll take it to him when I'm done eating."

Her cheeks flushed.

I suppressed a smile. "How are things going there?"

She nodded slightly. "Fine, great. I needed to go slow and he's been understanding about that." Her eyes lit up. "He's a really sweet guy."

I thought about my sweet guy. "Hey, do you have meatloaf today?"

"Yes."

"Save me two servings, with all the trimmings. I'll pick them up around six."

To make up for the lack of in-restaurant income, Jess had extended her carryout hours to seven p.m. "You realize you'll probably have to stay open for supper after things are better."

"That'll be what my mom calls 'good trouble,'" she said, then lowered her gaze to the table. "Can I ask a personal question?"

"Shoot," I said.

"What finally made you decide to have kids?"

Startled, I blew out air. "Kid, singular, I doubt we'll have time to squeeze in more than one. I'll be thirty-seven by the time number one is born."

I paused to gather my thoughts and, in that moment, realized I'd already made up my mind. On some level, I'd always wanted my own kids—my own warm, close family like the one I grew up in. But that covert undercurrent of anxiety, planted by the old biddies at church and nurtured by my ex, had kept me stuck in self-doubt.

"I'm sorry." Jess ducked her head. "I'm being too nosy."

"No, no, it's fine." I cleared my throat. "I've waffled a lot on the subject. But I've gotten a taste of the joy kids can bring into your life with my godchildren. And I've realized recently that fear was confusing the issue for me."

Her eyebrows shot up. "Why? You'll make a great mom. Look at how you are with the dogs. If you do the same with a kid, you'll be fine."

My chest warmed. "Thanks for the vote of confidence, but I was more afraid of how bad it would be if something happened to them." I chuckled. "I've been worrying about the worrying that comes with parenting."

Then the penny dropped inside my brain. "Johnny wants kids?"

She nodded, her gaze on the table again.

They're not going all that slow anymore, Ms. Snark observed internally, *if they're talking about kids.*

Jess looked up. "I don't think he gets the risks involved, because of my age. He's a bit younger."

Butterflies fluttered in my stomach. She was only a year older than me.

No, I am not *going there,* I told myself.

"How much younger?" I asked.

"He's thirty-two."

"Six years. That's the same gap between Will and me. It's not that big a deal."

She shrugged. "Somehow it feels more like a big deal when it's the man who's younger."

"But it shouldn't. Gender equality is, well, *equality.*"

She snorted slightly. "Tell that to Johnny. The only fight we've had so far is when he accused me of acting like I was his mother."

"Ironically, that was the subject of Will's and my last fight, only in reverse. But I get what you mean. Being fatherly toward your wife is more in sync with accepted gender roles than a man seeing his wife as his mother." I gave a mock shudder.

Jess actually giggled. "So is that the only issue you've had that's related to the age gap?"

I thought about that for a second. "Yeah, pretty much. That and my investigating things—that sometimes annoyed him."

Sometimes? Ms. Snark and inner Mom chorused.

I ignored them. "Those are really the only issues we've had, period. And that's getting resolved. Hey, I haven't told you yet."

I leaned forward and filled her in on our plans to start our own P.I. agency. "Keep that under your hat for now, though."

She patted her head. "Or under my hairnet, in my case."

The screech of tires interrupted our laughter, followed by a siren.

We jumped up and ran around the corner of the diner, almost colliding with Lisa and my lunch. We ducked around her.

Johnny's cruiser was racing down Main Street, toward my house, his lights flashing and the siren wailing.

Jess and I ran after. I caught glimpses of a vehicle in front of him.

A white SUV.

"Is that the guy?" Jess huffed out from beside me.

"Likely." I wanted to say more, but had no breath to spare.

The SUV raced past Sherie and Sybil's house, and my breath came a little easier.

Anger surged, red hot in my chest, trumping my fear. How dare this man invade my town?

"Johnny has him trapped at the dead end," Jess yelled.

But the SUV abruptly veered across the road and into the woods just past our property. It entered a narrow dirt path not designed for cars, its four-wheel drive spewing dirt in an arch that rattled on Johnny's hood.

Where he'd been forced to stop the cruiser, at the edge of the paved road.

The anger in my chest was joined by a sick feeling in my stomach. SUV guy was getting away!

I detoured toward the pasture fence.

Johnny was out of his cruiser and running full out onto the dirt path.

I whistled for Niña as I slipped under the fence. Thank heavens, she's an easy horse to catch. She came running.

I led her at a jog into the barn and slipped her bridle on over her halter. No time for a saddle. Climbing onto a hay bale, I hoisted myself onto her bare back.

Then we were out of the barn and racing toward the gate. A frisson of panic ran through me. I'd never ridden Niña bareback before. But her gaits were so smooth… I told myself I'd be okay.

Jess had figured out my intentions and was at the gate. She swung it open. Niña, Buddy and I took off after Johnny.

The SUV, on rough terrain, might or might not be able to outrun a man on foot, but the odds were better for a galloping horse.

Except that once we were into the woods, I had to slow Niña. Too many things to trip her up underfoot, and low-hanging branches eager to swipe me off her back.

We rounded a turn in the path and Niña screeched to a halt. I lurched forward onto her neck, almost falling off.

The SUV was stopped in front of a huge clump of bamboo blocking the path. Johnny was behind it, bent over, trying to catch his breath.

A narrow ray of sunlight shown through the SUV's windshield, lighting up an empty interior.

"Which way did he go?"

Johnny shook his head. "Don't know."

But from my perspective on horseback, I could make out a faint trail of bent-over palmettos. They led away from the open driver's door.

CHAPTER TWENTY-THREE

I pointed Niña's head toward the faint trail and squeezed my knees. We plowed through underbrush up to her withers, while I fervently prayed there weren't any snakes, gators or holes under those disturbed weeds. I was wishing I'd left Buddy back with Jess.

After a minute or two that felt much longer, we came out of the woods at the far end of the field behind Sherie's and my houses, about two hundred feet from State Road 200.

On its shoulder, a figure was climbing into the backseat of a big white car.

I squeezed my knees tighter and Niña extended her gait. I glanced over my shoulder. Buddy was losing ground, his tongue hanging out.

The car was pulling out onto the road, and we were still too far away for me to read the license plate. But it was a pale blue one I'd never seen before. The car was long, with an odd-looking rear end.

It roared away.

Disappointment hollowed out my stomach. My throat hurt as I reined Niña in.

Johnny had followed the trail we'd plowed. He met us at the edge of the field, talking into his radio. "Here she is now," he said.

"A white car picked him up," I reported.

"Tag number?" Johnny asked.

I shook my head. "Too far away. But it had those old-fashioned fins on the back. It might be a vintage car. A Cadillac or Pontiac, maybe? The tag was light blue."

He repeated all that into his radio. Staticky noise answered him. But he must have been able to make it out. "Will do. Your husband said to tell his crazy wife to stay put until he gets here."

"Tell him that his *partner* is fine and he should finish what he needs to do today." I slid off of Niña and stroked her sweaty neck by way of a thank you.

Giving me a curious look, Johnny did as I'd asked. More garble static responded.

Johnny grinned. "He said to tell you, 'yes, ma'am.'"

"Thanks." I turned to lead Niña toward home through the field.

Johnny jogged up next to me. In a teasing voice, he said, "You know, that really was crazy. You are–"

I cut him off. "Determined and courageous?"

He grinned again. "Sure, that's what I was going to say."

Will looked exhausted when he got home—shoulders slouched and eyes bloodshot—but he was smiling.

"You forgot to wear your sunglasses while driving again, didn't you?"

He ignored my fussing and grabbed me up in a bear hug. "I think we're about to break this case wide open."

I squeezed him back, then gestured toward the table by the slider, where I'd laid out silverware and a napkin at his normal spot.

"Tell me," I called back over my shoulder. In the kitchen, I grabbed potholders and pulled a heaping plate of food out of the oven, where it had been staying warm for the last hour.

"Wow, that looks great."

"Compliments of Jess Randall." I sat down across from him at the table. "Tell me!"

"Best cook in town." He shoveled in some mashed potatoes and gravy. "Aren't you gonna get yours?"

"I already ate, got too hungry. Tell. Me!"

"Okay." He quickly chewed and swallowed a bite of meatloaf. "First the lab. You were right. Totally different kind of sheet, more like an upscale hotel would use."

I tamped down the bubbles of excitement erupting in my chest. "Could've been a mix-up at the linen supply company. I'm sure they serve hotels as well."

He chewed and swallowed another mouthful of food. "Could be, but the next part is more definitive. My buddy, Jake, examined the ends of the strips of sheet. On one end they were torn, but on the other end there were two clean cuts, about an inch long."

"Somebody cut the end of the sheet with scissors or a knife, to get it started. Then tore the strips from there."

"Jake said most likely scissors. Now where would an inmate on suicide watch get scissors?" His grin lit up his tired face.

"Anything else from the lab?"

He shook his head, ate another bite of meatloaf. "Not yet. Jake's gonna analyze the sheet for trace evidence and DNA." More food went into his mouth.

You shouldn't have fed him until he told all, Ms. Snark commented internally.

Will swallowed and said, "Since it wasn't all that out of the way, I dropped in on Godwin in Gainesville on my way back, at his house."

He stabbed some green beans. I tried not to glare as he chewed and swallowed.

"He got kinda freaked out because his wife was there. He quickly shuttled me off to his study. I told him point blank that the Marion County Sheriff's Department was looking at him for a possible attempted murder. He got really freaked out then, was almost blubbering. He admitted that maybe he bent the rules a little to 'test the waters.'" Will made air quotes, his fork dangling from one hand.

I was tempted to snatch it away from him. "Test the waters, as in with charter clients?"

He nodded, swallowed another bite of food. "Yeah, but he still adamantly denies stealing fuel. And it turns out he has an alibi for the entire week when the sabotage happened. He was flying a client and his family around the Bahamas."

"He could've paid somebody to sabotage the plane?"

Will shoveled in more food, shaking his head. "I don't think he's our guy. He's less than an honest businessman, but he doesn't seem to be the violent type. And he seemed genuinely shocked that he was suspected of attempted murder."

"Wouldn't it be actual murder, since Charlie Butler died?"

"Yes. But I was trying not to freak him out too much, didn't want him to shut down and call his lawyer."

"Speaking of Charlie, I forgot to tell you. There's a memorial service planned for him for tomorrow night, six-thirty. I was going to go."

"I'll go too. His killer may show up, since he, or she, is likely associated with the airport in some way."

"But Godwin was our only good lead there."

Will stabbed another green bean. "I know, but I've saved the best for last." Then he put the green bean in his mouth and chewed it very, very slowly, grinning the whole time.

"Grrr."

He laughed. "I went to talk to the guard, Grimes. I asked him where a suicidal inmate could've gotten a high quality sheet and a pair of scissors, and I thought he was gonna faint right there in his doorway. He made denial noises for a few minutes, but eventually he admitted to setting the whole thing up."

"Wow! Why'd he do it?"

"Somebody called him, pressured him to do it. They provided the sheet, already torn into strips and tied together, left it in a bag under one of the benches outside the jail. He takes a break, goes outside, retrieves the bag, and sets it up. Waits a couple of minutes, goes back to Russ's cell, and then sounds the alarm."

"But why would Grimes go along with that?"

"He wouldn't tell me that part. My guess is that the person on the phone had something on him, knew something that wouldn't be good if it came out. The guy told him he didn't want Russ dead, only discredited. That's part of why he went along with it."

"So it was definitely a guy?"

"That's what Grimes said."

"Did you arrest him?" I asked.

"Yes. That's why I was late. Had to process him, but I didn't do the arrest report for my boss yet. I'm gonna do a little digging into Grimes's background and talk to him again tomorrow, see if I can get more out of him after he's spent a night in jail."

"Maybe you should let Elise do the digging. Under the radar remember?"

"Good idea. Have her run a background check on him, see if she can find out what he's got to hide."

I quickly texted her, flagging the request as top priority. I winced at the thought of the bill she would eventually send me, which I would have to pass on to Russ. But he'd said to spend what was necessary in order to get this resolved.

I frowned, still not able to get all the pieces to fit. "You implied Grimes was somehow connected to the airport. How?"

"That's the big question at this point, how does it all connect? We've got three things." He held up fingers and ticked them off with the tines of his fork. "The sabotage of Russ's plane, the attacks on you, Carla and Sybil, and now the faked suicide attempt. The last one says to me that the plane sabotage is not independent from the other events. First someone tried to kill Russ, then went after you and Sybil, and now they're trying to discredit Russ, once and for all."

"But what if the saboteur set up the fake suicide just to reinforce the idea that Russ sabotaged his own plane? To make sure they don't get caught."

"Maybe," Will said, "but Russ has already been arrested for the sabotage. Why not leave well enough alone? No, I think stopping the fraud investigation is the motive that connects those three things. If Russ, you and Sybil were out of the picture, how likely would it be that someone would keep looking at that hospital?"

"Whoever it is doesn't know about our contact at the VA then." But it was little comfort to know Wes might eventually help find our killer, after the three of us were already dead.

"Now," Will said, "we need to find out *who* is connected to all three things."

"So if someone shows up at the memorial service who is also connected to the hospital…"

"Yup," Will said, pushing his empty plate away. "Now, tell me about the guy you all chased this afternoon."

I shrugged. "Not much to tell. He was too far away to see details. I figured he was a man from the way he moved. Men tend to climb into the backseat of a vehicle head first, butt in the air, then they twist around and sit and bring their feet inside. Women either sit first and swing their feet in, or they approach it sideways, put one foot in first, then duck their head in as they sit. Those are the best ways to do it if you're wearing a skirt, so it becomes habit."

"It could've been a woman, though, who usually wears pants?" He grinned. "Like you."

I felt a tad annoyed. "Yeah, I guess."

His grin faded. "Sorry, I shouldn't be teasing you. That's actually an astute observation. The kind of little thing that can really help sometimes in an investigation."

"So you're admitting that I might be good investigator material?"

"Yeah, I guess I am."

My turn to grin at him.

"And your observations about the car on Route 200 were helpful. Light blue tags are for antiques. The traffic guys are going to comb through the owners of white vintage cars with rear fins in this county to see what they can dig up."

I shook my head. "What did SUV guy think he would accomplish, coming into town like that?" An ember of that earlier red-hot anger smoldered in my chest.

"Probably checking to see if you and/or Sybil were home. If he's never lived in a tiny town like this, he wouldn't have anticipated that his vehicle would be recognized."

"Especially a white SUV. They're a dime a dozen in Florida."

Will smiled at my old-fashioned saying. He called them *motherisms*. "A tech dusted the SUV for prints. It had been wiped clean. It's been towed to our lab, but it'll be Monday at the earliest before we get anything back on it. I should have Grimes's phone records by then as well. Although his anonymous caller may have used an untraceable cell. One way or another, I'm betting this case will be solved by Monday afternoon."

"I hope so."

"The SUV's VIN was filed off as well, but there are other ways to identify a vehicle. My guess is it will turn out to be stolen, though."

"Like the plates."

"Yes, which reminds me, I never got a chance to call the Porsche owner today. Gotta do that tomorrow."

"Does your captain still believe this is all about road rage?"

"I don't know. I was off duty today, remember?" Will grinned at me.

Sunday was one of my barn days. Will was just beginning to stir as I got up.

Susanna showed up to check on Queenie as I was finishing the last stall. "Hey, Marcia," she called from the middle of the barn's aisle, keeping a safe distance.

"I'm good to go now," I said. "It's been two weeks since my second dose."

"Awesome." She bounced the rest of the way down the aisle.

Queenie greeted her with a soft nicker. We stood outside the mini's stall for a few minutes, having a good old-fashioned gabfest.

I recruited her to come over later and be a "stranger" for Dolly's training. "And bring Dexter and Edna, if they're not busy."

"Dexter's no problem, but Aunt Edna…" She trailed off, shaking her head.

My throat closed. "What's wrong?"

"No, no, she's not sick," she quickly said. "Not physically, at least. It's more like she's down."

Susanna ran a hand through her graying strawberry-blonde hair. "When we had to close the motel and she didn't have anything to do, she just seemed to wind down. And now she's not gettin' wound back up again."

"But she's got plenty to do now, with the motel reopened, right?"

She shook her head. "Me and Dexter have been doing most of it, but now he's gettin' more hours again at the veterinarian hospital. I may need to hire somebody to help. Most all Aunt Edna does is lie around out on the back deck and read. She does some laundry and a little sewin'. That's it."

"Sure sounds like depression."

"I feel like I should be doin' something to get her goin' again, but I don't know what."

"Let me give it some thought, see if I can come up with an intervention strategy."

"That'd be great if you can think of something."

We hugged, which felt so good, and Buddy and I headed home.

The rest of the morning was more impatient waiting. I'd called Wes Sullivan and gotten his voicemail.

It would be Monday at the earliest before we got results on the sheet or from the tox screen of Russ's blood. But I was hoping Elise would come through with the report on Grimes today.

Despite it being Sunday, Will had gone in to follow up on a lead in one of his legitimately assigned cases.

Shortly after one, I was reading a short text from Gloria Vargas—*Mr. Fortham may be getting out of jail soon*—when Will texted.

God bless that woman!

I called instead of texting back. "You talking about Vargas?"

"Yup. She lit a fire under the jail's shrink to do a new eval on Russ and put the wheels in motion for a new bail hearing. He should be out by Tuesday."

"What if that doctor shows up again to Baker-Act him?"

"I hope he does. I'll be there with some questions for him."

"I suspect he's the psychiatrist the sanitarium has on contract. Elise found his name, James Woodrow. She's running a background check on him as well."

"Good. I didn't get anything more out of Grimes."

"Was your captain mad that you jumped into the situation at the jail like that?"

"Only until I told him I already had a person in custody. And Russ will stay in the infirmary until his hearing, with his own personal guard."

I said a silent prayer that whoever was behind all this didn't have any more contacts inside the jail.

"Oh," Will said, "and the captain has officially reopened the Butler case."

"Bet that made Joe Brown's day," Ms. Snark blurted out. I didn't feel at all bad about not stopping her.

"To give Joe credit, he isn't lazy. It's more that he's…"

"Bullheaded," I supplied.

A low chuckle.

"If you say it takes one to know one," I said, "you're not getting any dinner tonight."

"I never get any dinner from you anyway. You don't cook."

"Says the man who had meatloaf last night."

"*Jess's* meatloaf. I rest my case. Hey, speaking of dinner, I've got yet another lead in one of my cases. I won't have time to come home to eat before Butler's service tonight. What's the address? I'll meet you there."

"Sonny said the church is hard to find. He's meeting me at the airport at six to lead me to it."

"Fine. I'll meet you there at six. Then we'll grab a late dinner afterwards. Are you taking Buddy with you?"

"Yes. It's an outside service."

"Good. Don't get out of the car until I get there."

I opened my mouth to protest.

"Marcia, I'm serious. There's good reason to believe the killer's associated with the airport in some way. I'll try to get there first, a little before six, but in case I get tied up–"

"Okay, got it."

At two, Susanna and Dexter arrived on my front porch. I explained what we were going to do and asked Dexter to wait in the study.

Since everyone in my living room was now fully vaccinated, we could forego masks. I smiled at yet another step toward normalcy.

Carla was still waiting out her two weeks after the second shot. She stayed outside with Dolly.

We ran through the routine with Susanna, and Dolly barked on cue. I sent her back out to Carla and brought Dexter into the living room.

When Dolly trotted in, he exclaimed, "Oh, she's so cute!" Bless his heart, he'd forgotten all about telling her to bark.

But Dolly ran over to him, sat, and barked once.

I held my breath as Dexter reached out to pet her.

She darted out from under his hand and went to sit in front of Susanna. No bark.

Carla stood in the doorway, her mask halfway off her chin, mouth hanging open.

I rushed over to Dolly, gave her a treat and told her she was the smartest dog ever.

Buddy raised his head from where he'd been lying on his bed under the window. He looked at me, head cocked.

"Okay," I laughed, "the second smartest dog ever."

"Border Collies are supposed to be the smartest breed," Carla commented as she adjusted her mask.

"Is she trained now?" Dexter asked.

"We need to keep reinforcing it," I said, "but yes. And you two helped a lot."

Dexter grinned at his mother. "Mama, we trained her!"

My phone rang a few minutes after everyone had left.

I checked caller ID. *Finally!*

"Hey Wes, whatever came of checking out the people you had told about the investigation, before the plane crash?"

"Um, I talked to them again. It was only two people." He sounded slightly annoyed.

I guess I should've said *Hello, how are you?* first. Sometimes my Northerner abruptness gets me in trouble.

"The one guy said he didn't tell anybody else. The other mentioned it at lunch with a couple of her coworkers, when they were talking about fraud cases in the past. But she didn't give any specifics, because *I hadn't given her* any specifics."

"So, could any of them be connected to the hospital?"

"Nah. None of them are involved in sending patients to specific facilities. The woman and her friends are all in accounting. The guy's in human resources."

"Can you give me their names?"

"Um, I'd rather not. I mean I checked them out thoroughly."

"Wes, did you know that somebody tried to fake Russ's suicide yesterday morning?"

"Say wha'? No, I hadn't heard about that. Is he okay?"

"Yes, but I'm concerned whoever's behind this will keep coming after him."

Connections, Will had been talking about connections.

"Wes, I need those names. One of them might be connected to the hospital in some way that we can't even imagine."

Or connected to the airport. That would give us a thread to pull on.

"I don't know," Wes said, obviously hesitant.

"Look, my husband's a sheriff's department detective. He's helping me look into this. He knows how to be discreet, but we need to check out every possible lead."

A pause. "Okay, but please try to keep me out of it. I like my job. And, well, the guy in HR, he's in a position to get me fired."

I suspected Wes was being a little paranoid, but I kept my mouth shut as he gave me the names and I jotted them down.

I sent them on to Elise and asked if she had anything on Grimes yet. An email came back right away. *Working on it.*

Restless, I started getting ready for the memorial service early, just to have something to do. Recalling Will's crack about me always wearing pants, I pulled my little black dress off its hanger. I paired it with simple gold jewelry this time and left my hair down.

"Not bad," I told the woman in the mirror.

I still had a half hour to kill. I decided to stop for a frozen yogurt on the way. That would tide me over until our late supper.

I grabbed my cardigan, and Buddy and I went out to my car. I winced at the sight of the dented fender. I needed to deal with that soon.

I loaded Buddy into the backseat, and put my laptop on the passenger seat, so I could check for an email from Elise again, before the service.

Unfortunately, the frozen yogurt place I'd frequented in the past had gone out of business.

There wasn't quite enough time to spare now to go looking elsewhere for a snack. Hoping my stomach would hold out, I drove on to the airport.

There were a few vehicles in the lot, which I found reassuring.

I opened my laptop on the passenger's seat, booted it up, and silently blessed Sonny when the airport's wifi showed as available. I hate trying to read emails on my phone.

Yay, there was a message from Elise.

Here's the report on Grimes, she wrote. *And I also did a first credit pass on Dr. Woodrow. He definitely is living beyond his means. I'm going to dig deeper on him next.*

There was more, but I impatiently clicked on the attachment labeled *Initial Report–Corrections Officer Edward Grimes.*

My chest ached as I skimmed down it. He was susceptible to black-mail because his wife had been brought into the country illegally at age ten, but she'd missed out on DACA protection because she'd been thirty-two when it was implemented, one year over the maximum age for eligibility. And being married to a U.S. citizen wouldn't necessarily protect her from deportation.

I called Will but it went straight to voicemail. I didn't bother leaving a message. I'd be seeing him in a few minutes.

I went back to the email from Elise.

I feel bad that I've been slow getting everything to you lately, so I'm throwing in, free of charge, some more in-depth info on some of the people on your list.

James Smith–

Who? Oh yeah, Sonny.

I can't get grades, but I discovered that he was thrown out of his fraternity, Alpha Psi Chi, for excessive drinking and fighting in the frat house. And then later, he was expelled from the University of Florida, in Spring, 1999, after additional similar offenses on campus.

He really was a troublemaker when he was drinking. But I had to give him credit for straightening out his life in recent years.

Wait, that fraternity rang a bell. I scrolled down through my emails, found the one I was searching for and opened the attached report. Yup, the timing overlapped. My heart rate ratcheted up a notch.

It was a connection, but it could be a coincidence. A lot of people in this part of the state went to UF. And lots of them joined fraternities and sororities.

I clicked back to the email. The words *vintage Cadillac* caught my eye, just as Buddy whined in the backseat. I turned my head. His eyes looked worried.

"You need to go, boy?"

He whined again.

I really wanted to read that email. *Who* owned a vintage Cadillac? But Buddy's worried look now had me worried. Did he have a bladder infection, or was aging making him need to go more often? That thought made my chest heavy.

I scanned the parking lot carefully. It was now completely deserted. I wasn't sure if that was a good or a bad thing.

I got out, opened the back door, and leaned in to release Buddy from his safety strap.

My hand was still on the hook when his ears twitched. His tail thumped against the seat.

And the hair stood up on my bare arms.

Someone was behind me.

I yanked my head out of the car, started to turn…

Slim fingers slid around my throat.

CHAPTER TWENTY-FOUR

My fingernails dug into long, slender hands, trying to loosen them enough to yell, to breathe.

"What a shame, doll," the hands' owner said in my ear, "that I've gotta squeeze your pretty little neck. But you had to keep poking around."

Poking around? I saw red—dancing red spots to be exact, which could've been from oxygen deprivation. I raised a foot and stomped on the top of his sneaker, a maneuver from one of Sophie's videos.

"Yow!" His fingers loosened.

"Bud–"

Hands clamped down again, cutting off my words.

"What are you doing, man?" A male voice behind us.

Limping, Sonny dragged me around in a circle, his hands still on my throat, but looser. "What does it look like? I'm getting rid of her."

I dragged in some air and stared at the man ten feet away. "Wes…" I croaked out.

He raised his arm in the air. "Not that way, you're not." He held a small pistol.

My knees went weak, while my brain tried to make sense of their words. What was going on here?

"How are you gonna get rid of the body?" Wes asked Sonny, his tone conversational.

"There's a sinkhole back in those woods, real deep, with a good twenty feet of water in the bottom."

What is it with these guys trying to drown us in sinkholes? Ms. Snark grumbled.

A chill ran through me. The *us* would include Buddy. I couldn't let that happen.

"And the car?" Wes asked.

"Got a buddy with a chop shop," Sonny said. "It'll be spare parts by morning."

A soft whine of confusion from behind me. Buddy had heard his name, but not from my lips.

"You're an idiot," Wes said, his tone disdainful. "Her husband's a sheriff's detective. You think he's not going to tear this county apart searching for her if she disappears? And when he finds her, he'll know she was strangled."

Crapola! My knees wobbled again.

"I wasn't gonna strangle her," Sonny said. "Just squeeze until she passed out."

"I've got a better idea." Wes raised his gun higher. "I shoot you, finish her off and tell the cops I couldn't stop you in time."

I sucked in air as Sonny jerked me around in front of him as a shield.

"Buddy, grab gun!" I yelled, as loud as my sore throat would let me.

My dog catapulted from the backseat, streaking past us, and lunged for Wes. He knocked him over, teeth sinking into the hand holding the gun.

With a roar, it discharged. The bullet pinged off my back fender.

Wes howled but Buddy hung on. The gun dropped to the ground.

"Hold, Buddy!" I didn't want Wes grabbing the weapon up again.

Buddy continued to hang on to Wes's hand, and Wes continued to howl.

Sonny's hands had moved from my neck to my shoulders. He whirled me around. "Thanks, doll. You look so pretty tonight. I really hate to do this, but…" He cranked back his fist to slug me.

I let my knees give out, sank from beneath the hand still gripping my shoulder.

He didn't let go, which was his mistake. My dead weight pulled him off balance and his haymaker became a windmill.

While he flailed and staggered a step, I dropped onto my side and cranked back my upper leg.

Like a piston! Kick 'im in the knee! At least this inner voice had an uber cool Irish accent.

"Police, don't move!" A familiar voice.

But my foot was already in motion.

Sonny screamed, collapsed to the ground.

Dang, it worked!

I scuttled backward, then scrambled to my feet.

"Buddy, let go. Get gun." My dog jumped away from Wes and picked the small pistol up in his teeth. He jogged toward me.

I turned, scanning for Will. He stood across the parking lot, next to his truck, the driver's door hanging open. The gun in his hand was aimed at the two men on the ground, curled in fetal positions, cradling different parts of their bodies.

My husband stared at me, then slowly shook his head. "Remind me to never worry about you again."

A bark of semi-hysterical laughter erupted from my raw throat. "Can I have that in writing?"

I leaned against a desk in the detectives' bullpen and tugged on the skirt of my little black dress, waiting for someone to officially take my statement. Buddy lay panting at my feet.

The dress was ruined, stretched out of shape, with a large tear on the side where I'd laid on the sidewalk and kicked my would-be killer in the knees.

I was considering framing the dress, like others frame the first dollar bill they make in some new enterprise.

Will brought me a cup of cop-shop coffee. It was awful but I took a couple of sips anyway, to warm myself up. Not that it was chilly in the room, anything but.

I was pretty sure I was having aftershocks from earlier events.

I rooted in my purse for something to kill the road-tar aftertaste. Nothing edible but I did come up with a slightly fuzzy ibuprofen. I swallowed it dry rather than endure more of the coffee.

My stomach grumbled unhappily.

"You didn't get my message, did you?" Will said.

"What message?" My voice was still a little hoarse, my larynx sore. *Come on, ibuprofen.* "Oh, you must've been calling me when I was calling you. I got some info on…" I trailed off, not sure I wanted to give anyone official the information about Grimes's wife. Not even Will. Although it would likely come out anyway, eventually.

"I was calling to warn you to stay away from the airport," Will was saying. "The Porsche owner finally emailed me the list of places he'd been and near the top was Pine Hills Airport."

"And that made you suspect Sonny?"

"Not really. It only confirmed that whoever ran you and Sybil off the road was associated with the airport. I didn't panic until Joe called me when I was almost there. He'd found out that Sonny—you're never gonna believe this… Guess who his mother is."

I stared at him for a beat. Then insight blossomed. "Mrs. Ratchette!" we said at the same time.

I shook my head. "Dang. How did Elise miss that?"

"Probably the same reason Joe did initially. The last names are different. And on his birth certificate, it just said *baby boy Hughes*, his mother's maiden name. But apparently his biological father, James Smith, Sr., did claim him, for a while at least. There should've been a new birth certificate issued but there must've been some snafu at the Bureau of Vital Statistics. The stepfather, William Ratchette, called him Sonny and the nickname stuck."

"Except with his mother." Some more pieces were falling into place. "She was talking to her son on the phone, that day I was at the sanitarium, when Doc Johnson and I came out of his office. She said, 'I gotta go, Jimmy.' And Johnson asked her how her son was doing. I don't know *how* he was doing, but *what* he was doing at the time was getting ready to follow me and run me off the road. She had called him to tell him that I was snooping around, asking Johnson questions."

Another thought made my empty stomach lurch a little. "*And* we were standing near the office door when I was talking to the doc about an employee who had seen Ratchette writing in the patients' charts. No doubt she was eavesdropping. She would've easily figured out that the employee was Sybil, because she'd seen us together, the day we snuck in to talk to Russ."

I remembered the email I'd been reading when everything started going sideways at the airport. "Hang on a sec. I may have some other tidbits for you." I pulled out my phone and called up my email, found the most recent one from Elise.

"Guess how Wes Sullivan has been laundering his share of the loot. His girlfriend has not one but two luxury cars registered in her name, and one of them is a 1961 white Cadillac."

Will's eyebrows shot up.

I read on. "Elise thinks he paid for them with his line of credit on his house, then he'd pay the loan down again with sizeable monthly payments, in cash. He'd buy something else, another car or big-ticket item, and pay the loan down again. *And* she found out that he only took some of the exotic vacations he talked about on social media. He'd borrow large chunks of money for these supposed vacations, but he never bought any plane tickets and such. Then he'd pay the loan off yet again, with cash."

Will had come around to look over my shoulder. "Oh, our forensic accountant is gonna love this."

"Elise also found out that Sonny and Wes were in the same fraternity for their freshman year at UF. Sonny got kicked out for fighting, and the following year, Russ joined the fraternity."

"So Wes was funneling VA patients to the sanitarium," Will said.

I thought back on my conversations with him. "Crapola! He was pumping me for information the whole time." And I'd actually felt happy to think I had an ally. I gave myself a mental kick in the keister.

Becky's words echoed in my head, *You go with the information you have about the person at the time and then trust your instincts.*

Russ had said they weren't bosom buddies but he'd seemed to trust Wes, which made me trust him. And the guy was a good actor—no, not good, he was excellent. He'd come across as so sincere.

"Wesley and Ratchette were apparently in on the fraud together," Will was saying, "and when Russ told his frat brother, Wes that he wanted to investigate the sanitarium–"

"Wes turned to his buddy, Sonny," I finished his sentence, "and got him to sabotage Russ's plane."

Buddy heard his name and sat up, still panting heavily.

Anxiety zinged through me. "It's been too long since he's had water. Where can I get him some?"

"I'll get it. And how about I call for a pizza, unless you still want to try to go out after all this?" He waved a hand around the bull pen, where Joe Brown was sitting at a desk, on the phone and taking notes, and another detective was typing on his computer keyboard.

"Pizza sounds lovely." My stomach rumbled. "The sooner, the better."

He grimaced. "Unfortunately, we have to wait for Joe to take your statement. If I take it, the defense attorneys may try to make something of that."

"It's okay. As long as you feed me, I don't mind waiting."

He left the room and came back a couple of minutes later, his phone to one ear and a styrofoam cup of water in his other hand.

He disconnected and pocketed the phone. "Pizza's on its way. Sorry, I couldn't find anything more shallow like a dog dish."

"He'll manage."

Will set the cup on the floor in front of Buddy. He carefully stuck his tongue into it and lapped up water.

"Something else interesting," Will said, "that we just found out. It's what Joe's double-checking now. The day of the crash, the 911 call for the fire department came in at five minutes after ten."

After a beat of silent suspense, I said, "So?"

"The crash didn't happen until ten-o-nine."

"No wonder the fire department got there so fast. Sonny'd already called them." I shook my head. "He didn't want any more damage to the airport or other planes than was necessary."

Will nodded grimly.

Buddy had managed to get most of the water out of the cup. Now he gingerly gripped its edge in his teeth and held it up in front of him, his eyes on Will.

We both broke up. "*More, please,*" Will said, in a fake Oliver Twist British accent. "Did you teach him that?"

"No, he figured it out for himself." I knelt down, took the cup and passed it to Will, then hugged Buddy's neck. "I called Dolly the smartest dog ever earlier today. I think he's trying to show me how wrong I was."

EPILOGUE

I was determined to talk to Edna Mayfair today. I'd been trying to catch up with her for a week, keeping an eye out for her walking the dogs, so I could "casually" run into her and stop for a chat.

But I hadn't seen her.

Then this morning, Susanna told me Edna wasn't even walking the dogs anymore. She and Dexter were taking care of them now.

That scared me. A lot.

I had my spiel ready. I'd even practiced it in front of a mirror.

I found Edna on the motel's back deck. She had a book on her lap but she was staring into space.

The "boys" were lying on either side of her chaise. They were loose and rose to greet us rambunctiously, but showed no signs of planning to take off.

"I had an invisible fence installed back here," Edna answered my unasked question, "so they can romp more on their own."

I dropped Buddy's leash. The three dogs took off across the yard, Bennie and Bo chasing each other. Buddy trotted sedately amidst their chaos.

The Springer Spaniels were now pushing seven, middle-aged in dog years. They had calmed down some from their younger years, but not a lot. Edna wasn't much of a disciplinarian with them.

And Buddy was nine, an "older gentleman." My heart squeezed at the thought that I would only have him for a few more years.

Good. That touch of grief would help with my acting.

I sat on the edge of the second chaise, next to hers. "So, how have you been?"

"I'm fine," she said, somewhat snappishly. But her slight shrug contradicted her words. "People keep askin' me that. Sherie was goin' on and on at me yesterday. Cain't a woman retire?"

"Is that what you've done?"

Another shrug. "Looks that way, don't it? Dex and Susie are doin' all the work now." There was a touch of resentment in her tone, as if they had forced her out. "They seem to be handlin' things just fine."

"Actually, Susanna was telling me she needs to hire someone to help."

Edna gaped at me for a moment, then glanced away, staring at the Southern pines lined up along the back of her property.

"And Jess tells me that you're still sending your guests to her with breakfast vouchers, when you could reopen your own kitchen now."

Yet another shrug. "She's a better cook than I am."

She really is depressed, Ms. Snark commented internally, minus her usual snide tone, *if she's admitting that.*

"And since when did you get so nosy, missy?" Edna said.

I let out a bark of laughter. "Edna, I've *always* been nosy. But I don't normally need to pry your news out of you like this."

"Well I ain't got no news. Nothin' happenin' in my life these days." And with that, she picked up her paperback and pretended to read. Except she had it upside down.

She quickly flipped it around, but I still wasn't fooled. Her eyes were on the book but the far-away look in them said her mind was not.

I leaned back in my chaise and put my feet up. "I'm kinda down today," I said conversationally.

"Harumph."

"The anniversary of my father's death is coming up." It was only a slight exaggeration. That anniversary *was* coming up, but not for another three months.

Edna flicked her gaze my way. "Sorry to hear that."

I heaved a sigh. "Normally I don't feel sad anymore when I remember him. He's been gone for years. But around this time, I can't help thinking about the things he missed out on. Watching his grandchildren grow up–"

Edna's head jerked around. "You got somethin' to tell me?" Her tone was considerably perkier.

No, don't go there, I reminded myself. Giving Edna any news was tantamount to telling the whole town.

I shook my head.

Her shoulders slumped, and I felt like a heel. She turned back to her book.

Here we go.

"Dad had been talking about retiring, before his heart attack. But he said someone had given him good advice, that one shouldn't retire *from* something, they should retire *to* something. He was still trying to figure out what he wanted to retire to—something that he could really get into, a true, new chapter of his life."

"Uh huh," Edna said, still looking at her book, pretending she wasn't listening.

"He was talking about getting more involved with a volunteer group he was in, said that nothing made him feel more vital than helping others." I sighed again. "But he never got a chance to retire."

"But he liked what he was doin', right? Bein' a preacher."

"Oh yes, he liked it a lot."

"So I'm guessing then, that he died a happy man."

It's working! Edna was trying to comfort me.

"True. But I still feel like he got cheated out of even more happiness." One more small sigh.

"Say, when are we going to have our next Mayfair extravaganza?" I pumped enthusiasm into my voice. In truth, I dreaded Edna's extravaganzas, because something drastic always went wrong. But if they gave Edna focus again…

"We need to make up for lost time," I said, "and get some tourists coming back here. People are starting to travel again."

She put her book down on her lap. "I don't know. I hadn't given it much thought yet."

Yet! I resisted the urge to grin.

I sat up on the side of the chaise so I could see her face better. Yup, she had lost the far-away gaze. Now her expression was thoughtful.

Time to quit before I laid it on too thick.

"Well, I gotta get going. Lots to do before Will gets home."

"Yeah, sure. Tell him I said hi."

"You got it."

I called Buddy to me and we headed for home. Once out of Edna's earshot, I said to him, "I think it worked, boy. Time will tell."

My phone rang as we walked down Main Street. Caller ID read *Janice Robinson.*

Who?

Oh yeah, the woman on the training agency's board, who'd first set things in motion to get Russ out of that hospital.

"Hello."

"Ms. Banks-Haines, this is Janice Robinson."

"Ms. Robinson, how are you?"

"Very good, thank you. I have a message from Mr. Pennington."

Who?

"He wanted me to convey to you his gratitude. I'm afraid his lawyers don't want him to contact you directly. But he's very distressed by the unlawful activities at one of his facilities and he's grateful to you for uncovering them."

"Um, okay, tell him he's welcome."

"I will do that." She disconnected.

I stared at the phone for a moment, processing a new sensation. Or rather the absence of an old one.

No flutters of anxiety. "Upper crust" people, like Janice and my ex-husband, no longer intimidated me.

As my mother would say, they put their pants on one leg at a time, like everybody else.

I did have a lot to do before Will got home, but miraculously I got it all done with time to spare. The pot roast, his favorite—and one of the few things I actually know how to cook—was in the oven.

I hadn't dressed up. That would make him suspicious. But I did change into fresh capris and my favorite red blouse. It brought out the auburn highlights in my hair.

I had set the table by the slider a little more carefully than usual, placing fancy cloth napkins on each plate, strategically arranging Will's.

Finally, I opened a bottle of our favorite red wine, to allow it to breathe, and put it on the breakfast bar, along with two glasses.

Their placement, that far away from the table, turned out to be a mistake.

At six-ten, Will came through the door, tossing his suit jacket in the general direction of the sofa and yanking his tie off. "Russ's car is out front. Did you train today?"

"Only with Dolly. We finished up with Bear and Russ last week." I had already told him that, but tonight he got a pass for not always listening. "He must be visiting Carla."

Will wiggled his eyebrows suggestively as he plunked himself down in his spot at the breakfast bar. Reaching for the wine, he said, "Boy, am I ready for this. What a day."

I stood on the kitchen side of the bar and leaned my elbows on the granite top. "Good or bad 'what a day?'"

"Good, ultimately." He poured wine in the two glasses. "Emily Ratchette confessed." He grabbed his glass and took a big sip.

"Wow, that is good news. No trial then?"

"Not for her, or Sonny. Wesley Sullivan is still claiming he was trying to rescue you."

I snorted. "What got Nurse Ratchette to confess?"

"She made a deal on Sonny's behalf. In addition to all the other evidence we have against him, the lab found Sonny's fingerprint on the white SUV. Guess where."

I pondered that for a moment as I took a tiny sip of wine. "On the back of the stolen license plate."

He grinned. "Yup. Sonny'll get twenty years at Raiford, and she also got a promise out of the deal that he wouldn't be moved anywhere else."

"Why?"

"Because she'll probably only get twelve to fifteen years, for health-care fraud and accessory to murder after the fact. With good behavior, she can be out in eight or ten. She wants him in this part of Florida so she can visit him readily after that." He pointed to my glass. "Hey, aren't you going to drink that?"

I took another small sip. Then I put the glass down and went to the fridge. Pulling out the salad, I said, "So, what's her story?"

"She did it to keep the airport afloat. She provided the money for the mortgage payments." His gaze followed me as I carried the salad to the table. He even swiveled around a little on his stool. But he made no move to shift to the table.

"Apparently it had been Sonny's dream." Will took another sip of wine, grabbed the bottle and topped off his glass. Mine was still mostly full. "She saw it as a way to keep him out of trouble. No drinking, no fight-ing, and he got to fly whenever he wanted and even have his own airport. And you'll never guess how she got the money out of the sanitarium."

I headed for the oven. "Falsified vendor bills."

Will's mouth fell open. "How'd you guess?"

"I've been thinking about it, and that's the only way that makes sense. She managed the business end of things, handled the accounting, and Johnson is a trusting soul." I slid the roast out of the oven and trans-ferred it to a platter.

"You *are* good at this detecting thing," Will said. "Johnson wasn't in on it, just as you thought. She had him sign checks for vendor bills from fake companies she'd set up. And Johnson did genuinely think that some patients took longer to get better than others. Because—also as you suspected—the psychiatrist, Woodrow, was in on it too."

I spooned carrots and new potatoes into a bowl. "No legit psychiatrist would have prescribed that sedative, nor would he keep prescribing an antidepressant that took so long to kick in." I carried the bowl of veggies to the table.

"Ratchette's going to testify against Wesley Sullivan. She's pretty pissed at him." Will sipped his wine more slowly now. "He was only supposed to send veterans to the sanitarium who had no family, no one to check up on them. Oh, and the airport is going to be sold, because she also has to make restitution to the Veterans' Administration." Still he didn't move from the bar to the table.

I returned to the kitchen for the roast.

"Sonny's pretty torn up about that, and about Charlie Butler. Apparently Butler normally took Russ's plane up every couple of weeks. He'd flown it the week before, so Sonny assumed he wouldn't take it up that day, just check it over."

"I have trouble feeling sorry for Sonny." My hand went to my neck. "Or Ratchette." Although my chest tightened at the thought of poor Charlie.

I carried the platter to the table.

"Sonny claims," Will said, "that he had nothing to do with the attack on Russ in jail. He said that was Sullivan's doing."

"I'll believe that. It's more Wes's style than Sonny's. Hey, Carla's two weeks were up yesterday. She's fully immunized now." Maybe if I turned the conversation to something else, he'd turn his attention to dinner and move to the table.

"That's great. Now she can get a new day job." He was still firmly planted on his stool.

"She already has one." I gestured toward the table and took my seat. "Jess hired her as her evening manager at the diner."

"Wow." He finally stood up. "That's great."

"Speaking of jobs, Sybil got hers back, with an apology from the nursing agency."

"Also great." Will brought our wineglasses over. "By the way, there's a real memorial service scheduled now for Charlie Butler, for this weekend. When his kids realized he hadn't crashed the plane because he'd been drinking, they came forward and claimed his body."

He placed the glasses on the table and went back to the breakfast bar for the bottle.

I resisted the urge to bite my lower lip and tried to arrange my face in a casual expression. I felt like I might faint.

Finally, he sat down and reached for his napkin.

I held my breath.

His hand froze halfway there. "And Sonny told us something else that's interesting."

Crapola! I struggled to look attentive.

"Wesley Sullivan hates Russ's guts," Will said. "Apparently, young Russell stole his girl back in college."

"Oh no! So when Jo Ann asked for a referral to a psychiatrist..."

"Wesley called the doc and told him he knew Russ, that he'd always had problems with depression and had tried to commit suicide a couple of times in college. Then when the doc panicked and Baker-Acted him, good ole Wes made sure he ended up at the sanitarium."

I groaned. "He set the whole thing up. And I never doubted him."

"But you checked him out anyway. That's what a good detective does. Trust but verify."

I shook my head and closed my eyes...and almost missed the big moment.

"Why so fancy tonight?" Will said.

My eyes flew open.

He grabbed his napkin and froze again, staring at the object on his plate. After a beat, he said, "There's no line. What does that mean?"

"What?" I dashed around the table. The blue line from earlier had faded, but it was still there. I pointed to it on the pregnancy test.

"Woot!" He jumped up and hugged me. Then he held me away from him, his face sober. "Wait, does this mean you were pregnant before you got vaccinated?"

"Most likely, we had a birth control malfunction shortly before my second shot. I called my doctor earlier. He's not concerned. He was being overly cautious when he said to wait a month. He told me the placenta and umbilical cord don't develop until about the fifth week, so baby and I have only been connected for a few days now."

A frisson of excitement, with a twinge of anxiety, ran through me. The baby—my baby—was connected to me!

Will was looking at the pregnancy test again. "Does blue mean it's a boy?"

I laughed. "No, it means it's a baby."

"Girls are good too." Grinning, he grabbed me and danced us around the living room.

Buddy rose from his bed under the window, cocking his head.

Will abruptly let go of me and knelt beside the dog. "Guess what, boy. You're gonna have a little brother or sister!"

AUTHOR'S NOTES

If you enjoyed this book, please take a moment to leave a short review on the ebook retailer of your choice. Reviews help with sales and sales keep the stories coming. You can readily find the links to these retailers at the *misterio press* bookstore (https://misteriopress.com/bookstore/one-flew-over-the-chow-chows-nest/).

I have plans for one more full-length novel in this series and another novella. The next full-length book is tentatively titled *To Bark or Not To Bark*, and of course, stars Dolly. The story just prior to this one is *My Funny Mayfair Valentine*. (All the books in this series are listed in order, as well as the rest of my books, at the beginning of this book.)

This book was proofread by multiple sets of eyes, but proofreaders are human. If you noticed any errors, please email me, so I can have them corrected, at lambkassandra3@gmail.com.

Heck, email me anyway. I love hearing from readers!

And you may want to sign up for my newsletter at https://kassandralamb.com to get a heads up about new releases, plus special offers and bonuses for subscribers. You will also receive a free novelette, *The Tell-Tale Bark*, the prequel to this series, AND a free novella, *Sweet Sanctuary*, the prequel to my traditional mystery series, the Kate Huntington Mysteries.

Also, misterio press now has a readers' group on Facebook where we chat with readers and also offer giveaways, contests and other goodies (https://www.facebook.com/groups/misteriopressmysteries). Please stop by and check it out!

I have the usual folks to thank for helping to bring this story to fruition, especially my sister authors at *misterio press*, Kirsten Weiss and Sasscer Hill, who critiqued and proofread it.

And to my wonderful editor, Marcy Kennedy, a huge thank you for walking beside me and advising me during this journey through Marcia's adventures.

Last but not least, much gratitude to my biggest supporter, my husband, who does the final proofreading. (Any typos you might have noticed are my fault; I tend to keep tweaking things right up to publication day, and sometimes introduce new errors.)

There has been much debate in the author groups online regarding how we should handle the Covid-19 pandemic in our writing. There are three schools of thought. One, that we should embrace it and incorporate people's struggles into our stories; the second, that we should ignore the pandemic completely and allow our readers to escape into a Covid-free environment in our books.

The third is somewhere in the middle, where the reality of the pandemic is acknowledged but it does not dominate the story.

I've elected to go with the third approach. I strive to make the settings and backdrop of society as realistic as possible in my books, and I just can't bring myself to ignore such a huge "elephant in the room."

But in this story, I've opted to focus, as much as possible, on the positives of the Spring of 2021—the sense of liberation and hope, and the joy of hugging friends again.

Border Collies are indeed deemed to be the smartest of dog breeds (although Black Labs are also up there on the list), but I have exaggerated a bit the speed at which Dolly would pick up new tasks. I wanted to include the training scenes, since so many readers say that they really like those, but I also did not want to bore you all with the minutia of training.

Complicated tasks like clearing a room of "enemies" to reassure an anxious veteran have to be broken down into small increments, and then each part of the task is repeated again and again and again.

I should point out that I am not a dog trainer. I do NOT have that level of patience! I combine my understanding of behavior modification as a psychologist with a lot of research.

You will meet up with Dolly again in the next book, *To Bark or Not To Bark*. That book will most likely be the last full-length novel in the Marcia Banks and Buddy series. Although, I am planning to do one more holiday novella after that, *Auld Lang Mayfair*, to give you all a peek into Marcia and Will's, and Buddy's, future.

I can hear you all screaming, "No!" I am so sorry, but eventually series do have to end.

Why am I ending this series now? Because Marcia has completed what we writers call a "character arc." She had certain challenges and neuroses at the beginning of the series that she has slowly, and sometimes haltingly, overcome. So it is time to give her some peace and move on.

Lord knows her life will be complicated enough with raising a child and partnering with Will as a private detective!

By the way, I am what is called a pantser in the writing world. I have a vague idea of the outline of a story before I start writing, but I basically let my muse and my characters take me wherever they will.

I never intended to have Marcia end up a private detective, but as the last few books panned out, that seemed to be the only direction that made sense. And retired/burned-out law enforcement officers do sometimes become private investigators, so that made perfect sense for Will.

I should point out that there is no Leesburg Sanitarium in Florida, nor is there a Pennington Group, to the best of my knowledge. They are both figments of my imagination.

I have also been intentionally vague about the location of the central Florida Veterans' Administration's office. There is such an office but I do not want to suggest that anyone like Wesley Sullivan actually works there.

And I have no idea if they have picnic tables outside nor a hard-to-find visitors' parking lot. All of the above come down to literary license. In other words, I get to make things up!

Although I have been in a county jail (as a visitor, I have not been in the Marion County jail. The bank-teller type mechanical drawer and the sally-port of doors are from my real experience. And I did research the Marion County jail to determine that suicidal inmates are housed in the "Medical Dorm" and that visits to them must be approved ahead of time.

But the layout of the Medical Dorm and Infirmary is, again, my imagination at work. I considered requesting a tour of that area of the jail, but decided I did not want to make already suicidal inmates feel like they were animals in a zoo.

Also, if there is a real Joseph Brown in the Marion County Sheriff's Department, my apologies for making your fictitious namesake incompetent.

And there is no fraternity, currently by the name of *Alpha Psi Chi*. I had a hard time finding a combination of Greek letters that wasn't in use by a fraternity or sorority. But I finally found a small fraternity at the College of New Jersey, with a website that had shown no activity in years, and they were no longer listed on the college's Greek page.

If any remaining brothers of that fraternity happen to read this book, my apologies for inserting two fictitious criminals in your ranks.

Unfortunately, I don't have *To Bark or Not To Bark*'s plot fleshed out enough to give you a synopsis, but I hope that the delightful Dolly will be sufficient enticement to stay tuned!

ABOUT THE AUTHOR

Kassandra Lamb has never been able to decide which she loves more, psychology or writing. In college, she realized that writers need a day job in order to eat, so she studied psychology. After a career as a psychotherapist and college professor, she is now retired and can pursue her passion for writing.

She spends most of her time in an alternate universe with her characters. The portal to that universe, aka her computer, is located in Florida, where her husband and dog catch occasional glimpses of her.

Kass has completed the ten-book, traditional mystery series, The Kate Huntington Mysteries (set in her native Maryland, about a psychotherapist/amateur sleuth), plus four Kate on Vacation novellas (with the same characters). She is also the author of the Marcia Banks and Buddy cozy mystery series, about a service dog trainer and her sidekick and mentor dog, Buddy. There are eleven stories out in that series, which is set in north central Florida. Book twelve is planned for late 2021/early 2022.

To read and see more about Kassandra and her books, please go to https://kassandralamb.com. Be sure to sign up for the newsletter there to get a heads up about new releases, plus special offers and bonuses for subscribers.

Kass's e-mail is lambkassandra3@gmail.com and she loves hearing from readers! She's also on Facebook (https://www.facebook.com/kassandralambauthor) and on Goodreads (https://www.goodreads.com/author/show/5624939.Kassandra_Lamb) and hangs out some on Twitter @KassandraLamb. And she blogs about psychological topics and other random things at https://misteriopress.com.

Kassandra also writes romantic suspense under the pen name of Jessica Dale (https://darkardorpublications.com).

**Please check out these other
great *misterio press* series:**

Karma's A Bitch: Pet Psychic Mysteries
by Shannon Esposito

Multiple Motives: Kate Huntington Mysteries
by Kassandra Lamb

The Metaphysical Detective: Riga Hayworth Paranormal Mysteries
by Kirsten Weiss

Dangerous and Unseemly: Concordia Wells Historical Mysteries
by K.B. Owen

Murder, Honey: Carol Sabala Mysteries
by Vinnie Hansen

Full Mortality: Nikki Latrelle Mysteries
by Sasscer Hill

To Kill A Labrador: Marcia Banks and Buddy Cozy Mysteries
by Kassandra Lamb

Never Sleep: Chronicles of a Lady Detective Historical Mysteries
by K.B. Owen

Bound: Witches of Doyle Cozy Mysteries
by Kirsten Weiss

At Wits' End Cozy Mysteries
by Kirsten Weiss

Payback: Unintended Consequences Romantic Suspense
by Jessica Dale

Steam and Sensibility: Sensibility Grey Steampunk Mysteries
by Kirsten Weiss

Steeped In Murder: Tea and Tarot Mysteries
by Kirsten Weiss

Travels of Quinn
by Sasscer Hill

The Perfectly Proper Paranormal Museum Mysteries
by Kirsten Weiss

The Henry "Whispering" Smith Mysteries
by Candace J. Carter
(coming 2021)

The Mocassin Cove Mysteries
by Liz Boeger
(coming 2021)

Blogging is Murder: Digital Detective Cozy Mysteries
by Gilian Baker

Maui Widow Waltz: Islands of Aloha Mysteries
by JoAnn Bassett

**Plus even more great mysteries/thrillers in the
misterio press bookstore**

CPSIA information can be obtained
at www.ICGtesting.com
Printed in the USA
LVHW030934280621
691317LV00004B/57